BITE

Laurell K. Hamilton
Charlaine Harris
MaryJanice Davidson
Angela Knight
Vickie Taylor

JOVE BOOKS, NEW YORK

THE BERKLEY PUBLISHING GROUP
Published by the Penguin Group
Penguin Group (USA) Inc.
375 Hudson Street, New York, New York 10014, USA
Penguin Group (Canada), 90 Eglinton Avenue East, Suite 700, Toronto, Ontario M4P 2Y3, Canada
(a division of Pearson Penguin Canada Inc.)
Penguin Books Ltd., 80 Strand, London WC2R 0RL, England
Penguin Group Ireland, 25 St. Stephen's Green, Dublin 2, Ireland (a division of Penguin Books Ltd.)
Penguin Group (Australia), 250 Camberwell Road, Camberwell, Victoria 3124, Australia
(a division of Pearson Australia Group Pty. Ltd.)
Penguin Books India Pvt. Ltd., 11 Community Centre, Panchsheel Park, New Delhi—110 017, India
Penguin Group (NZ), 67 Apollo Drive, Rosedale, North Shore 0632, New Zealand
(a division of Pearson New Zealand Ltd.)
Penguin Books (South Africa) (Pty.) Ltd., 24 Sturdee Avenue, Rosebank, Johannesburg 2196,
South Africa

Penguin Books Ltd., Registered Offices: 80 Strand, London WC2R 0RL, England

This is a work of fiction. Names, characters, places, and incidents either are the product of the authors' imaginations or are used fictitiously, and any resemblance to actual persons, living or dead, business establishments, events, or locales is entirely coincidental. The publisher does not have any control over and does not assume any responsibility for author or third-party websites or their content.

BITE

A Jove Book / published by arrangement with the authors

PRINTING HISTORY
Jove mass-market edition / January 2005

Copyright © 2005 by The Berkley Publishing Group.
"The Girl Who Was Infatuated with Death" copyright © 2005 by Laurell K. Hamilton.
"One Word Answer" copyright © 2005 by Charlaine Harris.
"Biting in Plain Sight" copyright © 2005 by MaryJanice Davidson.
"Galahad" by Angela Knight copyright © 2005 by Julie Woodcock.
"Blood Lust" by Vickie Taylor copyright © 2005 by Vickie Spears.
Text design by Kristin del Rosario.

ISBN: 978-0-515-13970-9

JOVE®
Jove Books are published by The Berkley Publishing Group,
a division of Penguin Group (USA) Inc.,
375 Hudson Street, New York, New York 10014.
JOVE is a registered trademark of Penguin Group (USA) Inc.
The "J" design is a trademark belonging to Penguin Group (USA) Inc.

PRINTED IN THE UNITED STATES OF AMERICA

14   13   12   11   10   9

Contents

THE GIRL WHO WAS
INFATUATED WITH DEATH

Laurell K. Hamilton

This short story occurs in the interval between BLUE MOON *and* OBSIDIAN BUTTERFLY.

IT was five days before Christmas, a quarter 'til midnight. I should have been asnooze in my bed dreaming of sugarplums, whatever the hell they were, but I wasn't. I was sitting across my desk sipping coffee and offering a box of Kleenexes to my client, Ms. Rhonda Mackenzie. She'd been crying for nearly the entire meeting, so that she'd wiped most of her careful eye makeup away, leaving her eyes pale and unfinished, younger, like what she must have looked like when she was in high school. The dark, perfect lipstick made the eyes look emptier, more vulnerable.

"I'm not usually like this, Ms. Blake. I am a very strong woman." Her voice took on a tone that said she believed this, and it might even be true. She raised those naked brown eyes to me and there was fierceness in them that might have made a weaker person flinch. Even I, tough-as-nails vampire-hunter that I am, had trouble meeting the rage in those eyes.

"It's alright, Ms. Mackenzie, you're not the first client that's cried. It's hard when you've lost someone."

She looked up startled. "I haven't lost anyone, not yet."

I sat my coffee cup back down without drinking from it and stared at her. "I'm an animator, Ms. Mackenzie. I raise the dead if the reason is good enough. I assumed this amount of grief was because you'd come to ask me to raise someone close to you."

She shook her head, her deep brown curls in disarray around her face as if she'd been running her hands through what was once a perfect perm. "My daughter, Amy, is very much alive and I want her to stay that way."

Now I was just plain confused. "I raise the dead and am a legal vampire executioner, Ms. Mackenzie. How do either of those jobs help you keep your daughter alive?"

"I want you to help me find her before she commits suicide."

I just stared at her, my face professionally blank, but inwardly, I was cursing my boss. He and I had had discussions about exactly what my job description was, and suicidal daughters weren't part of that description.

"Have you gone to the police?" I asked.

"They won't do anything for twenty-four hours, but by then it will be too late."

"I have a friend who is a private detective. This sounds much more up her alley than mine, Ms. Mackenzie." I was already reaching for the phone. "I'll call her at home for you."

"No," she said, "only you can help me."

I sighed and clasped my hands across the clean top of my desk. Most of my work wasn't indoor office work, so the desk didn't really see much use. "You're daughter is alive, Ms. Mackenzie, so you don't need me to raise her.

She's not a rogue vampire, so you don't need an executioner. How can I be of any help to you?"

She leaned forward; the Kleenex waded in her hands, her eyes fierce again. "If you don't help me by morning she will be a vampire."

"What do you mean?" I asked.

"She's determined to become one of them tonight."

"It takes three bites to become a vampire, Ms. Mackenzie, and they all have to be from the same vampire. You can't become one in a single night, and you can't become one if you're just being casual with more than one."

"She has two bites on her thighs. I accidentally walked in on her when she was getting out of the shower and I saw them."

"Are you sure they were vampire bites?" I asked.

She nodded. "I made a scene. I grabbed her, wrestled with her so I could see them clearly. They are vampire bites, just like the pictures they passed around at the last PTA meeting so we could recognize it. You know one of those people lecturing on how to know if your kids are involved with the monsters."

I nodded. I knew the kind of person she meant. Some of it was valuable information, some of it was just scare tactics, and some of it was racist, if that was the term. Prejudiced at least.

"How old is your daughter?"

"She's seventeen."

"That's only a year away from being legal, Ms. Mackenzie. Once she turns eighteen, if she wants to become a vampire, you can't stop her legally."

"You say that so calmly. Do you approve?"

I took in a deep breath and let it out, slow. "I'd be willing to talk to your daughter, try to talk her out of it. But how do you know that tonight is the night? It has to be three bites within a very short space of time or the body fights off the infection, or whatever the hell it is." Scientists were still arguing about exactly what made someone become a vampire. There were biological differences before and after, but there was also a certain level of mysticism involved, and science has always been bad at deciphering that kind of thing.

"The bites were fresh, Ms. Blake. I called the man who gave the lecture at our school and he said to come to you."

"Who was he?"

"Jeremy Ruebens."

I frowned now. "I didn't know he'd gotten out of jail," I said.

Her eyes went wide. "Jail?"

"He didn't mention in his talk that he was jailed for conspiracy to commit murder—over a dozen counts, maybe hundreds. He was head of Humans First when they tried to wipe out all the vampires and some of the shape-shifters in St. Louis."

"He talked about that," she said. "He said he would never have condoned such violence and that it was done without his knowledge."

I smiled and knew from the feel of it that it was unpleasant. "Jeremy Ruebens once sat in the chair you're in now and told me that Humans First's goal was to destroy every vampire in the United States."

She just looked at me, and I let it go. She would believe what she wanted to believe, most people did.

"Ms. Mackenzie, whether you, or I, or Jeremy Ruebens, approve, or not, vampires are legal citizens with legal rights in this country. That's just the way it is."

"Amy is seventeen, if that thing brings her over underage it's murder and I will prosecute him for murder. If he kills my Amy, I will see him dead."

"You know for certain that it is a he?"

"The bites were very, very high up on her thigh." She looked down at her lap. "Her inner thigh."

I would have liked to have let the female vamp angle go, but I couldn't because I was finally beginning to see what Ms. Mackenzie wanted me to do, and why Jeremy Ruebens had sent her to me. "You want me to find your daughter before she's got that third bite, right?"

She nodded. "Mr. Ruebens seemed to think if anyone could find her in time, it would be you."

Since Humans First had also tried to kill me during their great cleansing of the city, Rueben's faith in me was a little odd. Accurate probably, but odd. "How long has she been missing?"

"Since nine, a little after. She was taking a shower to get ready to go out with friends tonight. We had an awful fight and she stormed up to her room. I grounded her until she got over this crazy idea about becoming a vampire."

"Then you went up to check on her and she was gone?" I made it a question.

"Yes." She sat back in her chair, smoothing her skirt. It looked like a nervous habit. "I called the friends she was supposed to be going out with and they wouldn't talk to me on the phone, so I went to her best friend's house in person and she talked to me." She smoothed the skirt down again, hands touching her knees as if the hose needed attention; everything looked in place to me. "They've got fake ID that says they're both over twenty-one. They've been going to the vampire clubs for weeks."

Ms. Mackenzie looked down at her lap, hands clasped tight. "My daughter has bone cancer. To save her life they're going to take her left leg from the knee down, next week. But this week she started having pains in her other leg just like the pains that started all this." She looked up then, and I expected tears, but her eyes were empty, not just of tears, but of everything. It was as if the horror of it all, the enormity of it, had drained her.

"I am sorry, Ms. Mackenzie, for both of you."

She shook her head. "Don't be sorry for me. She's seventeen, beautiful, intelligent, honor society, and, at the very least, she's going to lose a leg next week. She has to use a cane now. Her friends chipped in and got her this amazing Goth cane, black wood and a silver skull on top. She loves it, but you can't use a cane if you don't have any legs at all."

There was a time when I thought being a vampire was worse than death, but now, I just wasn't sure. I just didn't have enough room to cast stones. "She won't lose the leg if she's a vampire."

"But she'll lose her soul."

I didn't even try to argue that one. I wasn't sure if vampires had souls, or not; I just didn't know. I'd known good ones and bad ones, just like good and bad people, but one thing was true: vampires had to feed off of humans to survive. No matter what you see in the movies, animal blood will not do the job. We are their food, no getting around that. Out loud, I said, "She's seventeen, Ms. Mackenzie, I think she probably believes in her leg more than her soul."

The woman nodded, too rapidly, head bobbing. "And that's my fault."

I sighed. I so did not want to get involved in this, but I believed Ms. Mackenzie would do exactly what she said she would do. It wasn't the girl I was worried about so much as the vampire that would be bringing her over. She was underage and that meant if he turned her, it was an automatic death sentence. Death sentences for humans usually mean life imprisonment, but for a vamp, it means death within days, weeks at the most. Some of the civil rights groups were complaining that the vampire trials were too quick to be fair. And maybe someday the

Supreme Court would reverse some of the decisions, but that wouldn't make the vampire "alive" again. Once a vamp is staked, beheaded and the heart cut out, all the parts are burned and scattered on running water. There is no coming back from the grave if you are itty-bits of ashy fish food.

"Does the friend know what the vampire looks like, maybe a name?"

She shook her head. "Barbara says that it's Amy's choice." Ms. Mackenzie shook her head. "It isn't, not until she's eighteen."

I sort of agreed with Barbara, but I wasn't a mother, so maybe my sympathies would have been elsewhere if I was. "So you don't know if the vampire is male or female."

"Male," she said, very firm, too firm.

"Amy's friend told you it was a guy vampire?"

Ms. Mackenzie shook her head, but too rapid, too jerky. "Amy would never let another girl do that to her, not . . . down there."

I was beginning not to like Ms. Mackenzie. There's something about someone who is so against all that is different that sets my teeth on edge. "If I knew for sure it was a guy, then that would narrow down the search."

"It was a male vampire, I'm sure of that." She was working too hard at this, which meant she wasn't sure at all.

I let it go; she wasn't going to budge. "I need to talk to Barbara, Amy's friend, without you or her parents present, and we need to start searching the clubs for Amy. Do you have a picture of her?"

She did, hallelujah, she'd come prepared. It was one of those standard yearbook shots. Amy had long straight hair in a rather nondescript brown color, neither dark enough to be rich, or pale enough to be anything else. She was smiling, face open, eyes sparkling; the picture of health and bright promise.

"The picture was taken last year," her mother said, as if she needed to explain why the picture looked the way it did.

"Nothing more recent?"

She drew another picture out of her purse. It was of two women in black with kohl eyeliner and full, pouting lips, one with purple lipstick and the other with black. It took me a second to recognize the girl on the right as Amy. The nondescript hair was piled on top of her head in a casual mass of loose curls that left the clean, high bone structure other face like an unadorned painting, something to be admired. The dramatic makeup suited her coloring. Her friend was blond and it didn't match her skin tone as well. The picture seemed more poised than the other one had, as if they were playing dress-up and knew it, but they both looked older, dramatic, seductive, lovely but almost indistinguishable from a thousand other teenage Goths.

I put the two pictures beside each other and looked from one to the other. "Which picture did she go out looking like?"

I don't know. She's got so much Goth clothing, I can't tell what's missing." She looked uncomfortable with that last remark, as if she should have known.

"You did good bringing both pictures, Ms. Mackenzie, most people wouldn't have thought of it."

She looked up at that, almost managed a smile. "She looks so different depending on what she wears."

"Most of us do," I said.

She nodded, not like she was agreeing, but as if it were polite.

"How old is Barbara, her friend?"

"Eighteen, why?"

"I'll send my friend, the private investigator over to talk to her, maybe meet me at the clubs."

"Barbara won't tell us who it is that's been . . ." She couldn't bring herself to finish the sentence.

"My friend can be very persuasive, but if you think Barbara will be a problem I might know someone who could help us out."

"She's very stubborn, just like my Amy."

I nodded and reached for the phone. I called Veronica (Ronnie) Sims, private detective and good friend first. Ms. Mackenzie gave me Barbara's address, which I gave to Ronnie over the phone. Ronnie said she'd page me when she had any news, or when she arrived at the club district.

I dialed Zerbrowski next. He was a police detective and really had no reason to get involved, but he had two kids and he didn't like the monsters, and he was my friend. He was actually at work, since he belonged to the Regional Preternatural Investigation Team and worked a lot of nights.

I explained the situation, and that I needed a little official muscle to flex. He said it was a slow night, and he'd be there.

"Thanks, Zerbrowski."

"You owe me."

"On this one, yeah."

"Hmm," he said, "I know how you could pay me back." His voice had dropped low and mock seductive. It had been a game with us since we met.

"Be careful what you say next, Zerbrowski, or I'll tell Katie on you."

"My darling wife knows I'm a letch."

"Don't we all. Thanks again, Zerbrowski."

"I've got kids, don't mention it," he said, and he hung up.

I left Ms. Mackenzie in the capable hands of our nighttime secretary Craig, and I went out to see if I could save her daughter's life, and the "life" of the vampire that was a close enough personal friend to have bitten Amy twice on the very upper thigh.

THE vampire district in St. Louis was one of the hottest tourist areas in the country. Some people credit the undead with the boom we've experienced in the last five years since vampires were declared living citizens with all the rights and privileges that entailed, except voting. There was a bill floating around Washington that would give them the vote, and another bill floating around that would take away their new status and make it legal to kill them on sight again, just because they were vampires. To say that the United States was not exactly united in its attitude toward the undead was an understatement.

Danse Macabre was one of the newest of the vampire-run clubs. It was the hottest dance spot in St. Louis. We'd had actors fly from the West Coast to grace the club with their presence. It had become chic to hob-knob with vampires, especially the beautiful ones, and St. Louis did have more than its fair share of gorgeous corpses.

The most gorgeous corpse of them all was dancing on the main floor of his newest club. The floor was so crowded there was barely room to dance, but somehow my gaze found Jean-Claude, picked him out of the crowd.

When I first spotted him, his long pale hands were above his head, the graceful movement of those hands brought my gaze down to the whirl of his black curls as they slid over his shoulders. From the back with all that long hair the shirt was just scarlet, eye-catching but nothing too special, then he turned and I caught a glimpse of the front.

The red satin scooped over his bare shoulders as if someone had cut out the shoulders with scissors; the sleeves were long, tight to his wrists. The high red collar framed his face, made his skin, his hair, his dark eyes look brighter, more alive.

The music turned him away from me, and I got to watch him dance. He was always graceful, but the pounding beat of the music demanded movements that were not graceful but powerful, provocative.

I finally realized, as he took the woman into his arms, as she plastered herself against the front of him, that he had a partner. I was instantly jealous and hated it.

I'd worn the clothes I'd had on at the office, and I was glad that it was a fashionably short black skirt with a royal blue button-up shirt. A long black leather coat that was way too hot for the inside of the club and sensible black pumps completed the outfit, oh, and the shoulder holster with the Browning Hi-Power 9mm, which was why I was still wearing the coat. People tended to get nervous if you flashed a gun, and it would show up very nicely against the deep blue of the blouse.

To other people it must have seemed like I was trying to look cool, wearing all that leather. Nope, just trying not to scare the tourists. But nothing I was wearing compared to the sparkling, skintight dress and spike heels the woman had on; nope, I was woefully under-dressed.

It had been my choice to stay away from Jean-Claude for these last few months. I'd let him mark me as his human servant to save his life and the life of the other boyfriend I wasn't seeing, Richard Zeeman, Ulfric, wolf-king of the local pack. I'd done it to save them both, but it had bound me closer to them, and every sexual act made that mystical tie tighter. We could think each other's thoughts, visit each other's dreams. I'd fallen into Richard's dreams where he was in wolf form chasing human prey. I'd tasted blood underneath a woman's skin because Jean-Claude had been sitting beside me when he thought of it. It had been too much for me so I'd fled to a friendly psychic who was teaching me how to shield myself metaphysically from the boys. I did okay, as long as I stayed the hell away from both of them.

Watching Jean-Claude move like he was wed to the music, to the room, to the energy, anticipating not just the music but the movements of the woman who was in his arms made me want to run screaming, because what I really wanted to do was march over there and grab her by her long hair and punch her out. I didn't have that right, besides they were only dancing. Sure.

But if anyone would be able to tell me who was about to bring Amy Mackenzie over to be the undead, it would be Jean-Claude. I needed to be here. I needed the information, but it was dangerous, dangerous in so many ways.

The music stopped for a few seconds, then a new song came on, just as fast, just as demanding. Jean-Claude kissed the woman's hand and tried to leave the dance floor. She took his arm, obviously trying to persuade him to have another dance. He shook his head, kissed her cheek and managed to extract himself, leaving her smiling. But as she watched him walk toward me, the look was not friendly. There was something familiar about her, as if I should have known her, but I was almost certain I didn't know her. It took me a second or two to realize she was an actress, and if I ever went to movies I would have known her name. A photographer knelt in front of her, and she instantly went from unpleasant to a perfect smile, posing, choosing another partner. A second photographer followed after Jean-Claude, not taking pictures, but alert for a photo opportunity. Shit.

I had two choices. I could either stand there and let him take pictures of Jean-Claude and myself, or I could flee to the back office and privacy. I wasn't news, but Jean-Claude was the vampire cover boy. The press had been amused that the woman the other vamps called the Executioner, because she had more vamp kills than any other vampire hunter in the country, had been dating the Master of the City. Even I could admit it was nicely ironic, but being followed around by paparazzi had gotten old very fast. Especially when they tried to take pictures of me while I was working on preternatural murders for the police. For the American media if you stood next to the gruesome remains they wouldn't air the pictures, or print them, but European papers would. Some of the European media makes American media look downright polite.

When I stopped dating Jean-Claude, they drifted away. I was not nearly as photogenic, or as friendly. I didn't have to worry about winning the press over; there wasn't a bill in Washington that was trying to get me killed. The vamps needed the good press, and Jean-Claude was tagged as the one to get it for them.

I decided not to watch Jean-Claude walk toward me because I'd seen what my face looked like when I did—in color on the front of the tabloids. I'd looked like some small prey animal, watching the tiger stalk toward it; that explained the fear, but the fearful fascination, the open . . . lust, that had been harder to see in print. So I kept my eyes on the circling photographer and tried not to watch Jean-Claude glide toward me, as I leaned against the far wall, right next to the door that would lead into the hallway that led to his office.

I could have fled and avoided the press, but it would have meant I would be alone with Jean-Claude, and I didn't want that. All right, truth, I did want that, and that was the problem. It wasn't Jean-Claude I didn't trust, it was me.

I'd been concentrating so hard on not watching him come toward me that it was almost a surprise when I realized I was staring into the red satin of his shirt. I looked up to meet his eyes. Most people couldn't meet the gaze of a vampire, let alone a master one, but I could. I was a necromancer and that gave me partial immunity to vampire powers, and I was Jean-Claude's human servant whether I wanted to be, or whether I didn't, and that gave me even more immunity. I wasn't vampire-proof by any means, but I was shut up pretty tight to most of their tricks.

It wasn't vampire powers that made it hard to meet those midnight blue eyes. No, nothing that . . . simple.

He said something, and I couldn't hear him over the beat of the music. I shook my head, and he stepped closer, close enough that the red of his shirt filled my vision, but it was better than meeting that swimming blue gaze. He leaned over me, and I felt him like a line of heat, close enough to kiss, close enough for so many things. I was already flat against the wall; there was nowhere else to go.

He had to lean his mouth next to my face, a fall of his long hair moving against my mouth, as he said, "*Ma petite*, it has been too long." His voice, even over the noise, caressed down my skin as if he'd touched me. He could do things with his voice that most men couldn't do with their hands.

I could smell his cologne, spicy, exotic, a hint of musk. I could almost taste his skin on my tongue. It took me two tries to say, "Not nearly long enough."

He laid his cheek against my hair, very lightly, "You are happy to see me, *ma petite*, I can feel your heart trembling."

"I'm here on business," I said, but my voice was breathy. I was usually better than this around him, but three months of celibacy, three months of nothing, and being around him was worse. Damn it, why did it have to be worse?

"Of course, you are."

I'd had enough. I put a hand on that satin-covered chest and pushed. Vampires can bench-press small trucks, so he didn't have to let me shove him, but he did. He gave me some room, then his mouth moved, as if he were saying something, but I couldn't hear him over the music and crowd noise.

I shook my head and sighed. We were going to have to go back into the office so I could hear him. Being alone with him was not the best idea, but I wanted to find Amy Mackenzie and the vampire she was going to get executed. I opened the door without looking at him. The photographer took pictures as we went through the door. He had to have been taking pictures when Jean-Claude had me practically pinned to the wall, I just hadn't noticed.

Jean-Claude shut the door behind us. The hallway was white with harsher lighting than anywhere else in the club. He'd told me once that he had made the hallway plain, ordinary so if a customer opened the door they'd know instantly that it wasn't part of the entertainment.

A group of waiters, vampires all, came out of the left-hand door, wearing vinyl short-shorts and no shirts. They'd spilled out of the door in a cloud of excited talk; it stopped abruptly when they saw us. One of them started to say something, and Jean-Claude said, "Go."

They fled out the door without a backward glance, almost as if they were scared. I'd have liked to think it was Jean-Claude that they were afraid of, but I was the Executioner, their version of the electric chair, so it might have been me.

"Shall we retire to my office, *ma petite?*"

I sighed, and in the silence of the hallway with the music only a distant thrum, my sigh sounded loud. "Sure."

He led the way down the hallway, gliding ahead of me. The pants were black satin and looked as if they'd been sewn on his body, tight as a second skin. A pair of black boots graced his legs. The boots laced up the back from ankle to upper thigh. I'd seen the boots before; they were really nice boots. Nice enough that I watched the way his legs moved in them rather than the way the satin fit across his butt. Very nice boots, indeed.

He started to hold the door for me, then smiled, almost

laughed, and just walked through. It had taken me awhile to break him of opening doors for me, but I'd finally managed to teach a very old dog a new trick.

The office was done in an Oriental motif complete with framed fans around a framed kimono. The colors in all three ran high to reds and blues. A red lacquer screen had a black castle sitting atop a black mountain. The desk was carved wood that looked like ebony and probably was. He leaned against that desk, long legs out in front of him, ankles crossed, hands in his lap, his eyes watching me as I shut the door.

"Please, be seated, *ma petite*." He motioned to a black and silver chair sitting in front of the desk.

"I'm fine where I am." I leaned against the wall; my arms crossed under my breasts, which put my hand comfortably close to the gun under my arm. I wouldn't really shoot Jean-Claude, but the gun being close made me feel better. It was like a small, lumpy security blanket. Besides, I never went anywhere after dark unarmed.

His smile was amused and condescending. "I do not think the wall will fall down if you cease to lean against it."

"We need to figure out who the vamp is that's been doing Amy Mackenzie."

"You said you had pictures of the girl. May I see them?" The smile had faded round the edges, but his eyes still held that amusement, faint and condescending, which he used as a mask to hide things.

I sighed and reached into the pocket of my leather coat. I held the two pictures out toward him. He held his hand out for them but made no move to come to me.

"I won't bite, *ma petite*."

"Only because I won't let you," I said.

He gave that graceful shrug that meant everything and nothing. "True, but still I will not ravish you because you stand a few feet in front of me."

He was right. I was being silly, but I could taste my pulse in my throat as I walked toward him, the new leather coat sighing around me, the way new leather always does. It was a replacement coat for one that a vampire had ripped off of me. I held the pictures out to him, and he had to lean forward to take them from me. I even sat down in the chair in front of the desk while he looked at them. We could be civilized about this. Of course we could. But I couldn't stop looking at the way his bare shoulders gleamed against the scarlet cloth, the way the high collar made his hair a pure blackness almost as dark as mine. His lips looked redder than I remembered them, as if he were wearing a light lipstick, and I wouldn't have put it past him. But he didn't need makeup to be beautiful; he just simply was.

He spoke without looking up from the pictures. "I do not recognize her, but then she could come here occasionally and I would have no reason to." He looked up meeting my eyes, catching me staring at his bare shoulders. The look in those eyes said he knew exactly what I'd been looking at. The look was enough to make me blush, and I hated that.

My voice came out angry, and I was pleased. Anger is better than embarrassment any day. "You said on the phone that you could help."

He laid the pictures on his desk and clasped his hands back in his lap. The placement of his hands was utterly polite, but they also framed a certain area of anatomy, and the satin was very tight, and I could tell that other things were tight as well.

It made me blush again, and it made me angrier, just like old times. I'd have liked to be a smart alec and say something like, that looked uncomfortable, but I didn't want to admit that I'd noticed, so out of options that were polite, I stood up and turned away.

"None of my vampires would dare bring over anyone without my permission," he said.

That made me turn around. "What do you mean?"

"I have ordered a . . . how will you say . . . hiring freeze on, until that nasty bill in Washington is defeated."

"*Hiring freeze*," I said, "you mean none of your vamps can make more of you until Senator Brewster's law goes down in flames?"

"*Exactement.*"

"So you're sure that none of your vamps is doing this?" I said.

"They would not risk the punishment."

"So you can't help me. Damn it, Jean-Claude, you could have told me that over the phone."

"I called Malcolm while you were en route," he said.

Malcolm was the head of the Church of Eternal Life, the vampire church. It was the only church I'd ever been in that had no holy objects displayed whatsoever, even the stain glass was abstract art. "Because if it's not one of your vamps, then it's one of his," I said.

"*Oui.*"

Truthfully, I had just assumed it was one of Jean-Claude's vampires because the church was very strict on when you brought your human followers over to the dead side, and the church also checked backgrounds thoroughly. "The girl's friend said she'd met the vampire at a club."

"Can you not go to church and go to a club on the weekends?"

I nodded. "Okay, you've made your point. What did Malcolm say?"

"That he would contact all his followers and give strict orders that this vampire and the girl are to be found."

"They'll need the picture," I said. My beeper went off, and I jumped. Shit. I checked the number and it was Ronnie's cell phone.

"Can I use your phone?"

"Whatever I have is yours, *ma petite*." He looked at the black phone sitting on the black desk and stood to one side so I could walk around the desk without him leaning over me. Considerate of him, which probably meant he was going to do something else even more irritating.

Ronnie answered on the first ring. "Anita?"

"It's me, what's up?"

She lowered her voice to a whisper. "Your detective friend convinced Barbara that if Amy got herself killed she'd be charged with conspiracy to commit murder."

"I don't think Zerbrowski could make that stick."

"Barbara thinks he can."

"What did she tell you?"

"The vampire's name is Bill Stucker." She spelled the last name for me.

"A vamp with a last name. He has to be really new," I said. The only other vamp I'd ever met with a last name had been dead less than a month.

"Don't know if he's old or new, just his name."

"She have an address for him?"

"No, and Zerbrowski pushed her pretty hard. She says she's never been there and I believe her."

"Okay, tell Zerbrowski thanks, I'll see you Saturday at the gym."

"Wouldn't miss it," she said.

"Oh, and thanks to you, too, Ronnie."

"Always happy to save someone from the monsters, which reminds me, are you with you know who?"

"If you mean Jean-Claude, yes, I am."

"Get out of there as soon as you can," she said.

"You're not my mother, Ronnie."

"No, just your friend."

"Good night, Ronnie."

"Don't stay," she said.

I hung up. Ronnie was one of my very bestest friends,

but her attitude toward Jean-Claude was beginning to get on my nerves, mainly because I agreed with her. I always hated being in the wrong.

"The name Bill Stucker mean anything to you?" I asked Jean-Claude.

"No, but I will call Malcolm and see if it means something to him."

I handed him the phone receiver and stepped back out of the way, i.e., out of touching distance. His side of the conversation consisted mainly of giving the name and, saying, "Of course," and "Yes." He handed the phone to me. "Malcolm wishes to speak to you."

I took the phone, and Jean-Claude actually moved away and gave me some room. "Ms. Blake, I am sorry for anything my church brethren may have done. He is in our computer with his address. I will have a deacon at his doorstep within minutes."

"Give me the address and I'll go down and check on the girl."

"That will not be necessary. The church sister that is attending to this was a nurse before she came over."

"I'm not sure what Amy Mackenzie needs is another vampire, no matter how well-meaning. Let me have the address."

"And I don't believe that my vampire needs the Executioner shooting down his door."

"I can give the name to the police. They'll find his address, and they'll knock on his door, and they may not be as polite as I would be."

"Now that last is hard to imagine."

I think he was making fun of me. "Give me the address, Malcolm." Anger was tightening across my shoulders, making me want to rotate my neck and try and clear it.

"Wait a moment." He put me on hold.

I looked at Jean-Claude and let the anger into my voice. "He put me on hold."

Jean-Claude had sat down in the chair that I'd vacated; he smiled, shrugged, trying to stay neutral. Probably wise of him. When I'm angry I have a tendency to spread it around, even over people who don't deserve it. I'm trying to cut down on my bad habits, but some habits are easier to break than others. My temper was one of the hard ones.

"Ms. Blake, that was the emergency line. The girl is alive, but barely, they are rushing her to the hospital. We are not sure if she will make it. We will turn Bill over to the police if she dies, I give you my word on that."

I had to take his word, because he was a centuries-old vampire and if you could ever get them to give their oath, they'd keep it.

"What hospital, so I can call her mom?"

He told me. I hung up and called Amy's mother. One hysterical phone call later I got to hang up and now it was my turn to sit on the edge of the desk and look down at him.

My feet didn't touch the ground and that made it hard to look graceful. But then I'd never tried to compete with Jean-Claude on gracefulness; some battles are made to be lost.

"There was a time, *ma petite*, that you would have insisted on riding to the rescue yourself, questioning the girl's friend, and refusing to bring in the police at all."

"If I thought threatening Barbara with violence or shooting her would have made her talk, I'd be perfect for the job. But I'm not going to shoot, or hurt, an eighteen-year-old girl who's trying to help her best friend save her leg, if not her life. Zerbrowski could threaten her with the law, jail time, I can't do that."

"And you never threaten anything that you cannot, or will not do," he said, softly.

"No, I don't."

We looked at each other. He at ease in the straight-backed chair, his ankle propped on the opposite knee, fingers steepled in front of his face so that what I mostly saw of him were those extraordinary eyes, huge, a blue so dark it treaded the edge of being black, but you never doubted his eyes were pure, unadulterated blue, like ocean water where it runs achingly deep and cold.

Ronnie was right, I should leave, but I didn't want to leave. I wanted to stay. I wanted to run my hands over his shirt, to caress the naked surprise of those shoulders. And because I wanted it so badly, I hopped off the desk, and said, "Thanks for your help."

"I am always willing to be of assistance, *ma petite*."

I could have walked wide past his chair, but that would be insulting to both of us. I just had to walk by the chair and out the door. Simple. I was almost past the chair, almost behind him, when he spoke, "Would you have ever called me if you hadn't needed to save some human?" His voice was as ordinary as it ever got. He wasn't trying to use vampire tricks to make the words more than they were and that stopped me. An honest question was harder to turn my back on than a seductive trick.

I sighed and turned back to find him staring straight at me. Looking full into his face from less than two feet away made me have to catch my breath. "You know why I'm staying away."

He twisted in the chair, putting one arm on the back of it, showing that flash of bare shoulder again. "I know that you find it difficult to control the powers of the vampire marks when we are together. It was something that should have bound us closer, not thrust us farther apart." Again his voice was as carefully neutral as he could make it.

I shook my head. "I've got to go."

He turned in the chair so that he leaned both arms on the

back, his chin resting on his hands, his hair framing all that red cloth, that pale flesh, those drowning eyes. Less than two feet apart, almost close enough that if I reached a hand out I could have touched him. I swallowed so hard it almost hurt. I balled my hands into fists, because I could feel the memory of his skin against my hands. All I had to do was close that distance, but I knew if I did, that I wouldn't be leaving, not for awhile anyway.

My voice came out breathy, "I should go."

"So you said."

I should have turned and walked out, but I couldn't quite bring myself to do it. Didn't want to do it. I wanted to stay. My body was tight with need; wet with it, just at the sight of him fully clothed, leaning on a chair. Damn it, why wasn't I walking away? But I wasn't reaching for him either; I got points for that. Sometimes you get points for just standing your ground.

Jean-Claude stood, very slowly, as if afraid I'd bolt, but I didn't. I stood there, my heart in my throat, my eyes a little wide, afraid, eager, wanting.

He stood inches away from me, staring down, but still not touching, hands at his sides, face neutral. He raised one hand, very slowly upward, and even that small movement sent his fingertips gliding along my leather coat. When I didn't pull away, he held the edge of the leather in his fingertips inside the open edge of the coat at the level of my waist. He began to slide his hand upward, above my waist, my stomach, then the back of his fingers brushed over my breasts, not hesitating, moving upward to the collar of the coat, but that one quick brush had tightened my body, stopped my breath in my throat.

His hand moved from my collar to my neck, fingers gliding underneath my hair until he cupped the back of my neck, his thumb resting on top of the big pulse in my neck. The weight of his hand on my skin was almost more than I could take, as if I could sink into him through that one hand.

"I have missed you, *ma petite*." His voice was low and caressing this time, gliding over my skin, bringing my breath in a shaking line.

I'd missed him, but I couldn't bring myself to say it out loud. What I could do was raise up on tiptoe, steadying myself with a hand on his chest, feeling his heart beat against the palm of my hand. He'd fed on someone, or he wouldn't have had a heartbeat, some willing donor, and even that thought wasn't enough to stop me from leaning my face back, offering my lips to him.

His lips brushed mine, the softest of caresses. I drew back from the kiss, my hands sliding over the satin of his shirt, feeling the firmness of him underneath. I did what I'd wanted to do since I saw him tonight. I passed my fingers over the bare skin of his shoulders, so smooth, so soft, so firm. I rolled my hands behind his shoulders, and the movement let our bodies fall together, lightly.

His hands found my waist, slid behind my back, pressed me against him, not lightly, hard, hard enough that I could feel him even through the satin of his pants, the cloth of my skirt, the lace of my panties. I could feel him pressed so tight and ready that I had to close my eyes, hide my face against his chest. I tried to let my feet flat to the floor, to move away from him, just a little, just enough to think again, but his hands kept me pinned to his body. I opened my eyes then, ready to tell him to let me the hell go, but I looked up and his face was so close, his lips half-parted, that no words came.

I kissed those half-parted lips almost as gently as he'd kissed me. His hands tightened at my back, my waist, pressing us tighter against each other, so tight, so close. My breath came out in a long sigh, and he kissed me. His mouth closing over mine, my body sinking against his, my mouth opening for his lips, his tongue, everything. I ran my tongue between the delicate tips of his fangs. There was an art to French kissing a vampire, and I hadn't lost it; I didn't pierce myself on those dainty points.

Without breaking the kiss, he bent and wrapped his arms around my upper thighs, lifted me, carried me effortlessly to the desk. He didn't lay me on it, which is what I half-expected. He turned and sat down on the desk, sliding my legs to either side, so that he was suddenly pressed between my legs with only two pieces of cloth between us. He lay back on the desk, and I rode him, rubbing our bodies together through the satin of his pants and my panties.

His hands rubbed up my leg tracing my hose, until his fingers found the top lace of the thigh-high hose. I pressed myself into him hard enough for his body to arch, spasming our bodies together. And there was a knock on the door. We both froze, then Jean-Claude said, "We are not to be disturbed!"

A voice I didn't recognize said, "I am sorry, master, but Malcolm is here. He insists that it is urgent."

Evidently Jean-Claude did know the voice, because he closed his eyes and cursed softly under his breath in French. "What does he want?"

I slid off of Jean-Claude, leaving him lying on his desk, with his legs dangling over the end.

Malcolm's smooth voice came next. "I have a present for Ms. Blake."

I checked my clothing to make sure it was presentable; strangely it was. Jean-Claude sat up, but stayed on the edge of his desk. "Enter."

The door opened and the tall, blond, dark-suited figure of Malcolm walked through. He always dressed like he was a television preacher, conservative, immaculate, expensive. Compared to Jean-Claude he always looked ordinary, but then so did most everyone. Still, there was a presence to

Malcolm, a calm, soothing power that filled every room around him. He was a master vampire and his power was a thrumming weight against my skin. He tried to pass for human, and I'd always wondered if the level of power he gave off was his version of toned-down, and if this was the toned-down version, then what must his power truly be like?

"Ms. Blake, Jean-Claude." He gave a small bow of his head, then moved from the door and two vampires in the dark suits and white shirts of his deacons came through carrying a chained vampire between them. He had short blond hair and blood drying on his mouth, as if they'd chained him before he'd had time to clean himself.

"This is Bill Stucker; the girl, I am sorry to say, passed over."

"She's one of you then," I said.

Malcolm nodded. "This one tried to run, but I gave you my word that he would be punished by your law if she died."

"You could have just dropped him off at the police station," I said.

His eyes flicked to Jean-Claude, to me, to my leather coat forgotten on the floor. "I am sorry to interrupt your evening, but I thought it would come better if the Executioner delivered the vampire to the police rather than us. I think the reporters will listen to you when you say we did not condone this, and you are honorable enough to tell the truth."

"Are you saying the rest of the police aren't?"

"I am saying that many of our law enforcement are distrustful of us and would be only too happy to see us lose our status as citizens."

I'd have liked to have argued, but I couldn't. "I'll drop him off for you and I'll make sure the press knows you delivered him."

"Thank you, Ms. Blake." He looked at Jean-Claude. "Again, my apologies; I was told that the two of you were no longer dating."

"We aren't dating," I said, a little too quickly.

He shrugged. "Of course." He looked back at Jean-Claude and gave a smile that said more than anything that they didn't quite like each other. He liked interrupting Jean-Claude's evening. They were two very different kinds of vampire and neither really approved completely of the other.

Malcolm stepped over the struggling, gagged form of the other vampire and went out the door with his deacons. None of them even looked back at the vampire chained on the floor.

There were a flock of waiters and waitresses in their skimpy uniforms, huddled in the doorway. "Take this vampire and load him in *ma petite*'s car."

He looked at me, and I got my keys out of the leather coat and tossed it to one of the vampires. One of the women picked the chained vamp off the floor and tossed him over her shoulder like he weighed nothing. They closed the door behind them without being told.

I picked my coat off the floor. "I have to go."

"Of course, you do." His voice held just a little bit of anger. "You have let your desire for me out and now you must cage it again, hide it away, be ashamed of it."

I started to be angry, but I looked at him sitting there, head down, hands limp in his lap, as dejected as I'd seen him in a while, and I wasn't angry. He was right, that was exactly how I treated him. I stayed where I was, the coat over one arm.

"I have to take him down to the police station and make sure the press gets the truth, not something that will make the vampires look worse than they already do in all this."

He nodded without looking up.

If he'd been his usual arrogant self I could have left him like that, but he was letting his pain show, and that I couldn't just walk away from. "Let's try an olive branch," I said.

He looked up at that, frowning. "Olive branch?"

"White flag?" I said.

He smiled then. "A truce." He laughed, and it danced over my skin, "I did not know we were at war."

That hit a little too close to home. "Are you going to let me say something nice, or not?"

"By all means, *ma petite*, far be it for me to interrupt your gentler urges."

"I am trying to ask you out on a date."

The smile widened, his eyes filling with such instant pleasure that it made me look away, because it made me want to smile back at him. "It must have been a very long time since you asked a man out; you seem to be out of practice."

I put on my coat. "Fine, be a smart alec. See where it gets you."

I was almost to the door when he said, "Not a war, *ma petite*, but a siege, and this poor soldier is feeling very left out in the cold."

I stopped and turned around. He was still sitting on the desk trying to look harmless, I think. He was many things: handsome, seductive, intelligent, cruel, but not harmless, not to body, mind, or soul.

"Tomorrow night, pick a restaurant." One of the side effects of being his human servant was that he could taste food through me. It was the first time he'd been able to taste food in centuries. It was a minor power to share but he adored it, and I adored watching him enjoying his first bite of steak in four hundred years.

"I will make reservations," he said, voice careful again, as if he were afraid I'd change my mind.

Looking at him, sitting on his desk all in red and black

and satin and leather, I didn't want to change my mind. I wanted to sit across the table from him. I wanted to drive him home and go inside and see what color of sheets he had on that big bed of his.

It wasn't just the sex; I wanted someone to hold me. I wanted some place safe, some place to be myself. And like it, or hate it, in Jean-Claude's arms I could be perfectly who and what I was. I could have called Richard up and he'd have been just as glad to hear from me, and there would have been as much heat, but Richard and I had some philosophical differences that went beyond him being a werewolf. Richard tried to be a good person, and he thought I killed too easily to be a good person. Jean-Claude had helped teach me the ultimate practicality that had kept me alive, helped me keep others alive. But the thought that Jean-Claude's arms were the closest thing I had to a refuge in this world was a sobering thought. Almost a depressing one.

He slid off the desk in one graceful movement as if his body were pulled by strings. He started to glide toward me, moving like some great cat. Just watching him walk toward me made my chest tight. He grabbed each side of the leather coat and drew me into the circle of his arms. "Would it be pushing the bounds of our truce too far to say, that it is hours until dawn?"

My voice came out breathy, "I have to take him to the police and deal with reporters, that will take hours."

"This time of year dawn comes very late." He whispered as he bent to lay his lips against mine.

We kissed, and I drew back enough to whisper, "I'll try to be back before dawn."

IT was four days before Christmas, an hour before dawn, when I knocked on Jean-Claude's bedroom door underneath the Circus of the Damned, one of his other clubs. His voice called, "Come in, *ma petite.*"

An hour. It wasn't much time, but time is what you make it. I had stopped by the grocery store on the way and picked up some ready-made chocolate icing in one of those flip-top canisters. He could taste the chocolate while I ate it, and if it just happened to be on him while I was eating it, well. . . . The silk sheets on his bed were white, and we laughed while we covered him in chocolate and stained the sheets. But when every inch of him that I wanted was covered in thick, sweet chocolate, the laughter stopped, and other noises began, noises even more precious to me than his laughter. Dawn caught us before he could take a bath and clean himself of the sticky sweetness. I left him in a pile of chocolate-smeared white silk sheets, his body still warm to the touch, but his heart no longer beating. Dawn had found him and stolen his life away, and lifeless he would remain for hours; then he would wake, and he would be "alive" again. He truly was a corpse. I knew that. But he had the sweetest skin I'd ever tasted, candy-covered or plain. He had no pulse, no breath, no movement, dead. It should have made a difference, and it did. I think the siege, as he called it, would have been over long ago if he'd been alive, or maybe not. Being a vampire was too large a part of who Jean-Claude was, for me to separate them out. It did make a difference, but I laid one last icing coated kiss on his forehead, and went home. We had a date tonight, and with the feel of his body still clinging to mine, I could hardly wait.

ONE WORD ANSWER

Charlaine Harris

BUBBA the Vampire and I were raking up clippings from my newly-trimmed bushes about midnight when the long black car pulled up. I'd been enjoying the gentle scent of the cut bushes and the songs of the crickets and frogs celebrating spring. Everything hushed with the arrival of the black limousine. Bubba vanished immediately, because he didn't recognize the car. Since he changed over to the vampire persuasion, Bubba's been on the shy side.

I leaned against my rake, trying to look nonchalant. In reality, I was far from relaxed. I live pretty far out in the country, and you have to want to be at my house to find the way. There's not a sign out at the parish road that points down my driveway reading "Stackhouse home." My home is not visible from the road, because the driveway meanders through some woods to arrive in the clearing where the core of the house has stood for a hundred and sixty years.

Visitors are not real frequent, and I didn't remember ever seeing a limousine before. No one got out of the long black car for a couple of minutes. I began to wonder if maybe I should have hidden myself, like Bubba. I had the outside lights on, of course, since I couldn't see in the dark like Bubba, but the limousine windows were heavily smoked. I was real tempted to whack the shiny bumper with my rake to find out what would happen. Fortunately, the door opened while I was still thinking about it.

A large gentleman emerged from the rear of the limousine. He was six feet tall, and he was made up of circles. The largest circle was his belly. The round head above it was almost bald, but a fringe of black hair circled it right above his ears. His little eyes were round, too, and black as the hair and his suit. His shirt was gleaming white, but his tie was black without a pattern. He looked like the director of a funeral home for the criminally insane.

"Not too many people do their yard work at midnight," he commented, in a surprisingly melodious voice. The true answer—that I liked to rake when I had someone to talk to, and I had company this night with Bubba, who couldn't come out in the sunlight—was better left unsaid. I just nodded. You couldn't argue with his statement.

"Would you be the woman known as Sookie Stackhouse?" asked the large gentleman. He said it as if he often addressed creatures that weren't men or women, but something else entirely.

"Yes, sir, I am," I said politely. My grandmother, God rest her soul, had raised me well. But she hadn't raised a fool; I wasn't about to invite him in. I wondered why the driver didn't get out.

"Then I have a legacy for you."

Legacy meant someone had died. I didn't have anyone left except for my brother Jason, and he was sitting down at Merlotte's Bar with his girlfriend Crystal. At least that's where he'd been when I'd gotten off my barmaid's job a couple of hours before.

The little night creatures were beginning to make their

sounds again, having decided the big night creatures weren't going to attack.

"A legacy from who?" I said. What makes me different from other people is that I'm telepathic. Vampires, whose minds are simply silent holes in a world made noisy to me by the cacophony of human brains, make restful companions for me, so I'd been enjoying Bubba's chatter. Now I needed to rev up my gift. This wasn't a casual drop-in. I opened my mind to my visitor. While the large, circular gentleman was wincing at my ungrammatical question, I was attempting to look inside his head. Instead of a stream of ideas and images (the usual human broadcast), his thoughts came to me in bursts of static. He was a supernatural creature of some sort.

"Whom," I corrected myself, and he smiled at me. His teeth were very sharp.

"Do you remember your cousin Hadley?"

Nothing could have surprised me more than this question. I leaned the rake against the mimosa tree and shook the plastic garbage bag that we'd already filled. I put the plastic band around the top before I spoke. I could only hope my voice wouldn't choke when I answered him. "Yes, I do." Though I sounded hoarse, my words were clear.

Hadley Delahoussaye, my only cousin, had vanished into the underworld of drugs and prostitution years before. I had her high school junior picture in my photo album. That was the last picture she'd had taken, because that year she'd run off to New Orleans to make her living by her wits and her body. My aunt Linda, her mother, had died of cancer during the second year after Hadley's departure.

"Is Hadley still alive?" I said, hardly able to get the words out.

"Alas, no," said the big man, absently polishing his black-framed glasses on a clean white handkerchief. His black shoes gleamed like mirrors. "Your cousin Hadley is dead,

I'm afraid." He seemed to relish saying it. He was a man—or whatever—who enjoyed the sound of his own voice.

Underneath the distrust and confusion I was feeling about this whole weird episode, I was aware of a sharp pang of grief. Hadley had been fun as a child, and we'd been together a lot, naturally. Since I'd been a weird kid, Hadley and my brother Jason had been the only children I'd had to play with for the most part. When Hadley hit puberty, the picture changed; but I had some good memories of my cousin.

"What happened to her?" I tried to keep my voice even, but I know it wasn't.

"She was involved in an Unfortunate Incident," he said.

That was the euphemism for a vampire killing. When it appeared in newspaper reports, it usually meant that some vampire had been unable to restrain his blood lust and had attacked a human. "A vampire killed her?" I was horrified.

"Ah, not exactly. Your cousin Hadley was the vampire. She got staked."

This was so much bad and startling news that I couldn't take it in. I held up a hand to indicate he shouldn't talk for a minute, while I absorbed what he'd said, bit by bit.

"What is your name, please?" I asked.

"Mr. Cataliades," he said. I repeated that to myself several times since it was a name I'd never encountered. Emphasis on the *tal*, I told myself. And a long *e*.

"Where might you hail from?"

"For many years, my home has been New Orleans."

New Orleans was at the other end of Louisiana from my little town, Bon Temps. Northern Louisiana is pretty darn different from southern Louisiana in several fundamental ways; it's the Bible Belt without the pizzazz of New Orleans, it's the older sister who stayed home and tended the farm while the younger sister went out partying. But it shares other things with the southern part of the state, too;

bad roads, corrupt politics, and a lot of people, both black and white, who live right on the poverty line.

"Who drove you?" I asked pointedly, looking at the front of the car.

"Waldo," called Mr. Cataliades, "the lady wants to see you."

I was sorry I'd expressed an interest after Waldo got out of the driver's seat of the limo and I'd had a look at him. Waldo was a vampire, as I'd already established in my own mind by identifying a typical vampire brain signature, which to me is like a photographic negative, one I "see" with my brain. Most vampires are good-looking or extremely talented in some way or another. Naturally, when a vamp brings a human over, the vamp's likely to pick a human who attracted him or her by beauty or some necessary skill. I didn't know who the heck had brought over Waldo, but I figured it was somebody crazy. Waldo had long, wispy white hair that was almost the same color as his skin. He was maybe five foot eight, but he looked taller because he was very thin. Waldo's eyes looked red under the light I'd had mounted on the electric pole. The vampire's face looked corpse-white with a faint greenish tinge, and his skin was wrinkled. I'd never seen a vampire who hadn't been taken in the prime of life.

"Waldo," I said, nodding. I felt lucky to have had such long training in keeping my face agreeable. "Can I get you anything? I think I have some bottled blood. And you, Mr. Cataliades? A beer? Some soda?"

The big man shuddered, and tried to cover it with a graceful half-bow. "Much too hot for coffee or alcohol for me, but perhaps we'll take refreshments later." It was maybe sixty-two degrees, but Mr. Cataliades was indeed sweating, I noticed. "May we come in?" he asked.

"I'm sorry," I said, without a bit of apology in my voice. "I think not." I was hoping that Bubba had had the sense to rush across the little valley between our properties to fetch my nearest neighbor, my former lover Bill Compton, known to the residents of Bon Temps as Vampire Bill.

"Then we'll conduct our business out here in your yard," Mr. Cataliades said coldly. He and Waldo came around the body of the limousine. I felt uneasy when it wasn't between us anymore, but they kept their distance. "Miss Stackhouse, you are your cousin's sole heir."

I understood what he said, but I was incredulous. "Not my brother Jason?" Jason and Hadley, both three years older than I, had been great buddies.

"No. In this document, Hadley says she called Jason Stackhouse once for help when she was very low on funds. He ignored her request, so she's ignoring him."

"When did Hadley get staked?" I was concentrating very hard on not getting any visuals. Since she was older than I by three years, Hadley had been a mere twenty-nine when she'd died. She'd been my physical opposite in most ways. I was robust and blond, she was thin and dark. I was strong, she was frail. She'd had big, thickly-lashed brown eyes, mine were blue; and now, this strange man was telling me, she had closed those eyes for good.

"A month ago." Mr. Cataliades had to think about it. "She died about a month ago."

"And you're just now letting me know?"

"Circumstances prevented."

I considered that.

"She died in New Orleans?"

"Yes. She was a handmaiden to the queen," he said, as though he were telling me she'd gotten her partnership at a big law firm, or managed to buy her own business.

"The queen of Louisiana," I said cautiously.

"I knew you would understand," he said, beaming at me. " 'This is a woman who knows her vampires,' I said to myself when I met you."

"She knows this vampire," Bill said, appearing at my side in that disconcerting way he had.

A flash of displeasure went across Mr. Cataliades's face like quick lightning across the sky.

"And you would be?" he asked with cold courtesy.

"I would be Bill Compton, resident of this parish and friend to Miss Stackhouse," Bill said ominously. "I'm also an employee of the queen, like you."

The queen had hired Bill so the computer database about vampires he was working on would be her property. Somehow, I thought Mr. Cataliades performed more personal services. He looked like he knew where all the bodies were buried, and Waldo looked like he had put them there.

Bubba was right behind Bill, and when he stepped out of Bill's shadow, for the first time I saw the vampire Waldo show an emotion. He was in awe.

"Oh my gracious! Is this El—" Mr. Cataliades blurted.

"Yes," said Bill. He shot the two strangers a significant glance. "This is *Bubba*. The past upsets him very much." He waited until the two had nodded in understanding. Then he looked down at me. His dark brown eyes looked black in the stark shadows cast by the overhead lights. His skin had the pale gleam that said *vampire*. "Sookie, what's happened?"

I gave him a condensed version of Mr. Cataliades's message. Since Bill and I had broken up when he was unfaithful to me, we'd been trying to establish some other workable relationship. He was proving to be a reliable friend, and I was grateful for his presence.

"Did the queen order Hadley's death?" Bill asked my visitors.

Mr. Cataliades gave a good impression of being shocked. "Oh, no!" he exclaimed. "Her Highness would never cause the death of someone she held so dear."

Okay, here came another shock. "Ah, what kind of dear . . . how dear did the queen hold my cousin?" I asked. I wanted to be sure I was interpreting the implication correctly.

Mr. Cataliades gave me an old-fashioned look. "She held Hadley dearly," he said.

Okay, I got it.

Every vampire territory had a king or queen, and with that title came power. But the queen of Louisiana had extra status, since she was seated in New Orleans, which was the most popular city in the United States if you were one of the undead. Since vampire tourism now accounted for so much of the city's revenue, even the humans of New Orleans listened to the queen's wants and wishes, in an unofficial way. "If Hadley was such a big favorite of the queen's, who'd be fool enough to stake her?" I asked.

"The Fellowship of the Sun," said Waldo, and I jumped. The vampire had been silent so long, I'd assumed he wasn't ever going to speak. The vampire's voice was as creaky and peculiar as his appearance. "Do you know the city well?"

I shook my head. I'd only been to the Big Easy once, on a school field trip.

"You are familiar, perhaps, with the cemeteries that are called the Cities of the Dead?"

I nodded. Bill said, "Yes," and Bubba muttered, "Uh-huh." Several cemeteries in New Orleans had above-ground crypts because the water table in southern Louisiana was too high to allow ordinary below-ground burials. The crypts look like small white houses, and they're decorated and carved in some cases, so these very old burial grounds are called the Cities of the Dead. The historic cemeteries are fascinating and sometimes dangerous. There are living predators to be feared in the Cities of the Dead, and tourists are cautioned to visit them in large guided parties, and to leave at the end of the day.

"Hadley and I had gone to St. Louis Number One that night, right after we rose, to conduct a ritual." Waldo's face looked quite expressionless. The thought that this man had been the chosen companion of my cousin, even if just for an evening's excursion, was simply astounding. "They leaped from behind the tombs around us. The Fellowship fanatics were armed with holy items, stakes, and garlic—the usual paraphernalia. They were stupid enough to have gold crosses."

The Fellowship refused to believe that all vampires could not be restrained by holy items, despite all the evidence. Holy items worked on the very old vampires, the ones who had been brought up to be devout believers. The newer vampires only suffered from crosses if they were silver. Silver would burn any vampire. Oh, a wooden cross might have an effect on a vamp—if it was driven through his heart.

"We fought valiantly, Hadley and I, but in the end, there were too many for us, and they killed Hadley. I escaped with some severe knife wounds." His paper-white face looked more regretful than tragic.

I tried not to think about Aunt Linda and what she would have had to say about her daughter becoming a vampire. Aunt Linda would have been even more shocked by the circumstances of Hadley's death: by assassination, in a famous cemetery reeking of Gothic atmosphere, in the company of this grotesque creature. Of course, all these exotic trappings wouldn't have devastated Aunt Linda as much as the stark fact of Hadley's murder.

I was more detached. I'd written Hadley off long ago. I'd never thought I would see her again, so I had a little spare emotional room to think of other things. I still wondered, painfully, why Hadley hadn't come home to see us. She might have been afraid, being a young vampire, that her blood lust would rise at an embarrassing time and she'd find herself yearning to suck on someone inappropriate. She might have been shocked by the change in her own nature; Bill had told me over and over that vampires were human no longer, that they were emotional about different things than humans. Their appetites and their need for secrecy had shaped the older vampires irrevocably.

But Hadley had never had to operate under those laws; she'd been made vampire after the Great Revelation, when vampires had revealed their presence to the world.

And the post-puberty Hadley, the one I was less fond of, wouldn't have been caught dead or alive with someone like Waldo. Hadley had been popular in high school, and she'd certainly been human enough then to fall prey to all the teenage stereotypes. She'd been mean to kids who weren't popular, or she'd just ignored them. Her life had been completely taken up by her clothes and her makeup and her own cute self.

She'd been a cheerleader, until she'd started adopting the Goth image.

"You said you two were in the cemetery to perform a ritual. What ritual?" I asked Waldo, just to gain some time to think. "Surely Hadley wasn't a witch as well." I'd run across a werewolf witch before, but never a vampire spellcaster.

"There are traditions among the vampires of New Orleans," Mr. Cataliades said carefully. "One of these traditions is that the blood of the dead can raise the dead, at least temporarily. For conversational purposes, you understand."

Mr. Cataliades certainly didn't have any throwaway lines. I had to think about every sentence that came out of his mouth. "Hadley wanted to talk to a dead person?" I asked, once I'd digested his latest bombshell.

"Yes," said Waldo, chipping in again. "She wanted to talk to Marie Laveau."

"The voodoo queen? Why?" You couldn't live in Louisiana and not know the legend of Marie Laveau, a woman whose magical power had fascinated both black and white people, at a time when black women had no power at all.

"Hadley thought she was related to her." Waldo seemed to be sneering.

Okay, now I knew he was making it up. "Duh! Marie Laveau was African-American, and my family is white," I pointed out.

"This would be through her father's side," Waldo said calmly.

Aunt Linda's husband, Carey Delahoussaye, had come from New Orleans, and he'd been of French descent. His family had been there for several generations. He'd bragged about it until my whole family had gotten sick of his pride. I wondered if Uncle Carey had realized that his Creole bloodline had been enriched by a little African-American DNA somewhere back in the day. I had only a child's memory of Uncle Carey, but I figured that piece of knowledge would have been his most closely guarded secret.

Hadley, on the other hand, would have thought being descended from the notorious Marie Laveau was really cool. I found myself giving Waldo a little more credence. Where Hadley would've gotten such information, I couldn't imagine. Of course, I also couldn't imagine her as a lover of women, but evidently that had been her choice. My cousin Hadley, the cheerleader, had become a vampire lesbian voodooienne. Who knew?

I felt glutted with information I hadn't had time to absorb, but I was anxious to hear the whole story. I gestured to the emaciated vampire to continue.

"We put the three X's on the tomb," Waldo said. "As people do. Voodoo devotees believe this ensures their wish will be granted. And then Hadley cut herself, and let the blood drip on the stone, and she called out the magic words."

"Abracadabra, please and thank you," I said automatically, and Waldo glared at me.

"You ought not to make fun," he said. With some notable exceptions, vampires are not known for their senses of humor, and Waldo was definitely a serious guy. His red-rimmed eyes glared at me.

"Is this really a tradition, Bill?" I asked. I no longer cared if the two men from New Orleans knew I didn't trust them.

"Yes," Bill said. "I haven't ever tried it myself, because I think the dead should be left alone. But I've seen it done."

"Does it work?" I was startled.

"Yes. Sometimes."

"Did it work for Hadley?" I asked Waldo.

The vampire glared at me. "No," he hissed. "Her intent was not pure enough."

"And these fanatics, they were just hiding among the tombs, waiting to jump out at you?"

"Yes," Waldo said. "I told you."

"And you, with your vampire hearing and smell, you didn't know there were people in the cemetery around you?" To my left, Bubba stirred. Even a vamp as dim as the too hastily recruited Bubba could see the sense of my question.

"Perhaps I knew there were people," Waldo said haughtily, "but those cemeteries are popular at night with criminals and whores. I didn't distinguish which people were making the noises."

"Waldo and Hadley were both favorites of the queen," Mr. Cataliades said admonishingly. His tone suggested that any favorite of the queen's was above reproach. But that wasn't what his words were saying. I looked at him thoughtfully. At the same moment, I felt Bill shift beside me. We hadn't been soul mates, I guess, since our relationship hadn't worked out, but at odd moments we seemed to think alike, and this was one of those moments. I wished I could read Bill's mind for once—though the great recommendation of Bill as a lover had been that I couldn't. Telepaths don't have an easy time of it when it comes to love affairs. In fact, Mr. Cataliades was the only one on the scene who had a brain I could scan, and he was none too human.

I thought about asking him what he was, but that seemed kind of tacky. Instead, I asked Bubba if he'd round up some folding yard chairs so we could all sit down, and while that was being arranged, I went in the house and heated up some TrueBlood for the three vampires and iced some Mountain Dew for Mr. Cataliades, who professed himself to be delighted with the offer.

While I was in the house, standing in front of the microwave and staring at it like it was some kind of oracle, I thought of just locking the door and letting them all do what they would. I had an ominous sense of the way the night was going, and I was tempted to let it take its course without me. But Hadley had been my cousin. On a whim, I took her picture down from the wall to give it a closer look.

All the pictures my grandmother had hung were still up; despite her death, I continued to think of the house as hers. The first picture was of Hadley at age six, with one front tooth. She was holding a big drawing of a dragon. I hung it back beside the picture of Hadley at ten, skinny and pigtailed, her arms around Jason and me. Next to it was the picture taken by the reporter for the parish paper, when Hadley had been crowed Miss Teen Bon Temps. At fifteen, she'd been radiantly happy in her rented white sequined gown, glittering crown on her head, flowers in her arms. The last picture had been taken during Hadley's junior year. By then, Hadley had begun using drugs, and she was all Goth: heavy eye makeup, black hair, crimson lips. Uncle Carey had left Aunt Linda some years before this incarnation, moved back to his proud New Orleans family; and by the time Hadley left, too, Aunt Linda had begun feeling bad. A few months after Hadley ran away, we'd finally gotten my father's sister to go to a doctor, and he'd found the cancer.

In the years since then, I'd often wondered if Hadley had ever found out her mother was sick. It made a difference to me; if she'd known but hadn't come home, that was a horse of one color. If she'd never known, that was a horse of a different one. Now that I knew she had crossed over and become the living dead, I had a new option. Maybe Hadley had known, but she just hadn't cared.

I wondered who had told Hadley she might be descended from Marie Laveau. It must have been someone who'd done enough research to sound convincing, someone who'd studied Hadley enough to know how much she'd enjoy the piquancy of being related to such a notorious woman.

I carried the drinks outside on a tray, and we all sat in a circle on my old lawn furniture. It was a bizarre gathering: the strange Mr. Cataliades, a telepath, and three vampires—though one of those was as addled as a vampire can be and still call himself undead.

When I was seated, Mr. Cataliades passed me a sheaf of papers, and I peered at them. The outside light was good enough for raking but not really good for reading. Bill's eyes were twenty times stronger than mine, so I passed the papers over to him.

"Your cousin left you some money and the contents of her apartment," Bill said. "You're her executor, too."

I shrugged. "Okay," I said. I knew Hadley couldn't have had much. Vampires are pretty good at amassing nest eggs, but Hadley could only have been a vampire for a very few years.

Mr. Cataliades raised his nearly invisible brows. "You don't seem excited."

"I'm a little more interested in how Hadley met her death."

Waldo looked offended. "I've described the circumstances to you. Do you want a blow-by-blow account of the fight? It was unpleasant, I assure you."

I looked at him for a few moments. "What happened to you?" I asked. This was very rude, to ask someone what on earth had made him so weird-looking, but common sense told me that there was more to learn. I had an obligation to my cousin, an obligation unaffected by any legacy she'd left me. Maybe this was why Hadley had left me something in her will. She knew I'd ask questions, and God love my brother, he wouldn't.

Rage flashed across Waldo's features, and then it was like he'd wiped his face with some kind of emotion eraser. The paper-white skin relaxed into calm lines and his eyes were calm. "When I was human, I was an albino," Waldo said stiffly, and I felt the knee-jerk horror of someone who's been unpardonably curious about a disability. Just as I was about to apologize, Mr. Cataliades intervened again.

"And, of course," the big man said smoothly, "he's been punished by the queen."

This time, Waldo didn't restrain his glare. "Yes," he said finally. "The queen immersed me in a tank for a few years."

"A tank of what?" I was all at sea.

"Saline solution," Bill said, very quietly. "I've heard of this punishment. That's why he's wrinkled, as you see."

Waldo pretended not to hear Bill's aside, but Bubba opened his mouth. "You're sure 'nuff wrinkled, man, but don't you worry. The chicks like a man who's different."

Bubba was a kind vampire and well-intentioned.

I tried to imagine being in a tank of seawater for years and years. Then I tried not to imagine it. I could only wonder what Waldo had done to merit such a punishment. "And you were a favorite?" I asked.

Waldo nodded, with a certain dignity. "I have that honor."

I hoped I'd never receive such an honor. "And Hadley was, too?"

Waldo's face remained placid, though a muscle twitched in his jaw. "For a time."

Mr. Cataliades said, "The queen was pleased with Hadley's enthusiasm and childlike ways. Hadley was only one of a series of favorites. Eventually, the queen's favor would have fallen on someone else, and Hadley would have had to carve out another place in the queen's entourage."

Waldo looked quite pleased at that and nodded. "That's the pattern."

I couldn't get why I was supposed to care, and Bill made a small movement that he instantly stilled. I caught it out of the corner of my eye, and I realized Bill didn't want me to speak. Pooh on him; I hadn't been going to, anyway.

Mr. Cataliades said, "Of course, your cousin was a little different from her predecessors. Wouldn't you say, Waldo?"

"No," Waldo said. "In time, it would have been just like before." He seemed to bite his lip to stop himself from talking; not a smart move for a vampire. A red drop of blood formed, sluggishly. "The queen would have tired of her. I know it. It was the girl's youth, it was the fact that she was one of the new vampires who has never known the shadows. Tell our queen that, Cataliades, when you return to New Orleans. If you hadn't kept the privacy glass up, the

whole trip, I could have discussed this with you as I drove.
You don't have to shun me, as though I were a leper."

Mr. Cataliades shrugged. "I didn't want your company,"
he said. "Now, we'll never know how long Hadley would
have reigned as favorite, will we, Waldo?"

We were on to something here, and we were being
goaded and prodded in that direction by Waldo's companion, Mr. Cataliades. I wondered why. For the moment,
I'd follow his lead. "Hadley was real pretty," I said.
"Maybe the queen would've given her a permanent position."

"Pretty girls glut the market," Waldo said. "Stupid humans. They don't know what our queen can do to them."

"If she wants to," Bill murmured. "If this Hadley had a
knack for delighting the queen, if she had Sookie's charm,
then she might have been happy and favored for many
years."

"And I guess you'd be out on your ass, Waldo," I said
prosaically. "So tell me, were there really fanatics in the
cemetery? Or just one skinny white wrinkled fanatic, jealous and desperate?"

Then, suddenly, we were all standing, all but Mr. Cataliades, who was reaching into the briefcase.

Before my eyes, Waldo turned into something even less
human. His fangs ran out and his eyes glowed red. He became even thinner, his body folding in on itself. Beside me,
Bill and Bubba changed, too. I didn't want to look at them
when they were angry. Seeing my friends change like that
was even worse than seeing my enemies do it. Full fighting
mode is just scary.

"You can't accuse a servant of the queen," Waldo said,
and he actually hissed.

Then Mr. Cataliades proved himself capable of some
surprises of his own, as if I'd doubted it. Moving quickly

and lightly, he rose from his lawn chair and tossed a silver lariat around the vampire's head, large enough in circumference to circle Waldo's shoulders. With a grace that startled me, he drew it tight at the critical moment, pinning Waldo's arms to his sides.

I thought Waldo would go berserk, but the vampire surprised me by holding still. "You'll die for this," Waldo said to the big round man, and Mr. Cataliades smiled at him.

"I think not," he said. "Here, Miss Stackhouse."

He tossed something in my direction, and quicker than I could watch, Bill's hand shot out to intercept it. We both stared at what Bill was holding in his hand. It was polished, sharp, and wooden; a hardwood stake.

"What's up with this?" I asked Mr. Cataliades, moving closer to the long black limo.

"My dear Miss Stackhouse, the queen wanted you to have the pleasure."

Waldo, who had been glaring with considerable defiance at everyone in the clearing, seemed to deflate when he heard what Mr. Cataliades had to say.

"She knows," the albino vampire said, and the only way I can describe his voice is *heartbroken*. I shivered. He loved his queen, really loved her.

"Yes," the big man said, almost gently. "She sent Valentine and Charity to the cemetery immediately, when you rushed in with your news. They found no traces of human attack on what was left of Hadley. Only your smell, Waldo"

"She sent me here with you," Waldo said, almost whispering.

"Our queen wanted Hadley's kin to have the right of execution," Mr. Cataliades said.

I came closer to Waldo, until I was as close as I could get. The silver had weakened the vampire, though I had a feeling that he wouldn't have struggled even if the chain hadn't been made of the metal that vampires can't tolerate. Some of the fire had gone out of Waldo, though his upper lip drew back from his fangs as I put the tip of the stake over his heart. I thought of Hadley, and I wondered, if she were in my shoes, could she do this?

"Can you drive the limo, Mr. Cataliades?" I asked.

"Yes, ma'am, I can."

"Could you drive yourself back to New Orleans?"

"That was always my plan."

I pressed down on the wood, until I could tell it was hurting him. His eyes were closed. I had staked a vampire before, but it had been to save my life and Bill's. Waldo was a pitiful thing. There was nothing romantic or dramatic about this vampire. He was simply vicious. I was sure he could do extreme damage when the situation called for it; and I was sure he had killed my cousin Hadley.

Bill said, "I'll do it for you, Sookie." His voice was smooth and cold, as always, and his hand on my arm was cool.

"I can help," Bubba offered. "You'd do it for me, Miss Sookie."

"Your cousin was a bitch and a whore," Waldo said, unexpectedly. I met his red eyes.

"I expect she was," I said. "I guess I just can't kill you." My hand, the one holding the stake, dropped to my side.

"You have to kill me," Waldo said, with the arrogance of surety. "The queen has sent me here to be killed."

"I'm just gonna have to ship you right back to the queen," I said. "I can't do it."

"Get your whoremonger to do it, he's more than willing."

Bill was looking more vampiric by the second, and he tugged the stake from my fingers.

"He's trying to commit suicide by cop, Bill," I said.

Bill looked puzzled, and so did Bubba. Mr. Cataliades's round face was unreadable.

"He's trying to make us mad enough, or scared enough, to kill him, because he can't kill himself," I said. "He's sure the queen will do something much, much worse to him than I would. And he's right."

"The queen was trying to give you the gift of vengeance," Mr. Cataliades said. "Won't you take it? She may not be happy with you if you send him back."

"That's really her problem," I said. "Isn't it?"

"I think it might be very much your problem," Bill said quietly.

"Well, that just bites," I said. "You . . ." I paused, and told myself not to be a fool. "You were very kind to bring Waldo down here, Mr. Cataliades, and you were very clever in steering me around to the truth." I took a deep breath and considered. "I appreciate your bringing down the legal papers, which I'll look over at a calmer moment." I thought I'd covered everything. "Now, if you'd be so good as to pop the trunk open, I'll ask Bill and Bubba to put him in there." I jerked my head toward the silver-bound vampire, standing in silence not a yard away.

At that moment, when we were all thinking of something else, Waldo threw himself at me, jaws open wide like a snake's, fangs fully extended. I threw myself backward, but I knew it wouldn't be enough. Those fangs would rip open my throat and I would bleed out here in my own yard. But Bubba and Bill were not bound with silver, and with a speed that was terrifying in itself, they gripped the old vampire and knocked him to the ground. Quicker than any human could wink, Bill's arm rose and fell, and Waldo's red eyes looked down at the stake in his chest with profound satisfaction. In the next second, those eyes caved in and his long thin body began the instant process of disintegration. You never have to bury a really dead vampire.

For a few long moments, we stayed frozen in the tableau; Mr. Cataliades was standing, I was on the ground on my butt, and Bubba and Bill were on their knees beside the thing that had been Waldo.

Then the limo door opened, and before Mr. Cataliades could scramble to help her out, the queen of Louisiana stepped out of the vehicle.

She was beautiful, of course, but not in a fairy-tale princess sort of way. I don't know what I expected, but she wasn't it. While Bill and Bubba scrambled to their feet and then bowed deeply, I gave her a good once-over. She was wearing a very expensive midnight-blue suit and high heels. Her hair was a rich reddish brown. Of course she was pale as milk, but her eyes were large, tilted, and almost the same brown as her hair. Her fingernails were polished red, and somehow that seemed very weird. She wore no jewelry.

Now I knew why Mr. Cataliades had kept the privacy glass up during the trip north. And I was sure that the queen had ways of masking her presence from Waldo's senses, as well as his sight.

"Hello," I said uncertainly. "I'm . . ."

"I know who you are," she said. She had a faint accent; I thought it might be French. "Bill. Bubba."

Oooh-kay. So much for polite chitchat. I huffed out a breath and shut my mouth. No point in talking until she explained her presence. Bill and Bubba stood upright. Bubba was smiling. Bill wasn't.

The queen examined me head to toe, in a way I thought was downright rude. Since she was a queen, she was an old vampire, and the oldest ones, the ones who sought power in the vampire infrastructure, were among the scariest. It had been so long since she'd been human that there might not be much remembrance of humanity left in her.

"I don't see what all the fuss is about," she said, shrugging.

My lips twitched. I just couldn't help it. My grin spread

across my face, and I tried to hide it with my hand. The queen eyed me quizzically.

"She smiles when she's nervous," Bill said.

I did, but that's not why I was smiling now.

"You were going to send Waldo back to me, for me to torture and kill," the queen said to me. Her face was quite blank. I couldn't tell if she approved or disapproved, thought I was clever or thought I was a fool.

"Yes," I said. The shortest answer was definitely the best.

"He forced your hand."

"Uh-huh."

"He was too frightened of me to risk returning to New Orleans with my friend Mr. Cataliades."

"Yes." I was getting good at one-word answers.

"I wonder if you engineered this whole thing."

"Yes" would not be the right answer, here. I maintained silence.

"I'll find out," she said, with absolute certainty. "We'll meet again, Sookie Stackhouse. I was fond of your cousin, but even she was foolish enough to go to a cemetery alone with her bitterest enemy. She counted too much on the power of my name alone to protect her."

"Did Waldo ever tell you if Marie Laveau actually rose?" I asked, too overwhelmed with curiosity to let the question go unanswered.

She was getting back in the car as I spoke, and she paused with one foot inside the limo and one foot in the yard. Anyone else would have looked awkward, but not the queen of Louisiana.

"Interesting," she said. "No, actually, he didn't. When you come to New Orleans, you and Bill can repeat the experiment."

I started to point out that unlike Hadley, I wasn't dead, but I had the sense to shut my mouth. She might have ordered me to become a vampire, and I was afraid, very afraid that then Bill and Bubba would have held me down and made me so. That was too awful to think about, so I smiled at her.

After the queen was all settled in the limo, Mr. Cataliades bowed to me. "It's been a pleasure, Miss Stackhouse. If you have any questions about your cousin's estate, call me at the number on my business card. It's clipped to the papers."

"Thanks," I said, not trusting myself to say more. Besides, one-word answers never hurt. Waldo was almost disintegrated. Bits of him would be in my yard for a while. Yuck. "Where's Waldo? All over my yard," I could say to anyone who asked.

The night had clearly been too much for me. The limo purred out of my yard. Bill put his hand to my cheek, but I didn't lean into it. I was grateful to him for coming, and I told him so.

"You shouldn't be in danger," he said. Bill had a habit of using a word that changed the meaning of his statements, made them something ambiguous and unsettling. His dark eyes were fathomless pools. I didn't think I would ever understand him.

"Did I do good, Miss Sookie?" Bubba asked.

"You did great, Bubba," I said. "You did the right thing without me even having to tell you."

"You knew all along she was in the limo," Bubba said. "Didn't you, Miss Sookie?"

Bill looked at me, startled. I didn't meet his eyes. "Yes, Bubba," I said gently. "I knew. Before Waldo got out, I listened with my other sense, and I found two blank spots in the limo." That could only mean two vampires. So I'd known Cataliades had had a companion in the back of the limousine.

"But you played it all out like she wasn't there." Bill couldn't seem to grasp this. Maybe he didn't think I'd learned anything since I'd met him. "Did you know ahead of time that Waldo would make a try for you?"

"I suspected he might. He didn't want to go back to her mercies."

"So." Bill caught my arms and looked down at me. "Were you trying to make sure he died all along, or were you trying to send him back to the queen?"

"Yes," I said.

One-word answers never hurt.

BITING IN PLAIN SIGHT

MaryJanice Davidson

For my son.

ACKNOWLEDGMENTS

Thanks to my editor, Cindy Hwang, for asking me. Thanks also to Laurell K. Hamilton, who so kindly shared a book signing (not to mention, two anthologies and counting!) with me. Thanks are also due to Patrice Michelle for a great title and, as always, thanks to my family for their support, blah–blah–blah, why are you reading this when you could be reading the story? Not that I mind. In fact, I appreciate it . . . I didn't think anyone read these things. So thanks. But seriously. You should check out the story.

AUTHOR'S NOTE

There is a town called Embarrass, Minnesota, but it's not as close to Babbitt Lake as I made it seem. However, vampires love the water and have been known to buy houseboats and even cruise ships.

Prologue

∗⊱⊰∗

THE town knew Sophie Tourneau was a creature of the night, but they were careful not to ask too many questions. Even the town gossips, who would rather speculate than eat, were careful to restrain themselves.

Embarrass, Minnesota, knew several things and, most important, knew there were some things best left unsaid. The town knew, for example, that Sophie Tourneau (called "Dr. Sophie" by everyone since time out of mind) had come to live among them sometime in the middle of the last century. Some of the old-timers were sure she had come in the spring of 1965; others swore up and down that she hadn't shown her pretty face until 1967.

They knew she lived in a houseboat down on Babbitt Lake, puttering to various islands on her days off, and her houseboat, *The Hymenoptera*, whatever the heck that meant, was often tied up on one of Babbitt's many sand beaches. They knew she carried a cell phone and would instantly return to land to tend to her work if called.

They knew she was short, about five feet, two inches

tall, and sweetly rounded in all the right places. They knew her hair was as black as blacktop and as straight as the path to hell, and that her eyes were a soft, velvety brown. They knew she was pale, and never had a tan, or even a sunburn, not even on the hottest nights. She didn't get sweaty on the hottest nights, either.

And they knew, argue about her year of coming until they were blue, that she had been among them for at least four decades, and had not aged a day in all that time. Dr. Sophie still looked twenty-five years old. Children who had been in kindergarten the year she came were now grown, with children, and in some cases grandchildren, of their own. They were covering their gray or letting it all hang out, while Dr. Sophie still got carded if she tried to buy wine in the Cities.

Oh, and the town knew one more thing . . . she was extraordinary with animals. In a farming community like Embarrass, that counted for a lot. There wasn't a dog with hay fever, a cow with mastitis, a cat with distemper, a horse with twins, that Dr. Sophie couldn't manage, couldn't gentle down and help.

Of course, she couldn't help *all* of them. But she helped a damn goodly number of them. They never bit her, never fought. The town knew if you took your kid's puppy to Dr. Sophie, you were likely to be able to put off the old "Scooter went to live on a farm with lots of other dogs" speech, often for years.

There were, of course, theories. Most of them were advanced by each generation's crop of little boys. There were the usual dares, but they fell flat when Dr. Sophie caught them sneaking up to her houseboat (she always caught them; the woman had eyes in the back of her head and the ears of a bobcat) and invited them aboard for cookies. The children always came back, and with stories no more fantastic than, "She served us chocolate chip."

But children did not disappear. Dr. Sophie was never spotted baying at the moon in the nude. She would come out at any time of the night, any night, to tend to an ailing animal, be it wild fox or prize bull. There were no cryptic messages left in blood, anywhere. If she didn't keep daylight hours, well, that's what they had Dr. Hayward for. If she didn't go to church, well, who could blame her? In Embarrass you had your choice: you could be a Presbyterian or a lapsed Presbyterian. Plenty of people—well, some people—didn't go to church. And if she wasn't a regular goer, she always contributed to the fund-raisers or made baked goods when the occasion called for it.

Of course, there was something wrong about Dr. Sophie. No question. A beautiful, exotic woman who, even after all this time retained a slight French accent, a beautiful woman who did not age, who picked some tinpot little town to live in . . . or hide in. That was wrong. *She* was wrong. But nobody asked questions. Nobody showed up with pitchforks. She was the best veterinarian in the tristate area; maybe even the country. Wrong or not, vampire or witch or gypsy queen or whatever she was, nobody wanted her to leave.

One person in particular.

1

❖

"DR. Sophie?" An urgent rap on the screen door of her houseboat. She recognized the voice. Thomas "Don't-call-me-Tommy" Carlson, the mechanic's son. "Dr. Sophie, can I come in?"

"Come on in, Thomas." She was checking her bag, having a good idea what the problem was. "Is Misty having trouble?"

In the manner of eight-year-old boys, Thomas slammed the screen door aside and jumped into the boat before it could rebound closed. The sound was not unlike rocks rolling across a parking lot. "She can't get started, doc. She tries and tries, and she's licking herself, like, all the time down there, yuck! But the kittens won't come."

"We'd better go give her a hand, then," Sophie replied. "Lead the way."

She followed the boy silently; the mechanic's family lived on an old farm just down the road; it was a brisk ten-minute walk. She wondered idly why he hadn't called her cell phone and saved himself a trip, then she remembered the indefatigable energy of children. She hadn't realized how lost in thought she was until the child spoke again. "You're missing Ed, are'ncha?"

"I—yes."

"Well, he was old," Thomas said in a tone that was both heartless and comforting.

"You," Sophie said, smiling. "You think you'll be eight forever."

The truth was, she missed Ed dreadfully. She had known him since she was a child in Paris, and after she had been turned, he had come with her to America. She had bought him, a former banker trapped in the city his entire life, the home of his dreams; an enormous farm and all the livestock he could play with. In return, he had let her feed whenever she wished. Theirs was a comfortable relationship, one based on mutual need and friendship. She supposed he had been her sheep, but she despised that vampiric term. It denoted a relationship that was not equal, when, in fact, Ed called the shots. If anything, she had been *his* sheep.

But she had been foolish to overlook the inevitable . . . that he would age and, someday, die. She had assumed her friend would be eternal, like her.

And now, she missed him dreadfully.

At the end, though she had begged, he had refused to let her turn him. "Yeah," he'd croaked derisively, "this country needs an eighty-six-year-old vampire like I need another plate in my head. You think I want arthritis in my knees for all eternity? Don't you touch me, young lady. You're not too big to spank." His raspy voice had softened as he looked into her dark eyes, took in her unlined face. He went on in French, their mother tongue. "You would not be doing it for me, anyway, yes? You're just afraid to be alone. As old as you are, it's time to learn. So don't touch me. Let me go, Sophie."

So she had acceded to his wish, and oh how bitter it was to watch him die, to see him buried in the cold earth. Worse than the steadily rising hunger was an even more basic need: she missed her friend.

Thomas, she noticed, was looking at her sideways. "Some of the guys were wondering."

"Some of the guys are always wondering."

"Yeah, but. Now that Ed's dead. You know, we . . . they . . . were wondering if you were staying."

"This is my home now," she replied quietly. "It's been my home for . . . for a long time."

"Yeah, that's what we think, too," the child replied comfortably. "My dad says he was a kid when . . . I mean, we're glad you're staying."

She glanced at the back of Thomas's neck, tan and healthy and as wide as two pork loins placed side by side. Then she jerked her gaze elsewhere. That was no way to be thinking. She would not throw away everything she had made. . . . The town was curious, but a third-grader was out in the dark with her, and no one would question it, question him. Ed would be furious if she put that in jeopardy, and he would be right.

But she was a realist, and Ed's death had presented special problems.

She sighed. She was old enough so it wasn't a matter of urgency . . . yet. Meanwhile, there was Thomas's cat. The work, the animals, the country, the people, those were always there, and worth staying for.

2

❖

LIAM Thompson looked out his window and saw Sophie and the mechanic's kid hurry by on the dirt road just outside his farm. Kid's preggo cat must be having a hard time. Or the dog ate something out of the trash again.

Well, all right. That meant she'd probably go back to the office after she fixed whatever pet was sick. Sophie kept late hours, to put it mildly.

Liam looked around, but all the house cats were annoyingly healthy. So was his dog, Gladiator. The blue-eyed pup looked up at him as Liam prowled the house searching for sickness, his long tail making muted thumps on the hardwood floor.

"Well, shit," Liam said in his deep radio announcer's voice (not that he talked on the radio, but everyone in town told him he could). He went outside and checked the barn. No, all the barn cats looked perky, too, dammit. Cripes, how hard was it to get a sick cat when a guy needed one?

What was that?! One of the barn cats sneezed. Excellent! Could be a cold. Or pneumonia. Or cat flu. Or rabies.

He scooped up the startled animal and hurried out of the barn.

WHEN Sophie returned to her office, she wasn't surprised to see Liam Thompson waiting for her with what appeared to be a perfectly healthy cat. The cat's ears were back and she looked resigned, as did all Liam's pets when dragged to her examining room.

"What is it, Liam?" she asked, smiling. "Distemper? Swine flu? Mad cat disease?"

"She's been sneezing and sneezing," Liam told her. He was a fine-looking man, about six feet tall, with prematurely gray hair cut to Army regulation shortness and eyes the exact color of the faded blue jeans he wore. He appeared to have laugh lines, except no one in town could recall hearing him laugh, and his mouth was firm, his nose long and straight. His tan work shirt was rolled to the elbows, and, as always, he gave off the delightful scent of cotton and soap. She vastly enjoyed his company, even though he wasn't much of a talker. That was all right. Neither was she.

"Well, bring her in," Sophie said. "Let's take a look." It would be, she knew, a rather large waste of her time. Liam's pets were hardly ever sick; she suspected he was a hypochondriac on their behalf. Still, it warmed her to see a man so concerned about animals. The few times one of his cats had been genuinely ill, she had caught it in plenty of time. The only thing Liam Thompson's cats ever died of was old age.

"So . . ." Liam said.

"Yes," Sophie replied. She quickly examined the cat, a pretty little mouse-colored shorthair, *felis domestica*, and found her to be in sound health, if . . .

"Well, you're going to have kittens again."

"Great," he said. "I guess you'll be around when her time comes, then."

"I guess I will." Liam always insisted she attend when his cats birthed. It wasn't necessary, because one of the many things a cat could do well was have kittens, but he seemed to appreciate her presence. He always paid his bills promptly, too. He even paid them in person; he did not trust the mail.

"You know the drill," she said. "I guess I will see you in about thirty days."

"Yeah," he replied, and scooped up the cat, and left.

"Good night," she called after him, and he waved a blocky hand back in reply.

HE had to lean against the door of his truck for a minute before putting the cat inside and climbing in. God! God! God! She got prettier every time he saw her. Well, that wasn't true; she looked exactly the same every time he saw her. Which was utterly, totally, completely beautiful.

Those velvety brown eyes! Those soft, red lips! Even the way she talked charmed the shit out of him. "You know zee drill." And the way she said his name: "LEE-um." Well, okay, everybody pronounced it like that, but Sophie gave it a special accented spin. He had been waiting twenty years—since he had become a legal adult—to declare his intentions, but he was as tongue-tied around her at thirty-eight as he had been when he was fifteen.

The thirty days stretched ahead of him like an endless tunnel.

He started the pickup and smiled down at the cat, which was busily grooming herself. "Good work," he told her. "Thanks for getting knocked up."

The cat, naturally, ignored him.

3

THIRTY DAYS LATER . . .

"THAT makes four," Sophie said. "And now I think she's done." Smiling, she looked down at the blind, squealing creatures. They were various shades of white, gray, and brown, all pink noses and gaping maws and wee claws, clambering all over each other in search of food. "And your cat . . . er . . . ?"

"Fred."

Sophie didn't miss a beat. Liam gave all his cats odd, thought-up-at-the-last-second names. "Fred seems fine. Call me, of course, if she seems to have any trouble."

"Yeah." Liam took a deep breath. "Would you . . . d'you want to come into the house? For something to drink?"

Sophie nearly winced. Although the blood and various mess of Fred's birthing hadn't tempted her, the way the pulse was beating quickly at Liam's throat—almost as if he were nervous—did. She had to, *had* to find a solution to this problem. Driving down to the Cities and preying on various muggers and panhandlers simply would not do. For one thing, her car couldn't take the extra mileage. She knew she should have bought a Ford.

"I guess you don't," Liam said, incorrectly reading her long silence.

"Oh. Oh! No, I would like to have a drink. Very much." Very, very, very, very, very much. "Please, lead the way."

She followed him inside the neatly kept farmhouse and stood admiring the large kitchen, done in blue and white, and smelling like bread. It reminded her of some of the country houses back home. Liam wasn't a farmer, though he lived on a farm. He had inherited the place, along with quite a bit of money, from his father, who had invented pocket calendars.

"Lemmee see," Liam said, bending into the open refrigerator. "I've got milk . . . two percent, whole, and skim. Diet Coke. Regular Pepsi. Lemonade. Cherry Kool-Aid. Ginger ale. Orange juice. Grape juice. Oh, and I can make chocolate milk," he added, straightening and showing her the bottle of Hershey's syrup. "If you want."

Her eyebrows arched in surprise . . . she'd expected water, or maybe a beer. He saw her expression and said, "I know you like to drink."

He had no idea, the silly man. But she had to smile. She supposed if a person only accepted drinks, and never food, over a period of four decades, a reputation was built. "I would love some orange juice," she said. "Low pulp, yes?"

"Yeah."

While he busied himself getting glasses, she wandered around the kitchen, finally thumbing the ON button for the small television in the corner. She supposed it was rude, but the heavy silence in the kitchen was beginning to make her nervous. The local news had just started. That would give them something to talk about, thank goodness. "I

wonder if we'll find out when there'll be an end to this vile
cold snap," she mused aloud.

"So, um, you going to the meeting next week?"

"No," she replied, scratching his husky, Gladiator, between the ears. Gladiator was a less-than-admirable guard
dog, getting up briefly to smell her skirt when she entered,
then flopping down on the rug with a groan and going back
to sleep. "I must work." In truth, the meeting was being
held at the church. So, naturally, she couldn't attend. Too
bad. She had plenty to say on the issue of tearing down the
schoolhouse that had been on the edge of town for over a
hundred years. So there were some rats? The thing was a
historical monument! Americans. They only wanted what
was new.

"Oh. That's too bad. Because I thought that we . . .
um . . . I . . . you know, the meeting . . . if you needed a
ride or whatever. . . . Here's your juice."

She took the glass and sipped, and smiled at him. He
didn't smile back, merely gulped his own juice thirstily.

He *was* nervous. She couldn't imagine why. She'd
known him almost his entire life. He'd grown into a fine
man, too. Tall . . . strong . . . responsible . . . if he was
teased about being the quietest man in the state, what did
she care? He was a good man. He took excellent care of his
pets. As she got older, she realized the simple things really
were the most important.

"It was kind of you to invite me inside," she said. And it
was. Although she had been accepted by the townspeople
years ago, she rarely received social invitations of any
kind. She was sure that, deep down, the population of Embarrass, Minnesota, knew exactly what she was.

Accepting a vampire on her own terms and allowing her
to take care of the pets and livestock was one thing. Invit-
ing a creature of the night into your own home where you

lived and slept and were vulnerable all the time was something else.

"I've, uh, been wanting . . . I mean, it's no big deal. You know, since you came out. To take care of Fred and all. It's, you know, the least I could do." He stared longingly at the bottle of vodka perched on top of the refrigerator. She wanted to suggest he pour himself a stiff shot, but felt that would be inappropriate.

". . . the fourth such suicide in five months," the announcer said, and she jerked her head around. "Officials maintain that the deaths were self-inflicted, but the parents of the girls, particularly the latest victim, are not so sure."

Cut to a bereaved father, his eyes rimmed in red, wearing a yellow shirt that was jarringly bright for the circumstances. "Shawna would never have done something like that," he said hoarsely. "She was so happy. She was staring at the U of M next month. Friends . . . she had friends. She was popular, really popular. And . . . and she even had a new boyfriend. She never would have killed herself."

Cut back to the news announcer, who had been so heavily BOTOXed it was difficult for her to maintain the expression of vague sympathy. "Regardless, tonight in Babbitt, Minnesota, a town mourns."

Sophie set her empty glass down so hard, it broke on the table. Liam jumped, and Gladiator woke up. "I have to go," she said abruptly. "Thank you for the juice. I must . . ." She fumbled in her bag for her cell phone, and quickly punched in Dr. Hayward's number.

"What's the matter?" Liam asked, staring at the broken glass. "Are you okay?"

"I'm—yes, Matt? It's Sophie. I'm sorry to bother you this late, but I must leave . . . yes, right now. Tonight . . . yes. It's a . . . family matter . . . don't laugh, I'm quite serious. Yes . . . yes, if you please . . . no, I have no idea. I beg your pardon . . . yes, I appreciate that, Matt. Good night."

She punched the OFF button and dropped it in her purse, and turned to go. To her surprise, Liam's hand closed over her arm, just above the elbow. "What's going on?"

Despite her alarm, she was surprised; she couldn't recall him ever touching her. She gestured vaguely toward the television. "It's something I must look into. And . . . I have to find someone. It's nothing for you to—"

"Is it a vampire thing?"

She nearly fell down. It was one thing to instinctively understand the townspeople knew what she was and tolerated it. And another thing to discuss it obliquely with a child, such as Tommy. But for someone to come right out and ask her . . . she was so surprised she answered him. "Yes, it's a vampire thing. In fact, I believe a vampire is killing those girls."

"So, you're gonna stop it?"

"Well, I'm going to try. And really, I must go. I—"

"Well . . ." he said, letting go of her arm and walking over to a kitchen chair and picking up his denim jacket— even though it was August, it was quite chilly in the evenings. "I'll go with you."

"Really, Liam, you—"

"I guess I should be more, you know, specific," he said slowly, in his careful way. "I guess that sounded like a question. Like, can I go with you? But it wasn't. I'm going with you. Besides," he added reasonably, "you're gonna need someone who can look after you during the daytime."

She was so amazed by this turn of events, she let him escort her out to the truck.

4
⁜

THEY had each agreed to pack a bag and meet back at Liam's farm in half an hour. Sophie raced to her houseboat, packed quickly but carefully; she would, in all probability, be meeting her sovereign the next evening and must be dressed appropriately. Then she called Tommy to make sure he would feed her parakeets and clean the cage while she was gone. Finally, she hurried back to Liam's place . . . and skidded to a stop on the gravel driveway, amazed.

He had put a brand-new topper on the back of his red truck and was just now finishing spray-painting the windows black. She stepped around to the back and, careful not to get wet paint on her fingers, pulled the window up. There was a fully inflated air mattress lying the length of the truck bed, piled high with comfortable quilts and pillows.

She heard Liam coming around the side and turned just as he reached her. He jumped a little—most people were surprised at how good her hearing was—and said, "In case we need to move during the day. I can drive and you can sleep."

She chewed on that one for a minute, and finally said, "You seem . . . well-prepared."

"Well," he said shyly, "I'd always hoped I'd get to drive you around sometime. I just wanted to be ready."

He was so big, and his voice was so soft, it was hard to process the change. Weirdly, he looked more cheerful than she had ever seen him. All because he was driving into the dark unknown . . . with her? She wrinkled her forehead as she tried to process this, and he laughed. "I'm confused," she admitted.

"Aw, but you sure look cute when you're trying to figure somethin' out." He tossed the now-empty paint can into the garbage, then walked around to the front door. "Let's go, Sophie. You can tell me what's going on during the drive."

"What if I don't tell you anything?" she countered, clambering up into the passenger's seat—dratted thing needed a step ladder! "What if I keep it all a deep dark secret?"

He shrugged and started the truck. "Then we'll have a nice drive."

"Touché," she muttered.

"So . . . you know I'm a vampire."

"Yup."

"You've always known."

"Mm—hmm."

"You and everybody else."

He looked over at her, surprised. "Well, I can't vouch for what *everybody* knows and doesn't know. I remember my daddy telling me you were good with animals and we should be nice to you so you didn't leave. That was when I was just a kid m'self." He chuckled. "Boy, you were the prettiest thing I ever saw."

She blushed. Tried to, anyway. Blood didn't rush anywhere in her body anymore. "That's very sweet."

"My point is, nobody ever out and out said, 'Dr. Sophie's a vampire.' But nobody ever got out the cross and pitchforks, either."

"Thank goodness! She turned, putting her arm across the back of the seat, the better to face his profile. "Weren't you afraid?"

"Heck, no!" He looked surprised. "Just afraid you'd leave. We all knew you didn't . . . I mean, that you hadn't come from Embarrass. Or even Minnesota. Or even America. We were afraid you'd go back. To where you came from, you know? In . . . how many years? In all that time, you never once griped about late nights or house calls. Didn't mind working holidays. Truth was, we were scared to let you go."

"That's so . . . sweet." So they liked her for her work ethic, eh? Well, what did she expect?

"Bunch of outsiders came to build a Catholic church up here," he mused. "Course, Reverend Reed put a stop to that right quick. We didn't know if you could stay, if—"

"So you are telling me, in this entire town, no one, no one at all, had a problem with the resident veterinarian being a vampire?" Too good to be true! There had to be a . . . what was the colloquialism? A trap? No. A catch.

"Well, sure." He glanced at her, then back at the road. "The ones who had a problem moved away."

"Oh." She sat back, feeling foolish. Of course, several families had moved away in the last forty years. But when no one came down to her houseboat with a teapot full of holy water, she had put it out of her mind. And her dear friend Ed had always kept his ear to the ground. He would have warned her if the town's mood had turned ugly. "Yes, I can see that."

"So, there you go," he said comfortably.

"There I go," she parroted. "Do *you* know where we're going?"

"I expect we're heading down to Tyler Falls."

She blinked. "Yes. That's right. I must know. How did—"

"That news story, the one that got your panties in a bunch. Gal who killed herself was from Tyler Falls."

"They aren't killing themselves," she snapped.

"All right, keep your shirt on. What, you guess another vampire is doing it?"

"Liam, has anyone ever told you, you're extremely astute?"

He shrugged.

"Well, you're right. It's not the girls. What I think is, a vampire is making them fall in love, then he no doubt breaks up with them in some brutal fashion, then enjoys their torment and their eventual deaths. Remember, how the girl's father told the news she had a new boyfriend? I'm willing to bet they *all* had new boyfriends. Bastard," she added in a mutter.

"So, they *are* killing themselves."

"But they wouldn't have, if not for *him*. Bastard," she said again.

"So, we find him. And stop his clock."

"One thing at a time. First we talk to the girls' fathers. I'm suspicious, but I would like to talk to at least one of the family members. Then we tell the queen what we know."

"Okay." Pause. "The queen?"

"Oh, you won't be there," she assured him. "You can just drop me off when we get to Minneapolis."

"Hell with *that*," he said.

"Liam . . ."

"Nope."

She didn't reply, but figured that could be dealt with when the time came.

5

❧

"No," the woman in the bathrobe said. She was probably in her late forties, but looked like she was on this side of sixty. Poor thing, Liam thought. Losin' her kid, and now strangers knocking on her door in the middle of the night. "I told you. No more reporters."

She started to swing the door closed, but quick as thought, Sophie brought her arm up and stopped her, her palm slamming into the glass pane so hard, Liam was afraid it would break. "I beg your pardon," she said in her gorgeous accent, "but we do insist. We will not take up much of your time." She smiled big—Liam almost got dizzy, she smiled so big—and looked dead into the woman's eyes. "And a mother knows things, yes? A mother *always* knows things."

As if in a trance, the woman stepped back, leaving the door open. Sophie walked right in, bold as you'd want, and Liam followed her. He noticed that though the woman was staring at Sophie with a rapt expression, she kept her hands up on the neckline of her powder blue robe. Keeping it closed. Hum.

"It's so good of you to see us," Sophie said sweetly, soothingly. "And we won't be a minute. Where is your husband?"

"Asleep. He took three Ambiens and he sleeps all the time."

"Of course. And soon you will be sleeping as well. We just want to hear about Shawna's boyfriend."

"No good," Shawna's mother said, shaking her auburn head, which was probably neat and pretty most times, but tonight it looked like a dirty mop. "He was no good."

"Because he was never around, correct?"

"Yuh."

"You asked and asked to meet him. Told her to invite him to dinner many times."

"He never came."

"That's right, he never ever did, and you never saw him during the day, did you?"

"He was in school," Sophie's mother said, fiddling with the neckline of her robe. Liam had the impression she was trying to break Sophie's gaze, but couldn't quite do it. "He was busy. She understood. But not me. If he really cared for her, he would have met us. He would . . ." She sighed, a dreadful, lost sound.

Liam's heart was almost breaking, listening to that. To distract himself, he looked around the small ranch house. Pictures of Shawna all over the place. He jerked his gaze elsewhere, finally settling on Sophie, who was holding the mother's hands with both of her small ones. Her dark eyes were intent and sad at the same time.

He couldn't believe the night's events so far, and felt ashamed that he was so happy in the middle of so much shit and sorrow. He'd finally screwed up his courage . . . and now they were after a bad guy together. She'd let him come along; shit, she was letting him *drive* her. He was afraid he'd wake up any minute. It was awful being in the dead girl's house, but it would have been more awful to watch Sophie leave.

"Then he quit calling, yes?" Sophie was still pulling information out of the dead girl's mom, as carefully and gently as he'd get a kitten out of the lilac bushes behind his place. "And she couldn't find him? To talk to him, find out what was wrong?"

"It was worse than that. He said she was a child, a little girl. He said he needed a woman. A grown-up woman. He said he hadn't liked her for a while, he was just . . ." Another dreadful sigh. "Playing."

"And Shawna couldn't take that, yes? She tried to hide it from you, but . . ."

"A mother always knows. Her dad thought . . . you know, high school stuff . . ."

"That she would get over it."

"But she couldn't. He was everything. He was . . ." Shawna's mother's fingers were fiddling faster. "Her dark sweetheart. Her everything. He was going to be a doctor. He was pre med. That's how they met. And . . ."

"And she waited until you were gone," Sophie prompted gently.

"And then we came home . . . and she had . . . but I think he came back. I think he came back and hurt her by saying more bad things to her. Hurt her until she did that. Hurt her until he got what he wanted."

"As a matter of fact," Sophie said, "so do I. And there's just one more thing . . . where is this awful creature staying? Did Shawna tell you?"

"He's at the B and B. How many college students do you know who stay at a B and B? He was no good."

"I agree totally. Madam, you will not remember this conversation."

"No," she agreed, "I won't remember it."

"And you'll go to your bed, and find solace with your darling husband. And you'll sleep and sleep."

"I'll sleep and sleep," she agreed, "for the first time since Shawna left."

"Yes. And tomorrow, you will still grieve, but you will start to imagine that perhaps someday, there will be something to live for again. It won't seem like a far-off impossibility."

"Someday there might be something to live for. Lots of kids need good homes." Then she added doubtfully, "But I doubt it. Shawna's death is too big. It takes over everything."

"Yes, but not forever. Go to bed, now, madam." Sophie stood on her toes and kissed the older woman on the cheek. "Shawna sees you."

The woman turned around without another word and shuffled toward the back of the house.

Sophie burst into tears, startling Liam. He put a clumsy arm around her and she leaned against him. She smelled like sweet, fresh straw. "Oh, the poor thing," she wept. "Did you see the pictures? Their only girl, dead. And for what?"

"I guess," he said slowly, "for a mean trick."

Sophie stopped crying at once—though there had been no tears, just a kind of hoarse sobbing—and her eyes took on a hard shine he had never seen before. It was dumb, but he almost felt like taking a step back from her. "That's right, Liam. That's just right. A mean trick. And we're going to stop his clock. We're going to gut him like a trout and take his head and bury it with the garlic bulbs. That's what we're going to do."

"All right," he replied. "Sounds like a good deal. But I gotta gas up the truck first."

She smiled at that, as he had meant for her to do. "Fair enough. Let's leave this place. Can we be in Minneapolis before dawn?"

"You bet."

She tucked her small hand into his and followed him back to the truck.

6

"I'M sorry," the reservations clerk at the Radisson told them. "The only rooms we have left have a king-sized bed in them. Non-smoking," he added helpfully.

"That will be fine," Sophie replied. Liam was his usual expressionless self, but she assumed he wouldn't mind, either. In fact, the thought of sharing a bed with him caused a pleasant tingle low in her stomach, usually the sort of tingle caused by strolling through a blood bank. If Liam *did* mind, she could always sleep under the bed. Or in the closet. "Do you take American Express?"

When the clerk, a short man with a freckled, egg-shaped, shaved head, turned away to run the card, Liam muttered, "You got a credit card?"

"You know all those 'Cardholder for ten years,' 'Cardholder for twenty years' ads?" she whispered back.

"Don't even tell me."

"Well, I've had one for a long time."

He snickered and, when the clerk came back, said, "Can we get a window facing west?"

The clerk blinked. "Oh, sure."

"Got to take care of my skin," Liam said, totally straight-faced. Sophie almost laughed; Liam looked like a farmer, which was to say he was deeply tanned, with wrinkles around his eyes and hands like leather blocks. He was the SPF association's nightmare.

"Oh, really," Sophie said, rolling her eyes a minute later when they were in the elevator.

"Well, didn't think it was too good to tell him the truth."

"Hotel employees have heard it all. He likely wouldn't have batted an eye."

Liam grunted and glanced down at the key card, which looked almost tiny in his large, capable hand. "We'll draw the drapes, should do the trick, yeah?"

"Yes."

"Or you can sleep with your whole self under the covers."

She almost laughed at the mental image of her deeply unconscious self swaddled in covers deep in the middle of a king-sized hotel bed. "I think closing the curtains will be fine." She followed him out of the elevator and down the hall. "But you don't . . . ah . . . I needn't . . . I don't have to sleep in the bed. With you."

He looked over his shoulder at her, surprised. "Well, where the hell you supposed to sleep? The tub?"

"I was only suggesting—you've been so kind—I do not wish to make you ill at ease."

"The clams we had will do that all by themselves."

She couldn't resist a small scold. "Well, Liam, it was a restaurant that specialized in chicken. What were you thinking?"

"That I like clams," he said cheerfully, opening their door. "Tough to get in northern Minnesota."

"There's a reason," she retorted, sidling past him. It was a standard hotel room, clean but not exceptional. She eyed the king-sized bed a little nervously . . . it had been a long, *long* time. "Do you wish to have something else? Shall I call room service?"

"Naw, naw. Listen, Sophie . . ." He sat down on the end of the bed and pulled his boots off, sighing and wiggling his toes in clean white socks. "How come you paid for the room? I mean, why didn't you use your, I dunno, your evil vampire powers and just hypnotize him or whatever?"

"But why? I have money." In fact, quite a bit of it, courtesy of her late great-great-grandfather. Sophie had been lucky enough to sell the vineyard before the blight that took more than half the grapes. But that was a long time ago. She forced herself back to the present, to Liam and the hotel room. "And why get the clerk in trouble? He would have to explain why he let someone stay for free. I don't mind paying."

"Oh. Uh-huh. Well, not that I'm sayin' you should have done it, I was just curious. If I could zap people like you do, I probably wouldn't pay for a damn thing." He paused for a minute, then chuckled. "And I love the way you talk. 'Why get zee clerk in trouble.' Heh. Didja know, when you get nervous, you don't use contractions?"

"Thank you. I did not know that." She cleared her throat, a harsh bark; she never had enough saliva to pull it off. "Ah. I need to go out for a bit. But if you change your mind about room service, please feel free to order whatever you wish. I should return shortly."

"Whoa, whoa." Quick as a flash, he was off the bed and gently grasping her wrist. "Where you off to? What's the matter?"

"I . . . uh . . . I need to . . . well, you've had your meal, and now I must—"

"Oh. Right!" He was silent for a moment, and she started prying his fingers off her arm, careful not to hurt him. She'd been doing this too long to be embarrassed, nor did she want to have a long discussion about it. She was what she was and there was no use talking about it. "Well, shoot, I'm right here. Why not me?"

She stopped in mid-pry, shocked. "Really? You'd do that? But . . . why in the world?"

"You're a good girl, Sophie," he said gruffly. "I'm not worried. And I don't think you should be wandering around Minneapolis by your lonesome."

"Liam . . . I don't want to hurt your feelings, because I'm incredibly flattered. You have no idea what a gift you've offered me—"

"I guess I do," he corrected her. "It's my blood, y'know."

She nodded and continued. "But I just don't think it's appropriate. . . . We live in the same town, but we don't really know each other. And you'll feel . . . when . . . *if* . . . I feed on you, it will be very . . . sexual. And I would never want to push you . . . in that way. My friend Ed—"

"—was a lucky man, that's what *I* think." He took her in his arms, carefully, as if she might crack like a china dish. "And the only way you could hurt me is if you sent me away and picked some stranger." Then he kissed her.

She clung to his shoulders and opened her mouth for him, glorying in the feel of his arms around her, his tongue exploring her. He smelled wonderful, like cotton sheets just out of the dryer (with a faint clam underhint). His hands moved restlessly over her back and she pulled his T-shirt up and stroked his hard stomach.

"As for the sex part . . . shoot, I've wanted you for years. I wanted you before I even knew what wanting really was."

She nearly swooned onto the bed . . . he was just *darling*! He looked like a hard-working eighteenth-century farmer, and he had the soul of a Renaissance poet. "It's been a long time," she whispered, marveling at the feel of his smooth skin. She had to be almost twice his age, though she didn't look it. Did he mind?

Did she?

"Yeah, I figure . . . Ed's been gone awhile . . ."

"Not with Ed. Ed and I were friends, nothing more." She smiled shakily. "We shared blood and friendship and that's all. It's been a *long* time."

"Well, I hear you on that one." He had pulled her cardigan off, unzipped the back of her simple summer dress, then stepped back as her clothes fell to the floor. "Oh, cripes, Sophie. I thought about this a million times, and you're about a zillion times prettier than I could have ever thought up on my own."

She reached behind and unsnapped her bra (even the undead liked support), and her small breasts bounced free. He sucked in a breath and then bent to her, kissing her neck and her cleavage, his tongue darting out to caress a nipple.

"A long time," she repeated, and ripped his shirt over his head so hard she almost threw him to the floor. "Oh! I beg your pardon."

He laughed and tackled her, bringing her to the bed, and they wrestled for a moment, their clothes the casualties.

She crept down the length of his sweetly muscled body, inhaling his musk, stroked his throbbing length for a moment and, when he groaned beneath her busy fingers, carefully sucked him into her mouth.

His hands fisted in her hair, tumbling it loose from the clips, and she pulled him into her throat with no trouble at all, pleasantly surprised to find that sex really *was* like riding a bicycle. But her growing hunger could not be denied much longer—*any* longer—so finally she pulled back, licked his thigh, then sank her fangs into his femoral artery. Salty sweetness flooded her mouth and she nearly rolled to the floor with the goodness of it, the rightness of it.

He groaned again, his hands still restless in her hair, and she fed, immediately contented. She could feel his penis, hot against her cheek, almost jerking as she took her pleasure from him, as he took pleasure in return.

Once she had enough—it never took much, thank goodness the movies were wrong about *that*, among other things—she could politely return to the festivities, so she sat up and straddled him.

"Oh, Jesus," he said, and she flinched. "Oh, *shit!*"

She laughed.

"Don't worry about it." He reached up and cupped her breasts in his hands. Sophie wriggled with delight as Liam stroked her dark nipples with his thumbs. She positioned herself more carefully and between one moment and the next, he was sliding inside her, filling her as she had wanted to be filled for too many years. His eyes, that vivid blue she had always admired, slipped closed.

Liam groaned again and shifted his hands to her hips, helping her find a rhythm they both liked. She bent forward and bit him at the neck; she couldn't help it. He shivered and moved against her faster and she met his thrusts with her own urgency. Oh, glory, it was wonderful to be with someone again, to have that connection, to feed, to be *fucked.* Liam was giving her everything she had longed for, all at once. It was almost too much; for a moment she was nearly delirious with happiness. Then she realized she had mistaken her orgasm for delirium.

She pulled away from his neck, almost laughing, and said aloud, "These things happen. Did you . . . ?"

"I'm gonna die now," he announced, answering her question. "That pretty much killed me."

"You look pretty lively to me," she teased. She started to climb off him but he tightened his grip in wordless denial, so she merely shifted and lay beside him.

"Have I mentioned I'm so damned glad you didn't go out tonight?"

"Well, no. I am, too."

"So, okay," he sighed, stroking her shoulders. "I guess this is where we do the pillow-talk, but I'm so friggin' tired . . ."

"It's been a long night," she told him. "For both of us. Go to sleep."

"You first," he yawned, but she didn't, of course, and finally he quit fighting it and she watched him sleep. For a long time.

7

"Do you think you should check with Jerry?"

"Huh?" He scraped off another inch of shaving cream and met her eyes in the mirror. "How come? Hey, you've got a reflection!"

"Of course I do," she said impatiently. "Did you make arrangements for your pets before we left?"

"Yeah, I dropped the Gladiator off with Tommy . . . kid's crazy for dogs and his mom said it was okay. Him and Rusher can eat garbage together."

"I hope you're talking about Gladiator and Rusher," she said, smirking. She stretched up and kissed him between the shoulder blades. He shivered, then scraped off more shaving cream.

"You keep that up," he said, "you'll have your hands full."

"Perish the thought." She kissed him again, to tease, then asked, "What about the cats?"

"The cats?"

Odd. He was a smart man, but he seemed to have trouble following the conversation this evening. "Yes, Liam, *your* cats."

"Right. They're, uh, not really . . . I mean, they show up, and I feed them . . ." He caught her expression in the mirror. "I'll just double-check with Jerry," he added hurriedly, then wiped his face with the towel. She followed him into the other room and watched as he dialed a phone number.

"It's much cheaper to use my cell phone," she commented.

"Eh, you got the bucks."

"Just because I have it, doesn't mean I wish to waste it."

"Cripes, are all vampires such nags?"

She almost laughed, but managed to keep looking stern.

"Yeah, Jerry? It's me, Liam . . . yeah, listen, you mind keeping an eye on my place for a couple days? Yeah, the cats pretty much take care of themselves . . . they keep the mice population down in the barn so you don't gotta worry about feeding them, and there's fresh water over by the pump, but just . . . uh . . . check in on 'em every day or so? You mind? Yeah, I'll be back—what? *No*, Sophie and me didn't run off together. I mean, we did, but we'll be back . . . right?" He raised his eyebrows at her. "We'll be back? Yeah, she's nodding . . . uh-huh. None of your damn business, and thanks for watching the cats." He hung up. "There, can I finish shaving now?"

"Yes, please," she said, still trying not to laugh. Embarrass was a small town; she could just imagine the storm of gossip that had arisen when she and Liam had disappeared together.

He muttered something as he passed her, but even her attuned vampire hearing didn't catch it. It sounded like, "Women." Such things, it seemed, transcended age.

"I just don't think—"

"I'm goin'."

"But I'm not sure you realize—"

"Goin'."

"But it isn't necessary for you to—"

"Sophie."

"But—"

"Sophie."

She slumped back against the seat and sighed, something she didn't often do. He was impossible. Implacable. Men! She'd forgotten how oddly protective they could get after a little hip-bumping.

The last thing she needed was to bring a sheep to the library; Marjorie was a little touchy on subjects like that. The head librarian was so old, and so infinitely crafty, most people were drooling idiots in comparison. Especially most humans, who had only a fraction of her life span and knowledge. Subsequently, the old vampire didn't suffer fools lightly. Liam wasn't a fool, but compared to Marjorie . . .

Well, this was for the greater good, and the thought of restraining Liam—knocking him out, somehow, like they did in the movies?—did not sit well with her. She would just have to . . .

Her truck door swung open and Liam stuck his head in. "You coming?"

"Yes," she replied through gritted teeth. "In fact, would you kindly follow me."

"No problem," he said, cheerful now that he saw he was getting his way. He pointedly ignored all her glares and sulks and followed her into the building, which looked like an abandoned warehouse.

Inside, of course, was a different story.

"Huh," Liam said, looking around. "Looks a lot smaller from the outside."

"Good evening, Sophie," Marjorie said, standing right beside the main desk, looking (as she always did) as if she had been waiting just for them.

"Marjorie," she replied, and they kissed on both cheeks. She didn't bother introducing Liam; Marjorie wouldn't have cared. "I'm not here to relax and read, I'm afraid. I need to meet with the queen tonight. Can you arrange it?"

Marjorie wrinkled her brow. She was a tallish woman with excellent posture and black hair streaked with gray. Her dark eyes were cold, though, and any resemblance to someone's youngish grandmother was strictly imaginary. "I don't keep her appointments, I'm afraid. But I can give you directions to her house."

"You mean just . . . go there?"

Marjorie shrugged apologetically. "It's how things are done now."

"Since Nostro was killed?"

"Yes. The new queen is somewhat . . . relaxed in her rules."

"Well, there's nothing for it," Sophie said, nibbling on her lower lip. "I must speak with her. It can't wait another night."

"Of course. You're in luck, too," she added, nodding in Liam's direction. "She's fond of sheep. She has a couple of them herself."

"Uh . . ."

"Excuse me," Liam said. "I was having a little trouble with that one. What's a *mouton*?"

Startled, Sophie realized she and Marjorie had been speaking in French the entire time. "Liam, I apologize. When Marjorie greeted us in French I just slipped into it—"

"That's okay. I was gettin' most of it. All those *For Dummies* books and tapes are really good," he added.

Sophie blinked. "You studied French on your own?" Of course he did, she realized. The high school didn't offer it. Only Spanish.

"Well . . . yeah. Because you . . . I mean, nobody in town knows anything about you, except that you're French.

And I thought, you know, if I knew your language, we could maybe . . ." He shrugged. "I dunno."

Overcome, Sophie was for a moment unable to speak. She merely gaped at him like a fish while Marjorie shifted her weight impatiently. Finally, she turned to the older woman and managed, "We'll take that map, thank you."

"I've got it right here for you."

Wordlessly, Sophie took the piece of paper. As Marjorie always looked as though she was waiting for whoever came to see her, she also always had exactly what that person needed. The older vampires were all used to it.

"Thank you for coming by," the librarian was saying. "And thank you for bringing your sheep. He smells divine."

"I ain't a sheep," Liam said flatly. His midwestern drawl, usually pleasant and unassuming, had hardened. "I'm a man. *Her* man."

Marjorie smirked, but Sophie was suddenly ashamed. Equally suddenly, she didn't care for the smile on Marjorie's face. "Of course, Liam. I—I—" She had no clue what to say. Should she apologize? But Marjorie had been the one who had given offense. Although she herself had referred to Liam as a sheep, in her mind. Should she—

"Really, that's charming," Marjorie said. Her smirk had widened until she looked like a gray-haired jack-o'-lantern. "If you get tired of this one, Sophie darling, I do hope—"

"You want to step outside and talk about it some more?" he interrupted.

"Liam!" Sophie nearly shrieked.

"What? I'm a feminist. 'Sides, she's probably got six hundred years on me."

"Eight hundred," Marjorie said dryly.

"Anyways, I'm an equal opportunity ass-kicker. Nobody talks to me that way. I might be a nobody from some small town, but I'm not . . . you know. A nobody."

Sophie fought the urge to bury her face in her hands.

Meanwhile, Marjorie's brow wrinkled as she digested that, and then she smiled, quite naturally. "I don't want to step outside with you. And I apologize if I offended you. I'm just used to things being . . . a certain way."

"Yes, well, just a simple misunderstanding, we must be going now," Sophie said, almost babbled, seizing Liam's arm so hard he winced. "Thank you for the information."

"You're so welcome." She shook Liam's hand. "So nice to meet you. Please stop by anytime. The library is not restricted to the undead." She said this with such total sincerity, Sophie almost believed her.

"Yeah, well. Guess I got a little hot under the collar."

"Yes, you did." Marjorie's eyes were veiled, and a smoky gray. "It was quite . . . interesting. As I said. Stop by anytime."

"Say, anybody ever tell you, you're kind of cute? I—ow!"

"Good-bye," Sophie called, and practically dragged him out by the hair.

8

SOPHIE was still crabbing away at him while they were going up the sidewalk. The gist of it was "Never pick fights with vampires," like any fool didn't know that. But there was a big difference between keeping your head down and letting someone pull it off and hand it to you. Maybe French people didn't get that.

". . . so unbelievably arrogant, so completely dangerous . . ."

He let her sweet, accented bitching fade out as he stared around at the place. Summit Avenue in St. Paul was pretty famous for big digs, but this! Every mansion on the street was nicer than the last, and the one they were standing in front of was the nicest of all. It was humongous, like something out of an old movie, a massive white structure with black shutters. It didn't feel evil, though Sophie told him the queen of the vampires lived there.

"I guess we should go knock," Sophie said timidly, which startled the hell out of him. He didn't think she was afraid of *anything*. Come to think of it, she'd been very deferential to the librarian, too. Maybe she just wasn't used to being around her own kind. Maybe she'd moved to Embarrass for more than a fresh start. "Yes. Let's do that. We'll knock."

"Okeydokey," he agreed.

As they stepped up to the gigantic, wraparound porch, the front door suddenly opened and a good-looking young man in his mid-twenties came out. He was wearing green scrubs and had a hospital ID around his neck with a terrible picture on it. His hair was dark and cut very short, and his green eyes were clear and friendly.

"Hi there," he said, jingling his car keys. "Come to visit? Go on in. I'd stay and, you know, do the polite intros, but I'm late and you're not here to see me anyway. Right? Right. So, 'bye."

He hurried down the steps, throwing a distracted wave over his shoulder, then disappeared around the corner toward the detached garage. They watched him go, bemused, then Sophie turned and looked back up at the house.

"We can just . . . go in?"

"Guess so," Liam replied and opened the front door. After seeing the outside of the house, he was a little more prepared for the beauty and opulence of the foyer. He could hear voices coming from a large room on their right, and turned in that direction. Sophie clutched his arm, pulling him back. "Sophie, what is *with* you?"

She was chewing on her lower lip so hard, he expected to see it start bleeding. If she could bleed. "It's just . . . I met Nostro. And he was horrible. Horrible. And if she beat him. . . . But we have to bring this to her," she added, seeming to straighten with remembered pride. "It's our— *my*—responsibility."

"Right," he said. "Calm down, ease up. You look great, don't worry about it." And she did. Her glossy brown hair was piled up on top of her head, being held in place by the miracle of a single hair clip. She was wearing a dark red suit, light-colored stockings, and black shoes. She was pale, but then, she was always pale. He thought she looked like a million bucks. In fact, as he'd watched her pull up her stockings in their hotel room (he didn't know gals even wore stockings and garter belts anymore), he'd been unable to resist jumping her bones again, and they'd had a wonderful time rolling around on the floor.

She hadn't bitten him that time, politely explaining afterward that she was still satisfied from the night before. He knew she was lying; he could tell by the way her gaze kept shifting from his eyes to the bruise forming on his neck. But he didn't push it, figuring she had other things on her mind.

"You look nice, too," she told him, which was a laugh, because he was wearing jeans (clean, at least) and an old blue flannel shirt (also clean). Well, he didn't think the big shot queen would much care *what* he was wearing.

He gripped Sophie's hand, surprised as always by its pleasant coolness, and practically pulled her into the next room.

". . . and they're doing really well, pretty well, I mean, they'll still kill and eat anybody who gets too close, anybody human I mean, but I'm keeping a pretty close watch and, um, I guess that's all."

The girl speaking was smaller than Sophie, which was pretty damn small. She had red hair and the skinniest, palest arms and legs Liam had ever seen. She was wearing a pleated black skirt and a white blouse, and little white socks and loafers, looking for all the world like a schoolgirl. In fact, she probably *was* a schoolgirl. Didn't look a day over fifteen.

"Very good, Alice," a deep voice said. Liam looked, then looked again. He'd thought it was a shadowy corner, but there was a man sitting in a tall wingbacked chair, a big man, tall and scary-looking and Liam wanted to turn around, cool as a cuke, and walk right of there and back to the truck and then drive all the way back to Embarrass, checking the rearview the entire time. "Once again, I must ask if you wish to be relieved of your duties. You've been at this for several months and—"

"Majesty, I love this job, and I wish to keep on doing it. Before I wanted to because, you know, with the new, uh, regime, I wasn't really sure of my place. So I figured, you know. But now . . . I—I kind of like them," she finished, staring down at her shoes.

"Them?" the man asked, distaste clear in his tone.

"Happy, Skippy, Trippy, Sandy, Benny, Clara, Jane, and George." She smiled weakly. "George's my favorite."

"You've *named* them?"

Liam wondered who *them* was. He bumped into something, and he suddenly realized he'd backed all the way up into the door, totally unconsciously. He told himself to get a grip. They were just vampires, for Christ's sake.

He forced himself to look around the room while the vampires talked about *them*, tearing his gaze away from the scary guy sitting in the corner. There were three other people in the room; the first one he noticed was a petite, great-looking blonde standing behind and slightly to the left of the guy's chair. Even from across the room, he could see how dark and pretty her big eyes were, fixed now on the girl. And she was so small, she easily fit behind the corner chair. The guy seemed totally unaware of her, but he'd cock his head when she'd bend down to whisper to him, and besides, Liam had the feeling no one snuck up on this guy.

There was also a dark-green couch (he supposed some fancy magazine would call it "moss green" or whatever) in the middle of the room, and two women were sitting on it, playing checkers. The one closest to him was a good-looking black gal (shit, he'd never seen this many gorgeous people outside of a Hollywood movie). She was way too thin, with her hair so tightly pulled back he could practically see her skull throbbing, but her skin was a gorgeous dark brown and she had a look about her he really liked, as if she didn't take a lot of shit.

The other one . . . he glanced at her, and then his gaze came back, as it had with the man.

She was as cute as a bug's butt, as Sophie would have said (when she got excited, Liam noticed she mixed up her metaphors). Her hair was blond, but much shorter than the other woman's, and the light tossed reddish glints into it. She was sitting cross-legged, in tan shorts and a navy blue sweater buttoned to her chin. She wore shoes the color of her sweater, shoes that had a little heel and emphasized the long, pretty shape of her foot. She was watching the other woman's hands and swung her foot while she waited her turn, occasionally peeking at her shoes and smiling.

She looked up at him (and, presumably, Sophie), and he saw her eyes were a cross between green and blue, the color of the ocean in a postcard. Her chin was pointed, giving her a sharp, foxlike appearance, and her cheekbones were high, emphasizing the prettiness of her eyes and the smoothness of her brow. He had an odd urge to stroke her forehead, which mercifully passed. It helped to glance back at Sophie now and again.

"Hey," she said casually, turning the full force of her sea-colored gaze on him, and he nearly fell down. Staring at her was like staring at the door to heaven. It promised delights beyond compare . . . but didja *really* want to leave everything you ever knew behind?

"So, anyway, Your Majesties," the schoolgirl was saying, "the Fiends are just fine, healthy as can be . . . I guess . . . and they—"

The spectacular blonde on the couch stood so fast, he

didn't actually see it. One second she was leaning over, about to get kinged, the next she was standing and pointing (uh-oh) at Sophie, and the redhead was cowering away from her.

"*What* . . ." she began, "is *on* . . . your *shoes*?"

Sophie looked down at her feet, then back up. "Ah . . . Your Majesty, my name is Dr. Sophie Tourneau, and this is—may I present my . . . uh . . . my friend, Mr. Liam—"

"Seriously. It looks like you plowed through—God, is that *shit*? Is that *shit* on your shoes?"

"Elizabeth," the man in the corner sighed.

"Oh, boy," the black gal said. "Here we go."

"They were, uh, a gift, uh . . ." Sophie sounded completely rattled and Liam almost smiled. Shoes, they were talking about shoes, of all the dumbest things! "And I— I'm a vet, an animal doctor, and sometimes I wear them on the job . . . and . . . and . . ."

"So you're telling me it *is* shit?" Liam thought the blonde was going to pass out. "Jesus Christ in an Easter parade!" Everyone (except him) visibly flinched. "How could you . . . *do* that? I mean, that's why God made Payless Shoes. You want to tromp around in the shit? I—I—" She put a hand to her brow, and Liam noticed she had pretty hands with long fingers. The nails were done in that what-do-you-call-it, with the white tips. French manicure. "You just can't—can't come in here—*dressed* like that—your poor *feet*—"

"Unless it's really important." The woman standing behind the fella piped up. It was the first time she'd spoken loud enough for him to hear. "As I'm sure it is."

"Aren't you French? You sound French. Aren't French people supposed to have style?"

"Uh-huh," the black gal said. "Also, African-Americans have rhythm, and white girls can't dance. Especially you, white girl."

"*You* stay out of this." The blonde—surely this wasn't the queen?—suddenly collapsed onto the couch, nearly kicking over the checkers game. "Well, I can't be expected to listen to this! The whole thing is stupid anyway, I was *totally* against it—"

"We know," everybody but Liam and Sophie said.

". . . and thought it was, just, *so* massively lame, but I put up with it without bitching—much—and all these dead people trooping through my house—"

"Excuse me," the black lady said, not looking up from the board. "Through *my* house."

"I told you to quit holding that over my head! Where the hell was I?"

"Dead people trooping through your house," Liam said helpfully.

"Right. Right! *Thank* you. And they're in and out of here like I'm fucking King Solomon—what, they can't solve their own problems?—and now I gotta see shoes abused and I can't take it!" She threw her arm over her face and lapsed into silence. Finally.

Sophie's mouth was opening and closing like a walleye, but she wasn't saying anything. And all the vampires—he guessed they were all vampires—were staring at them. Except for the guy. He was staring at the blonde and smiling, a little. So finally Liam coughed and said, "Well, there's a bad vampire and he's killing girls up north." *Now* the guy was looking at him, along with everybody else. Even the blonde was peeking at him from under her arm. "We just, y'know, thought you oughta know."

The queen sat up. "Oh, *fuck.*"

"Yup," Liam agreed.

9

※

"YOU'RE kidding me. Right? You're kidding. I mean, that's nasty. That's just . . . yerrggh."

"Yup," Liam agreed. He took another drink of his smoothie. They had trooped into an enormous kitchen, the guy had fired up two blenders and brought a ton of fruit and orange juice out of the fridge, and now they were sitting around like old friends, slurping down strawberry smoothies. Except for him. His was strawberry-banana. "That's what we thought. Sohpie figured it out."

"When?" the guy asked. He had introduced himself as Eric Sinclair, but everybody except Jessica (the black gal) called him Majesty or My King or Shitheap (the spunky blonde, it appeared, didn't like him). Speaking of the blonde, her name was Betsy and, yup, she *was* the queen. The other blonde's name was Tina and she was very deferential to Shitheap and Betsy. Alice, the schoolgirl, had politely excused herself and left.

"I beg your pardon?" Sophie asked, her glass rattling as she set it down. She was a little more relaxed than when they'd arrived, but not much. Liam couldn't blame her. It wasn't every day you met a king and queen. Luckily, they weren't *his* king and queen, so he could be his regular old self. "Your Majesty, did you ask me when?"

"Last night," Liam began, helping her out a little, "we were watching the news and Sophie saw this story and put it all together.

"She's really smart," he added. "Smartest person in Embarrass."

"I'm sure that's true," Shitheap said, smiling at Sophie, which seemed to calm her down a little.

"Up by Babbitt Lake?" Jessica asked.

Liam chewed a small piece of banana that had escaped the blender's whirring blades. "Yeah, you know it?"

"My dad used to take me fishing there when I was little."

"Well, we, me and Sophie, live there. She's our vet."

"And you saw this man on the news . . ." Sinclair prompted.

". . . and decided to come up and wreck my night," the queen finished. When they all stared at her, she had the grace to look embarrassed. "Sorry. That sounded less jerky in my head."

"We didn't see *him*," Sophie said. "We saw the father of one of the girls on the news. So Liam drove me down—"

"You didn't feel the need to keep this in the, uh, community?" Tina asked.

"She tried," Liam said simply.

There was a short silence, broken by the queen's muffled giggle, then Sophie continued. "We drove down and spoke to the girl's mother. I don't think there's much doubt, or I certainly would not be bothering you with this."

"Ugh! He dates these girls, makes them love him, then *dumps* them to watch them go all suicidal with despair?"

"Yup."

"What a shit!" Betsy was on her feet. "Let's go up to Embarrass and kick his ass!"

"It's not in Embarrass," Sophie began, but Sinclair interrupted her.

"I quite agree. This behavior is not acceptable in the least. Also, it's messy and people are bound to notice."

"Here we go," Jessica said into her smoothie.

"Messy? It's messy?" The queen looked around, but Jessica and Tina were hurriedly clearing all the empty glasses off the small table. Nothing was within throwing reach. "How about, 'He's a shit and we're gonna stake his ass.' How about, 'Those poor girls, let's avenge them.' How about *anything* besides messy?"

"He did say anything besides messy," Liam pointed out. "He said it wasn't acceptable behavior. Which I guess it's not."

"Dude: so not talking to you." The queen gave him a good glare, so he hung tight to his glass. "I don't—"

"So, you're the queen of all the vampires, huh?"

That took the wind out of her sails. "Yeah, I guess," she replied, and her shoulders slumped.

"So all the vampires have to do what you say?"

"No," Eric Sinclair said.

"And I'm not a vampire," Jessica said. "I'm just a hanger-on."

"Me, too, I guess," he joked.

"You shut up, too. Everybody shut up. And to answer your question . . . uh, I'm sorry, your friend told me your name but I—"

"Liam."

"Right. Anyway, they're supposed to, but I don't want 'em to, and a lot of them don't listen anyway."

"But that's not because you're resisting your destiny or anything," Jessica said, smirking at him.

"Jess! Repeat after me: not helpful."

"With all due respect, Your Majesties, shouldn't we be driving north? He could be seducing another girl this minute." Sophie's expression darkened. "He could be breaking up with another girl this minute."

"He could feel the tip of my shoe up his ass in another minute," the queen vowed, slipping off of her stool. "Jess, you stay here."

"Oh, come on," she protested. "I always miss out on the good stuff."

"If by *good* you mean hideously dangerous, then yeah, you do. Look, it's vampire business, anyway. And last I looked, you were alive."

"Then *he* shouldn't go, either," Jessica said, pointing at Liam.

"It's my truck," he said mildly.

"Shit, it's my *house*," she said, starting to pout. Some women couldn't pull it off, and some looked charming as hell when they tried. Jessica was one of the latter. "That doesn't stop them from leaving me out all the time."

"What is the sound of one woman bitching?" Betsy asked the air. "If nobody's around to hear the sound of Jessica bitching, does she actually bitch?"

"Oh, you're so evicted."

"She's right, though," Sinclair said mildly. "It's inappropriate for Liam to come with us if we leave Jessica behind."

"Tough shit," he said. "I'm going."

Betsy's eyebrows arched but, shockingly, she said nothing.

"Sophie's not facing down some bad killer vampire without me, and that's how it is."

"So there, Sinclair." To Liam, Betsy said, "Good for you. It's kind of romantic. Totally annoying, but romantic."

"You're right, yes, you certainly are," Sinclair said smoothly. Liam was having trouble looking away from the man's deep, dark gaze. "However, I—"

Suddenly, he couldn't see Sinclair anymore. After a second, he realized Sophie's hands had shot out, covering his eyes.

"Sir," she was saying, "please don't. He's been so good to me. So helpful. And it *is* his truck. And he wasn't afraid to come. He's known about me and he . . . he deserves to come."

"If he's going, I'm going," Jessica said crossly. "I've earned the right to come, too."

Gently, Liam pushed Sophie's hands down. He guessed the guy was going to hypnotize him or whatever, and he was grateful for her intervention. "Come or stay, but let's get going. Sophie's right. Time's wasting."

"You guys!" Jessica wailed.

Betsy shook her head. "Too dangerous."

Tina nodded hers. "She's right, Jessica."

"But inconsistent and annoying if we take him and not her," Sinclair added.

"Look, Jess, let's settle this fair and fast, okay? Rock, paper, scissors?" Betsy asked.

Jessica brightened. "Sure."

Both women's left hands fisted. "Rock, paper, scissors," they chanted in unison.

Then, "Shit!"

10

⚜

"POOR Jessica." Betsy was gloating. "She always goes for scissors."

"I'm sorry about your shoe," Sophie said. They were on cell phones. Sophie and Liam were in his truck. The vampire king and queen were following in an electric blue GT Mustang convertible. Odd that such a cool and controlled man had such a flashy car, but it was none of Sophie's business. "I do think she shouldn't have thrown the left one in the blender."

"She's got a temper," Betsy agreed, "and she knew just where to stick it to me. That's okay. I'll steal her credit card and get it fixed at the leather shop. Worry about *your* shoes. Seriously." Sophie heard the queen laugh, then the click of a disconnect.

"Well, I guess they'll follow us up there and we'll . . . you know." Sophie paused, then sighed. "Are you not speaking to me?"

"That was the plan. I guess with all the lecturing, you

didn't notice. Then we were talking to the other vampires and I forgot I wasn't talking to you."

"It's the sheep thing, isn't it?"

"Yes, it's the sheep thing," he said, sounding annoyed. "Shit, what else would it be?"

"I promise, I won't refer to you like that again, and I won't allow anyone to—"

"It's not that, Sophie. *Sheep* is just a word. It's *you*. I'm sure you're older than I am . . . I just don't know how much older. And I don't care. But you do. Right?"

"It's not that I . . . care, exactly," she said slowly. "I'm just used to things being a certain way."

"Yeah, well, I love you."

"What?"

"I figured, best to get that out of the way," he explained, as if he hadn't just said a shocking thing, as if he hadn't changed everything. "You know, being in love with you. The thing is, I've always loved you. And I've always wanted you. And I knew you were a vampire and I knew you were pretty old—"

"Not *that* old," she said, her vanity pricking her. "Not for a vampire. I'm not even a hundred yet."

"Yeah, well, I'm just saying, I don't care about any of that, I care about *you*. But this won't work unless you don't care, either."

"Liam, you drop this bombshell on me—"

"Yep," he said cheerfully.

"—all in the last forty-eight hours . . . do you realize that before Tuesday, we'd never spent any time together that wasn't pet-related? You have to admit, this is all very fast."

"Yep. I have to admit that."

"Well, you have to give me some time." She folded her arms across her chest, feeling stupid and happy and annoyed and afraid.

"How much time?"

"More than two days," she snapped. "It shouldn't be a problem, since you've been waiting your entire life to be with me, right? So you can give me another forty-eight hours?"

"I'm glad you hit me over the head with that right away," he retorted. "I wouldn't want you to wait."

"I'm just saying." If she could have blushed, she would have. That had sounded much worse out loud than she had meant. She was just . . . surprised. She hadn't a clue he had such deep feelings for her. All this time, and he never told her.

"You never told me."

"Well, I was waiting for exactly the right time."

"A vampire serial killer throwing us together? That was the right time?"

"Well, yeah."

"And there's a lot more to it than love, you know." She said this with triumph, as if she were thinking of reasons to make him be wrong about loving her.

"Sophie, what the hell are you talking about?"

"There's the issue of how I need blood to survive."

"Yeah, I know."

"Liam: I drink blood from living donors in order to function. I have to do it a *lot*."

"So? I have to eat regular food to survive."

"It's not the same thing."

"But it doesn't make you a bad person, right?

"No," she said slowly. "Feeding . . . biting and taking blood . . . it's like any weapon, I think. You've got a shotgun at home, yes? Well, is it a good shotgun or a bad shotgun?"

"Guess that depends," he replied. "If I use it to blow the head off a serial vampire scumbag killer, it's a good one. If I used it to, I dunno, hurt a kid or whatever, it's a bad one."

"Well, I think feeding is much the same. I could have hurt you. I could have killed you."

"I think you *did* kill me," he said cheerfully.

She didn't smile. "I'm being serious, Liam."

"Yeah, I can tell by the way you're sucking all the enjoyment out of this moment."

"And I'll outlive you," she continued doggedly, "unless we take steps."

"I know."

"I don't think you do."

"There it is again."

"What?"

"That I'm a vampire and a lot older, and so I'm smarter and just in general better than you."

"That's ridiculous!" she cried, freshly stung.

"Ha!"

"Ha yourself."

They didn't say another word until they got to the town where the last girl, Shawna, had lived and died. Then Liam said, "I'd prefer to ride with Betsy."

"You took the words right out of my head," she snapped, her idioms suffering, as always, when she was angry. She swung her door open and jumped out of the truck. "I'll send her over."

"Good."

"Good!" She stomped over to the king and queen, who looked to be in the middle of their own lover's spat.

"You don't suck like ordinary people suck, by the way. You suck like Academy Award–sucking. If there was an Oscar handed out for Most Sucking, you'd have it locked."

"You've got to come up with something new. Anything new."

"Excuse me, Majesties," she interrupted, her nervousness in their presence evaporating. She could be angry or she could be nervous, but apparently she couldn't be both. "Liam would like the queen to ride with him."

"Ride with . . . oh, right. The B and B thing." Shawna's mother had told them the killer was staying at a local bed-and-breakfast. There were two in town; they didn't know which one she had meant. So they had decided to split up. Originally each couple would make a team. Not any longer. "That's fine with me. Later, Sinclair." She walked over to Liam, who had gotten out and was standing beside the truck. "Hey, can I drive?"

He wordlessly handed her the keys, then walked around to the passenger's side. Sophie waited for a moment. For an apology? Whose?

"Dr. Trudeau, we need to be going," Sinclair told her.

"Sir," she replied miserably, and fell into step behind him.

11

⚜

"WHAT'S the matter?" Betsy asked him. She was so tall, she didn't have to adjust the seat, just the rearview mirror. "Did you guys have a big wicked fight, or what?"

"Something like that."

"I know what that's like."

"Mmm," he replied, secretly doubting she had the tiniest clue. Nice enough gal, and super-pretty, but a regular guy like him didn't have much in common with the queen of the vampires. "Okay."

"Dude, seriously. I'm supposed to be the consort of a guy who's totally arrogant and sneaky and has, like, eighty hidden agendas."

"You're supposed to be?"

"Don't even get me started. It's a whole long story, and I come off really bad in it. But so does Sinclair! Anyway—"

"You've got something . . ." He pointed to her neck, where three mosquitoes were currently having a party. He guessed . . . did mosquitoes bother vampires?

"What?" She brushed in the wrong spot, as people always did when told they had something on them. "What? Did I get it?"

"Here, I—" He brushed at her neck, and was startled when something snagged his finger. Well, he was pretty bad at this stuff. "Aw, shit, now I'm caught on something . . ." He pulled back, surprised to find a gold chain entwined on the end of his finger, and even more surprised to find a cross dangling from the end of the chain.

"Oh, crap! The chain broke!"

"I can fix it," he told her, since she seemed pretty upset about it.

"It's just, Sinclair gave it to me. I wouldn't want anything . . . it's nice, right?"

"Right." He stared at it in wonder . . . she *was* a vampire, correct? "Let me hold on to it for you, and I'll fix it when we're done tonight."

"Thanks. It used to belong to his sister, I guess it's a family heirloom thing. I wouldn't want anything to happen to it, is all. Anyway, where was I?"

"I'm sorry," Liam said. "But I've just gotta know. You're a vampire, right? The queen of them? What are you doing carrying around a cross? And if Sinclair gave it to you . . . I guess it's just an old wives' tale, huh?"

"Oh no, no," she assured him, stomping on the clutch and shifting into third. "Sorry, didn't mean to go all Bela Lugosi mysterious-ee on you. I haven't been a vampire very long . . . just a few months."

"That's why crosses don't work on you?"

"No, no. Nothing works on me. Crosses normally burn the crap out of a regular vampire, but I guess I'm special." She said it glumly, as if it wasn't a good thing at all. "Crosses don't burn me, and holy water makes me sneeze, and stakes through the chest don't work, but they sure wreck my clothes."

"That's too bad," he said, because he had to say some-thing. "About your clothes, I mean."

"Tell me. My dry cleaner totally freaks out when I come near him these days. Anyway, crosses would burn Sinclair, except he got that one way back when his sister died, be-fore he was a vampire."

"Oh."

"Okay? Everything cleared up?"

"Uh, sure," he said, pretending he heard this sort of thing all the time. Of course, very little had been cleared up. Why was this woman so special? Why had Eric Sin-clair, whom she professed to dislike, given her a family heirloom, a religious symbol, no less? Could she be killed? *Should* she be killed?

He guessed he'd never know, and wasn't sure if that was good news, or bad.

"Now where was I? Oh, right, the jerkiness of Eric Sin-clair."

"And the whole consort thing," he prompted her, pock-eting the necklace.

"So, I'm supposed to just throw all my doubts aside and be his wife for, like, a thousand years or whatever. And no-body can understand why I'm not getting with the pro-gram." She laughed, sounding a little bitter. "Just forget everything I've ever learned and trust some guy who's as scary as he is good-looking."

Hmm. Wasn't that what he expected Sophie to do? Toss aside all she had learned, all she was, because he was mor-tal and he demanded it? Maybe her *thing* was more his problem than hers.

"Hellooooooo?" Betsy was saying, waving a hand in front of her face and steadying the steering wheel with the other. "My lips are moving; it's polite to pretend to listen."

"I heard every word," he assured her.

*   *   *

"IT seems your evening has been almost as stressful as mine."

"Sir, you have no idea." She glanced over at him and was surprised to see a compassionate expression on his face. "I've had a lot thrown at me in the last few hours, that's all. I'm certainly not going to bore you with it."

"I'm interested," was all he said, so she found herself telling him the entire story . . . her loneliness since her friend had died; how wonderful Liam was; how she didn't know he had loved her in secret all those years; how wonderful Liam was (when he wasn't being a tiresome pighead); how he seemingly accepted her vampire nature; how wonderful Liam was . . . all of it.

"It sounds like a *wonderful* problem to have."

"Sir, it's not that simple."

"No?"

"Sometimes it's . . . easier to stay by yourself."

"Keep the status quo, you mean."

"Yes."

"It's certainly safer."

"Yes." She saw where he was going and gave voice to her biggest fear. "He's a child with a crush."

"He looked full-grown to me. He also looks like a man who knows what he wants."

"Hmph."

They had finished searching the bed-and-breakfast, which was free of guests except for a couple on their honeymoon, currently enjoying themselves behind a closed bedroom door. No serial killers in *that* room.

Sophie was embarrassed; for a while she'd completely forgotten that there was quite a bit more at stake than her love life. But she and the king were almost half-hearted about the search; their enhanced senses had already told them the B and B was virtually deserted, but it was always best to make sure.

"Thank you for listening," she said, following him back out the front door. "I appreciate your advice and will think hard about what you've said."

"I didn't say much," he replied mildly. "Compared to my queen, I'm not much of a talker."

"Is that some kind of slam, pal? Because if you wanna go, we'll go." Betsy was walking through the front yard, Liam on her heels. "No luck at the other place. They've got a full house, and none of them are our guy. It's all couples."

"Couples like the killer with his new girlfriend?" Sophie asked.

"Naw," Liam said. "Couples like retired people on vacation. You guys didn't have any luck?"

"How could you search an entire house, then drive across town and be here just as we finished?" Sinclair asked.

"Dude: have you *seen* this town? It's, like, a mile long. Is it our fault we're way more efficient at looking for killers than you two are? I'm telling you, our guy's not there."

"Well, he isn't here either," Sophie said. "Damn it all. We'll have to go back and talk to Shawna's mother some more, poor thing. I was hoping we could leave her out of it."

Liam was looking at the wooden sign over the front door. "This is the Rose Manor. But The Garden Bed-and-Breakfast is the one we're looking for. We just assumed this was The Garden, because it's the other B and B you can see from the road. But . . ."

"There's another one," Sinclair said immediately. "Probably called The Iris or something tiresome like that. But since the same people own and run them both, they're considered one business. We checked the one across town, and we checked this one, because those are the two businesses."

A quick trip inside to speak with the owner confirmed

their suspicions; there was indeed one other B and B called The Garden.

"Stupid," Liam said disgustedly. "We should have checked. Never assume, that's what my mom always said."

"I don't understand," Sophie said. "We checked the two in town. What are you talking about?"

"There's three in town, and they're all under the business name The Garden, because they're all owned by the same family. We checked two of them . . . you and Sinclair checked The Rose, Betsy and I checked The Tulip." At her mystified expression, he continued. "Those are the names of the *individual* houses, though they're all under the same business name. But there's one more, like the guy said inside. And it'll have another flower name, like Sinclair said."

"I guess it makes sense for the bad guy to make it hard for us to track him down," Betsy said. "I know I'm totally confused. But if there's another one, there's another one. Let's go check it out."

Five minutes later, they were standing at the end of a long driveway outside a third Victorian with yet another flower motif.

"The Sweetheart Rose," Sinclair said. "I was close."

"We're *assuming* he's even still there," Betsy said. "If it was me, I'd be long gone."

"He's not going anywhere," Sophie said as Sinclair nodded agreement. "With the funeral, and the reporters, and all the mourners . . . there's too much here for him still."

"Prick," Betsy commented, and this time, everyone nodded.

12

⁂

THE villain met them on the front steps.

This was startling, to say the least.

"Hello," he said cheerfully. "I was just leaving to go break another girl's heart, so I only have a minute."

Sophie felt like hitting him. With luck, she would soon be doing exactly that. "You *what*?"

"Dude, you are so busted," Betsy told him. Then, to Sinclair, "This kind of takes of fun out of it. No big showdown scene. Unless this is it."

"You killed all those girls," Sophie said, beginning to recover. She had a horrible feeling she knew why the youngish-looking man seemed so unconcerned. "It's the same as if you had . . ." She groped for the words. "Shot them or used a knife on them."

"Yes, I know." She could see why he passed for a premed student; he didn't look a day over twenty-five. He was short, only a few inches taller than she was, with hair that was exactly between blond and brown. He had pleasant features and looked rather like anyone else on the street, in his denim jacket and khaki slacks. His eyes were wide-set and brown. They were the only feature that gave him away. They glittered like a snake's. "I've been meaning to get down to Minneapolis and . . ." He cut himself off and laughed. "Okay, that's a lie. I've been up here having some fun, for a change."

Sophie was staring at him. They were all, she realized, staring at him. Betsy was right. This was a very odd way to go about catching a killer. "For a change?" she finally asked, when no one else said anything.

"Sure. I mean, working for Nostro, talk about all work and no play making me a dull boy. I actually missed the big fight, when this guy here"—he nodded at Sinclair—"took control of the whole shebang. I was out getting Nostro some more girls."

"You brought him victims."

"Sure."

"And when he wasn't holding your leash any longer," Sinclair went on with terrifying pleasantness, "you decided to come and . . . how did you put it? Have some fun?"

"Sure." The killer looked puzzled. "Look, I know I should have come down and paid my respects, but you haven't been in power that long, and I figured I had time—"

"We're not here about *that*," Betsy said, exasperated. "Jeez. Like we care if you come down to the cities and kiss our asses, or pretend to kiss our asses, which is way worse. We're here to stop you from killing anybody else."

The killer's brow wrinkled as he struggled with the alien concept. "But . . . why? Do you need my help with something? I'll be glad to go back to Minneapolis—"

"Dude . . . We. Don't. Want. You. To. Kill. Anybody. Else."

"Because. It's. Wrong," Sophie added.

"Do you mean, it's wrong because I'm not letting you have a crack at the girls? I could—"

"Stop talking now," Sinclair said.

"Do you believe this guy?" Betsy cried, turning to the group. "He's not getting this at *all*. He—" Her eyes narrowed as she took in the expression on Sophie's face, and the identical one on Sinclair's. "You guys totally expected this!"

"Well . . ." Sophie began, but had no idea where to go from there.

"This is a regular thing for vampires?" Liam asked, his displeasure evident.

"*No*," Sophie said. "Er . . . all right, sometimes. Not the making the girls fall in love with him part. But the, ah, other part."

"See? See? *This* is why I'm not getting on board with the whole consort thing," Betsy told him triumphantly. "And why being a vampire makes my skin crawl. Just when I think it might not be a totally insane idea, something like this happens. And you're all, 'Ho hum, another vampire who's a total psycho killer, oh well.' "

"You guys have lost me," the killer interrupted. "You're mad because of the girls? What, you had your eye on one of them? Because if I crossed territory, I really apologize."

"I guess they aren't people to you," Liam said. "They're . . . what? Sheep?"

The killer laughed. "Not hardly! You're supposed to cherish and protect your sheep. The girls are more like . . . hors d'oeuvres."

Betsy carefully pushed the sleeve of her sweater up, almost to her elbow, then socked the killer in the face.

"Ow!" he cried, clapping a hand to his nose. "What was that for?"

"Where to begin?" Sophie replied.

"That was a good start," Sinclair said, "but start in the groin area next time. And use knives instead of your hands."

Betsy shuddered. "Ick. Though if anybody deserves it,

it's this punk. So, what? Do we arrest him? Can we do that?"

"Can this wait until after Theresa kills herself?" the killer asked nasally. "I was leaving to go watch, but—"

"You mean you're doing it again? Right now? But Shawna's barely a week in her grave!"

"Yeah, well, I thought it'd be fun to do a two-fer, you know, play them off each other, but Shawna was a little more fragile than I thought, she kind of jumped the gun on me—" Then he stopped, because Sinclair had picked him up by the throat.

"Where does Theresa live?" Silence, followed by Sinclair adding, "Oh, good, I can beat it out of you. Several times."

"Sinclair, he can't talk, you're squishing his vocal cords," Betsy pointed out. "Not that we want you to stop or anything."

Sinclair let go, and the killer fell to the lawn and gurgled a street address. "We'll tend to the girl," the king said, grabbing Betsy's hand and pulling her toward the car. She yelped, but let herself be dragged away. "You two take care of him. Frankly, if I have to look at him for another ten seconds. . . . you two deal with it."

"What's *that* mean?" Liam asked as Sinclair tore out of the small driveway.

"Drown him, stab him, choke him, slice him, squeeze him, starve him, burn him," Sophie suggested.

"What is everybody's problem tonight?" the killer bitched, standing and trying to brush grass stains off his pants. "You'd think this was about something important."

"Oh, boy," Sophie said. "You're a disgrace to all of us, you wretched horrible thing, and it will be the greatest pleasure of my life to kill you."

"The greatest?" Liam asked.

"Not now, Liam."

"If you saw Shawna's mother," he told the killer, "you might not be so, what's the word?"

"Cavalier," Sophie suggested.

"Asshole. You might not be such an asshole about it."

"I don't have to talk to you, sheep."

"Don't you call him that."

"Don't sweat it, darlin'," Liam said. "I've kind of changed my mind about a couple of things in the last five minutes. I thought you had a thing. Well, you don't. *This* guy does. Whatever problems you and I have, we can work it out."

"That's really touching," the killer said. "I haven't puked in eighty years, but I might right now."

"Oh, Liam, really?" Try to stay focused, you silly cow, she told herself, but it was impossible to deny how incredibly happy those words had made her. "You don't think I'm some vampire snob who can't relate to a mortal because she's seen too much?"

"I do still think that," he admitted, "but, like I said, we can work it out. Doncha think?"

"I do think," she admitted. "I agree, comparably speaking, our troubles don't seem so insurmountable now, do they?"

"I'm still here, you know," the killer reminded them. "Shit, this is why I'm up here in the first place. Decades of being the go-to guy, the guy who can get you what you need, but nobody ever saw me. I was just one of Nostro's stooges."

"I'm sorry for the mean things I said," Sophie said, looking up into Liam's blue, blue eyes. "I was angry, and I was afaid."

He smiled down at her. "That's okay. I said some things, too. Mostly because I was mad."

"Will you guys pay some attention to me? Don't you remember? I'm the guy everybody's mad at?"

"Think they're still holding our room downtown?"

"Probably not. But we could get one up here," she said, reaching up and stroking the new bruise on his neck. Liam shivered and she smiled back at him.

"Dammit!" Abruptly, annoyingly, the killer lunged at them, interrupting what was going to be a wonderful clinch. Liam put up an arm to fling him off . . . and the killer lunged again.

"Ow! Little son of a bitch bit me." Liam was staring at his now-bloody arm. "Broke the skin, too. Can vampires transmit rabies?"

"How dare you touch him! Nobody bites him but me!"

"You tell him, honey," he added, shaking the blood off his wrist.

Screaming, the killer lunged at them again. Liam, who had been digging in his pocket for a clean handkerchief, again warded him off.

Sophie didn't understand until later what happened next; it was too quick, and it hurt her to watch. Liam had swiped back at the killer, and the killer's screams heightened in pitch until she thought her ear drums might rupture. The killer had actually staggered back—why, Sophie didn't know—and Liam followed up, this time swiping down.

The killer looked down at himself, which was understandable, because he was glowing. Sophie looked at him, and the light hurt her . . . it had been like trying to see into the middle of the sun.

Liam, either by accident or design, had drawn a line on the killer: from nipple to nipple. And then, from neck to belt buckle.

A cross.

The killer watched in horror—Sophie felt a little horrified, too, in truth—as the lines Liam had drawn on him first glowed, then sank *into* him, like a foot into mud. And, five seconds later, the screaming was cut short as the killer's vocal cords turned into ash . . . as the killer's entire body turned to ash.

"This never happens," Sophie said, staring. "It's just a movie legend. I've never seen anybody turn into dust before. It just doesn't happen these days."

Liam held out . . . a necklace? A fine gold chain, with a cross—a cross! Sophie hurriedly looked away from it. "I took it from Betsy. Promised to fix it for her. And I will, too," he added. "Just as soon as we finish some other business." He kicked through the three-foot mound of ashes, scattering it. Then he took her into his arms. "So, I guess I'm your sheep."

"No," she told him. "You're . . . yourself. Liam. You're Liam."

"I'm a lucky fellow, is what I am." He kissed her.

She kissed him back, then looked at the foot-wide black smudge on the grass, all that was left of Shawna's tormenter. "I'd say so, yes."

Epilogue

✢

"LET me get this straight. You drew a cross on the bad guy with *my* cross? And he turned into dust and went to Hell, or wherever bad vampires go when they turn into dust?"

"Yup."

"Well, shoot. And we missed it!" Betsy dumped more sugar in her coffee. They had come, by mutual agreement, to the Country Kitchen on Highway Six. "Though, we did save Theresa," she admitted, brightening. "That was pretty cool. Sinclair zapped her with his mojo. Made her forget she'd ever met Fuckface. And a good thing, too, because she was starting to get into her dad's gun collection in a really unhealthy way."

"Excellent," Sophie said. "Just excellent."

"And you fixed my necklace! What, you found an all-night jewelry store?"

"I had some tools in the truck," Liam said, looking modest.

"Thank you again for bringing this distasteful business

to our attention, Dr. Trudeau," Sinclair said. "If not for your conscientiousness, he might have done a great deal more damage."

She shook her head. "I wish I'd caught on sooner."

"You did everything you could. More than most people would have done, I bet," Liam told her, squeezing her hand. She squeezed back, carefully, and smiled at him. "Oh, man. I ever tell you, you've got the prettiest smile?"

"No. It seems to be one of many things you've been keeping to yourself," she teased.

"Not anymore."

"I have things to tell you, too," she admitted. "Many things."

"Well, we've got plenty of time now. We can tell each other everything."

"I can't wait. Liam, I—I don't think you're a child with a crush."

"I think that might be as close to 'I love you, too' as you will get," Sinclair said.

"Seriously. You guys. We're *right* here." Betsy waved at them from across the table. "I mean, make with the goo-goo eyes a little more, why don't you? Get a room!"

"We did. And we'd better get there pretty quick, or my new girlfriend is going to go up in smoke like that little prick."

"Horrible thought. Dr. Trudeau." Sinclair nodded at her, and she stood beside the booth and bowed back. Liam slid out behind her. "Liam." Since he wasn't a subject, the king shook his hand. "Thank you again."

"It was nice meeting you," Betsy said, shaking their hands. Sophie started to bow to her, then thought better of it (the warning glare was a tip-off). "Thanks for figuring it out, tracking down the bad guy, and killing him. I'm trying to figure out what you needed us for," she joked.

"It's nice to make new friends, if nothing else," she

replied, smiling shyly at the queen. "I've been alone for a while, but it was by choice . . . a poor one, I'm thinking now."

"Yeah, well, nice to meet you, too."

Sophie was looking at the new queen with a thoughtful expression. "I avoided this area when Nostro was in power, but now things seem very different. I'd like to stay in touch."

"Nothing would please us more," Sinclair said. "Good night."

"One more thing," Liam said, as he and Sophie went back out to the truck. "Since I'm telling you all the deep dark secrets I've been keeping, I've got another one."

"Yes?"

"I hate cats."

She laughed. "Be serious."

"Sophie. I hate 'em. That's why I don't have any."

"You have a dozen!"

"Well, they aren't mine. I just feed them and look after them."

"I thought you loved cats," she said, confused. "You're always bringing them to me and—oh."

"Yeah."

"Oh!"

"Uh-huh. You know, you're not as smart as you think you are."

"I guess not," she admitted, and laughed, and kissed him.

GALAHAD

Angela Knight

1

❖

SHE came out of it curled on the living room rug, sweating and nauseated. Caroline Lang swallowed hard, trying not to heave up the pint of magic, calorie-free Ben and Jerry's she'd had for dinner. The copper taste of blood drowned out any lingering chocolate, accompanied by a pulsing throb in her lower lip. She must have bitten it.

Groaning, she rolled onto her hands and knees and watched her arms shake. Her muscles were still jumping in the aftermath of the vision, and her head throbbed. The television didn't exactly help, blaring a used car commercial loud enough to wake Elvis. "Off!" Caroline gasped, casting a quick spell.

The TV instantly went silent. She sighed in the blessed stillness.

One minute she'd been licking a spoonful of Chunky Monkey and yelling answers at a particularly witless *Jeopardy* contestant. She'd just told him the capital of Lithuania when all hell broke loose in her brain. Blinded by the storm of images, Caroline had reeled to her feet, tripped over the coffee table, and fallen flat on her face.

After that, she'd been subjected to fifteen solid minutes of the Vision from Hell. None of which made a damn bit of sense. There'd been a seven-foot devil and cups of human blood, women sacrificed on stone altars, vampires grinning while they did stuff no vampire had any business doing. She'd even seen herself, flinging magic around like something out of *The Lord of the Rings*. But what really worried her was the guy with the sword, his handsome face cold with determination as he fought at her side.

That was all she needed. Another flipping vampire, sinking his fangs into various parts of her anatomy, including her heart. Unfortunately, she was going to need all the help she could get.

This being a witch thing was starting to seriously suck.

No way, Caroline thought, beginning to panic as the implications of her vision became painfully clear. *This is a really bad idea. I haven't had the training. I'll screw it up. I'll get somebody killed. I'll get* me *killed.* She climbed to her feet, longing to crawl into bed and pull the covers over her face. *I'm only an English teacher. They can't seriously expect me to . . .*

Yes, they could. Caroline had only been in Avalon a month, but she already knew these lunatics took the Maja's Oath seriously.

But what if she didn't tell anybody? What if she just ignored it? Nobody had to know.

Except her.

Caroline groaned, knowing there was no way she'd just stand around with her thumb up her butt and let people die without trying to do something about it. Of course, she didn't have a clue what *to* do, but one step at a time.

Okay then. She straightened her shoulders, the decision to act steadying her. Much as she hated the thought, she had to find the vampire swordsman. Luckily, that shouldn't be a problem. It felt as if the vision had tied a mystical cord around her neck, and he was somewhere out there on the other end.

She'd just have to make sure he didn't get too close. She wasn't up to another game of Bite-and-Run, not after her glorious month with Count Rat Bastard, otherwise known as Dominic Bonnhome, who'd gotten her into this mess to begin with.

Just before she stepped outside, Caroline took one last longing look around. Over the past couple of weeks, she'd consoled her broken heart by playing with her new powers, including conjuring a houseful of French antiques. She'd since decided they were a little much for her tiny brick ranch, so when she'd seen this cool cream leather living room set on *Queer Eye*, she'd magicked herself a copy. She liked the results. The cream set off the gold in the cheer-leading trophies tastefully displayed on top of the TV.

Now, whether a twenty-eight-year-old woman should actually display her cheerleading trophies was a different question. She'd think about that one if she survived.

Enough stalling. Time to find the vampire.

Caroline opened the door and stepped out into an alien world. To the east, a Scottish castle towered over an expansive golf course that was a dead ringer for Augusta. Just across the cobblestone street, the neighbors' Roman villa lazed in the moonlight, surrounded by an olive grove. Something tiny and glowing zipped around in the trees, reminding Caroline of the lightning bugs back home.

It was probably a fairy.

Next to those displays of conspicuous magical consumption, her pretty brick ranch looked like a double wide. It was a good thing witches and vampires didn't form homeowners' associations, or she'd be in deep trouble for dragging down the neighborhood's property values.

When she got a little stronger in the magic department, Caroline fully intended to ditch the magical duplicate of her house in Georgia and replace it with something that would let her keep up with the Draculas. Disneyland, maybe.

Crossing her postage-stamp of a yard to the cobblestone street, she paused a moment to get her bearings. Ahead, the magical city of Avalon sprawled in all its shimmering, other-worldly glory beneath a sky spread with alien constellations.

Pretty as it was, it was a little unnerving.

In the space of eight weeks, she'd gone from grading papers to losing her job to living on an alternate Earth in a parallel magical universe. Sometimes she got mental whiplash so bad, she had to create a dimensional gate back to Realspace Earth, where her parents had a house in At-lanta. An evening spent listening to Dad bitch about the Braves made her feel almost normal again.

One of these days she was going to have to tell them what she'd become. But any conversation that began, "Well, Dad, I picked up this vampire in a bar . . ." couldn't go anywhere but downhill.

CAROLINE tracked the swordsman down in an elegant brick Georgian that looked like a set in *My Fair Lady*. The massive double doors opened automatically when she stepped up to them, but once inside, the building seemed as empty as the rest of Avalon. She wondered where the heck everybody was. The place had seemed crowded enough when she'd arrived with Dominic. Then, *poof!* Instant ghost town.

Was it something she said?

He was here, though. This close, Caroline could feel him—strength and masculinity, powerful and dark and frightening.

Her favorite flavor.

Cut that out, Caroline, she told herself sternly. *You're on a fangfree diet, remember?*

Following that psychic pull, she walked down a short corridor past stained glass windows, heavily carved wainscoting, and a chandelier dripping with crystals shaped like daggers. Yet another set of intimidating doors swung slowly open. Caroline resisted the temptation to give them a magical creak.

The first thing she saw was a walnut bar the length of an aircraft carrier, equipped with more brass than the Boston Pops and more crystal than Tiffany's. Around it stood walnut tables and massive armchairs upholstered in oxblood leather. Other than the swordsman, there was no one in sight.

He sat in an armchair wearing a full suit of plate armor that gleamed gold in the dim lighting. A great helm sat on the table at his elbow, next to a pair of gauntlets. His long sword leaned against the arm of the chair, its hilt encrusted with gems.

Damn, he looked more gorgeous and romantic than he had in the vision. Black hair lay tangled around shoulders broad enough for an Olympic gymnast. His face was equally broad and exotic, with an arrogant Roman nose and cheekbones so high and sharp, they could grate female hearts into pâté.

He turned to look at her as she entered, one brow lifted, his eyes a smoky blue that gave his harshly handsome face a hint of the poet.

All of which provided a marked contrast to the bottle of Jack Daniels he balanced on one knee.

"You just sit around in full armor?" Damn, she'd kill for a can opener. "Doesn't it chafe?"

"It's enchanted. I've worn less comfortable Armani." The swordsman squinted at her through the smoke curling from his thick black stogie. Instead of the usual cigar reek, it smelled masculine and exotic, a hint of magic giving the smoke a faint glow. "Don't believe I know you, kid. And I thought I knew every Maja in the Mageverse." White teeth flashed. "Most of 'em in the biblical sense." Flicking ashes into a crystal ashtray sitting beside his helm, he took another puff. His hand was big, square, and scarred, but his lips looked impossibly erotic as they closed around the cigar.

She dragged her wandering attention away from all the carnal ideas that mouth gave her. "I'm Caroline Lang." And how was she supposed to explain the situation without sounding like an even bigger idiot than usual? "I'm new here."

The swordsman stood to shake her extended hand. His touch did devastating things to her concentration. "Hell of a time to join the business." He nodded at the nearest chair. "I'm Galahad. Have a seat."

"Galahad? *The* Galahad?" When he lifted an amused brow, she mechanically moved to take the chair he'd indicated.

Gorgeous old tales spun through her memory. Sir Galahad, son of Lancelot and knight of the Round Table. So pure of spirit, he alone of all Arthur's knights was fit to find the Holy Grail, the cup of Christ.

The legends had neglected to mention he was a vampire.

They'd gotten the part about the Holy Grail wrong, too, according to the vamp who'd made her a witch. Assuming Count Rat Bastard hadn't lied about that the way he had about everything else. For one thing, it wasn't holy.

According to Dominic, the cup actually belonged to Merlin himself, who used a series of tests to determine the worthiness of the knights and ladies of Camelot. Those who passed were allowed to drink from the Grail, which magically transformed them. The women became magic-using witches—Majae—while the men became warrior vampires, or Magi. Collectively, they were known as Magekind, the immortal guardians of Man.

The Magekind were a fertile lot, but their children were born mortal. The Latents, as they were called, carried a genetic trait called Merlin's Gift that could transform them into Magekind.

If, that is, the adult Latent made love to a Maja or Magus at least three times. Repeated sexual contact triggered the Gift, transforming the Latent in an explosion of magic. Without that contact, the child grew old and died like anybody else, except for passing the trait on to his own Latent descendants. Sometimes the Gift passed unused through so many generations, the Latents themselves forgot its existence.

Which is how Caroline became a witch after meeting Dominic Bonnhome in a bar. He'd spent the next month romancing her—wine, roses, expensive dinners. She'd just lost her teaching job to state education cutbacks, and she was feeling all too vulnerable. Dominic seemed the perfect antidote: handsome, seductive, fantastic in bed. A dream lover who anticipated her every need and fulfilled each and every one of them. What more could a girl want?

Then he told her he was a vampire. Didn't it just figure? The man of her dreams was a nutball. What was worse, he swore she was a descendent of one of the knights of the Round Table. She was getting ready to call the little men in white coats when he turned into a wolf.

What a relief.

So when he'd offered her immortality, measureless power, and a role in saving the world with him by her side forever, she'd jumped at it like the lovesick idiot she'd been. The next thing she knew, it felt like the power of the cosmos was pouring into her on the end of Dominic's dick. Suddenly she was a Maja, mistress of mind-blowing magical powers. Scary as hell, but what a kick.

It only got better when he showed her how to create a magic gate to Avalon. She thought she'd died and gone to cheerleader heaven.

Which was when her dream lover dropped her like a coyote-ugly sorority girl the morning after a drunken frat party. Ooops. Her Maja trainer later told her Dominic was a professional seducer whose job was romancing promising Latents. She'd been suckered.

Now the latest vampire in her life was watching her through the smoke of his cigar. Sir Galahad himself. She could tell just by looking at him that he was going to be bigger trouble than Dominic.

"Ninety percent of what you've heard about me is bullshit," Galahad told her.

"Yeah? My trainer said you Round Table guys are stone killers who go through women like toilet paper." *Keep your distance, Sir Fangsalot.*

He stuck the cigar between his fangs and grinned around it. "You got me on the first part. Not sure about the second." Puffing, he allowed an artistic pause to develop. "I've never used toilet paper. Last time I took a dump, Europe was sliding into the Dark Ages." Before she could think of a suitable response to that one, he flicked his cigar into the ashtray. "So what brings you to the Lords' Club, Caroline? You do realize the Ladies' Club is across the street, right?"

Apparently Sir Galahad was a sexist jerk. That made things a lot easier. "I guess you didn't get the memo. Men and women are equal now."

He gave her a long look that somehow made her feel like a bitch. "Maybe, but witches are better than everybody. Which is why there are two clubs. All that blood and sex is *so* distasteful."

And maybe she needed to quit being so defensive before she alienated the only guy who could help her. "That's what I get for making assumptions."

"I forgive you." He stretched out his long legs, mailed heels clanking on the hardwood floor as he studied her. "Mostly because of those shorts. Is that fabric, or just a layer of magical spray paint?"

Caroline glanced down. She wore the same snug denim cutoffs and cropped T-shirt she'd had on when she sat down to watch TV. "I forgot I was wearing these. I came right over when I had the vision."

"Yeah, I figured I didn't owe this little encounter to good Karma." He rolled out of his chair with a boneless grace that suggested he wasn't kidding about the enchanted armor. Caroline followed as he sauntered over to the bar and pulled a glass down from an overhead rack. "I assume this vision did not involve you, me, and a pair of fur-lined handcuffs."

She had to admit she was tempted, Dominic notwithstanding. "If I said yes, could we pretend it did?"

He looked up at her, lifting a brow. "I'd love to, but I get the distinct impression we have a more pressing engagement." Pouring two fingers of whiskey into a glass, he handed it to her. "Spit it out, Caroline. Who am I supposed to kill now?"

2

❖

CAROLINE reached past Galahad to claim the glass of whiskey. She had the feeling she was going to need it. "Actually, I think they're vampires."

"Figures. Geirolf's bunch?"

"Who's Geirolf?"

"You *are* new." He shrugged those impressive gold-clad shoulders. "It's complicated. Why don't you tell me what you saw?"

She hesitated, not sure where to start. "Well, you're not going to believe this, but I think I saw the devil."

"Big guy? Red skin, huge horns?"

"I'm not making this up."

"I don't doubt it, but that wasn't the devil. *That* was Geirolf."

"You're kidding. Horns?"

"He only had horns part of the time. The rest of the time, he looked kind of like Richard Gere." Galahad took another swig from his bottle and grimaced at the fire.

"Both forms were probably illusions. He was actually an alien from another planet in the Mageverse."

Dominic had mentioned Mageverse aliens, too. Apparently Merlin and his lover Nimue had also been from another planet; they'd come to Realspace Earth like old-style missionaries visiting Africa. After transforming the humans they'd chosen as champions, they'd jaunted off to the next world on their list. "Geirolf is one of Merlin's people?"

"God, no." Galahad leaned a mailed elbow against the bar, armor creaking as he settled in to tell his story. "Geirolf and his kind—they're called the Dark Ones—are psychic parasites."

Caroline snorted. "Sounds like Dominic."

"Guy that turned you?"

"Yeah."

"I figured. You've got that skittish look. Court seducers don't have a whole lot of scruples when it comes to recruitment." He met her gaze. "Not all of us are like that, Caroline."

Those blue eyes were so direct and level, she found herself relaxing. Maybe he could be trusted. "That's good to hear. So what's this with these killer aliens?"

He puffed his cigar a few times, eying her thoughtfully through the smoke before continuing. "The Dark Ones came to Earth about five thousand years ago and started passing themselves off as gods. They'd con the locals into making human sacrifices, then they'd feed on the life force of the victims. When Merlin and Nimue showed up, they declared war on the Dark Ones and kicked their collective butts."

She toasted him with her glass. "Yay, Merlin."

He grinned and flicked his ashes into the crystal ashtray at his elbow. "After the battle, Merlin and Nimue banished the Dark Ones and imprisoned their ringleader, Geirolf, in a cell on Mageverse Earth."

"Why didn't they kill him?"

"Evidently they're not real big on killing. Personally, I think it's the only real way to thin the asshole population."

Caroline instantly thought of a principal or two she'd like him to meet. "That could work."

"Yeah, but they won't let me do it. Anyway, Geirolf stayed locked up for the next sixteen centuries before escaping a year ago. The bastard managed to create a vampire army before we killed him last month."

"You sure he's dead? Because I saw him making magical cups in my vision."

Galahad shook his head. "Nope, he's dead. You must have seen something that's already happened. I never heard anything about any cups, though."

"Well, he made them. Three of them. He gave them to these . . . I guess they were his priests. They wore these really loud robes. Anyway, thousands of worshipers lined up to drink from those cups. As soon as they took a sip, they turned into vampires." She sipped her whiskey and frowned. "Some of whom were female. I thought only men became vamps."

"Geriolf's vamps have different rules than we do." Galahad scratched his jaw thoughtfully. "So that's how he transformed all those idiots. We wondered. Sounds like he stole a couple of pages from Merlin's book."

"Presumably. Next I saw him getting ready to sacrifice a naked man and woman on this stone altar . . ."

"Right. That was a Magekind couple, Erin Grayson and Reece Champion. Geirolf intended to use their deaths to power a spell designed to wipe us all out."

"Sounds ugly."

"That's putting it mildly. We'd have all cashed in our chips if he'd pulled that spell off. Luckily Erin and Reece managed to kill him first. But before we could wipe out Geirolf's worshippers, his second-in-command scattered them all over the planet. We've been hunting vampires ever since." Galahad grimaced. "And what a pain in the ass that's been."

"Oh, so that's what that was. I wondered what the hell was going on when I saw all those vampires vanish." Caroline sighed and took another sip. "Anyway, it's going to get worse."

"Figures. Why?"

"Geirolf's priests took the cups with them when they gated away. I saw this one in particular make his own little nest after looking up twenty of his followers. And since he's got his very own cup—"

Galahad winced. "—He's going to use it to create more vampires."

She nodded. "His own private army."

"Jesu, that's all we need." He sighed. "Looks like we're going on a cup hunt."

IT had always annoyed Galahad that Magekind vampires couldn't work spells beyond healing their own wounds or turning into wolves. If you needed anything magical done, you had to go to a witch, particularly for complex spells. However, for relatively simple ones—protection or communication, for example—you could get her to make you an enchanted object, like armor, swords or gems. You could then use that object to work that specific spell.

Which was why Galahad was forced to put his helm on to contact Morgana Le Fay. When he closed his visor and called her name, her image instantly appeared in his mind.

Normally, Morgana favored slinky lingerie or designer suits, but this time she was clad in a glittering suit of plate mail, heavily engraved with runes and set with enchanted gems. A chain mail coif framed her long-boned, elegant face. Even in her current grim mood, she was one of the most beautiful women he'd ever seen. "Your timing leaves much to be desired, Galahad," she growled. "We found that nest in Peru, and I'm getting ready to lead an attack. I don't have time to chat."

"Make time," he snapped, and quickly filled her in.

When he finished, she cursed in a fluid, profane blend of a dozen dead languages. "Enchanted cups. No wonder there seem to be so many more of these Goddess-cursed vampires."

"We've got to get that cup, Morgana."

"Obviously. I'll want a look at it, if I'm supposed to create a counter-spell."

"Then Caroline and I are going to need reinforcements. She estimates there were a good twenty vamps in that nest she saw."

"Then you'll just have to figure something out, because I can't spare anyone." When he started to protest, Morgana held up a ringed hand. "Galahad, we're about to fight a force of two thousand with one barely half that size. Arthur has his hands full with odds just as bad in Turkey, and Lancelot and Grace are leading a force against a heavily fortified nest in Montana. Then we've got another hundred agents going after individual killers, with Merlin knows how many innocents at risk." She broke off. "Speaking of killers, I gather you tracked your assignment down."

"Took him out just after sunset." He grimaced, remembering the carnage he'd seen. "Son of a bitch was lucky I hadn't found the bodies before I killed him, or I'd have gotten artistic."

She winced. "How bad was it?"

"Bad as it gets. I counted twenty kids, all under eleven. Did save three of 'em he had in a cage, though. They're going to need a Maja to do psychic repairs, or they'll be screwed up for the rest of their lives."

Actually, he wouldn't mind being put under a spell or two himself. Otherwise he'd be seeing that pit full of little corpses in his nightmares for the next couple of centuries. At least until he saw something worse.

Morgana sighed. "Let me get through this fight and I'll attend to it. What did you do with the survivors?"

"Called the police after I killed the bastard. They'll see the boys get home."

She stiffened. "You didn't let the mortals find his body?"

"I'm not an idiot, Morgana. Nobody's going to find him. Ever."

"Good." The witch studied his face, her own softening fractionally. "Before you go after that cup, get something to drink. And I'm not talking about that mortal poison you love. You look drained."

Galahad gave her a taunting smile. "So gate on over. You know I don't drink *that* from a bottle."

Morgana lifted an elegantly aloof brow. "I seem to have a prior engagement. Why don't you nibble on your new friend instead? She probably needs it as much as you do. By the way, be careful with her. She hasn't had combat training."

He straightened. "*Any?* Merlin's Cup, Morgana!"

"Why do you think she's not here fighting? We're so short-handed, I had to pull her trainer in. And I could hardly throw Caroline into a battle like this when she's only had about a week's instruction."

"Let me get this straight. You left a brand-new Maja alone in Avalon with nobody to instruct her in the use of her powers? You're lucky she hasn't turned the city into a crater."

Morgana snorted. "That kind of spell would require more knowledge and power than she has."

"And you want me to take her into combat?"

"Not particularly, but we don't seem to have a choice."

"Morgana . . ."

"What do you want me to do about it, Galahad?" she snapped. "Yes, I'm aware the situation is far from ideal, but you're just going to have to make the best of it. Keep a close eye on the girl, kill as many vampires as you can, and don't let her blow up anything important."

He was about to tell her just how asinine that order was when something boomed, almost knocking her off her feet. Morgana ducked with a vile Latin curse. "Take care of it, Galahad. I've got vampires to kill."

The image vanished.

Galahad glowered into his darkened visor. Perfect. Just perfect. Thrown to the wolves with no backup except a grass-green Maja who'd probably blast him by mistake. He jerked off his helm and cursed.

"I gather they're not sending reinforcements," Caroline said.

Galahad turned to see her sprawled in a chair, long, silken legs crossed at the ankle. The view was almost enough to take him mind off their current situation. "They don't have any to send. We're stretched too thin, and Geirolf's vampires seem to be creating new recruits. If we don't get a handle on this, we're screwed."

"I was afraid of that. In my vision, I didn't see anybody else on our side." She flipped her long, silken hair off one shoulder. It reached to the center of her back, as mink brown as those big dark eyes of hers. They dominated her oval face, though that exotic full-lipped mouth did a good job of balancing them out. Add a round chin and high cheekbones, and you had a girl-next-door prettiness Galahad found more than a little intriguing.

Caroline's body was just as mouth-watering, with a lean, elegantly muscled build that suggested she did a lot more than grade papers. Her cropped shirt clung to perfect breasts the size of brandy snifters, while those spray-paint shorts revealed long, sleek legs.

Except . . . Galahad looked closer and frowned. There was a hectic flush across her high cheekbones, one he knew a little too well. "How long has it been since you were milked?"

She lifted a brow. "Is that a reference to breast size? Because if it is . . ."

"No, when was the last time anybody fed from you?" He hated that term. The Majae considered *milk* demeaning, but at least it didn't make them sound like Happy Meals.

"That would have been Dominic. I didn't much notice, since I was busy getting barbecued at the time." She rolled her eyes. " 'Merlin's Gift,' my ass. Hell of a way to ruin a good climax."

"How long have you been here?"

She shrugged. "A month or so."

"And you haven't fed anybody in all that time? Didn't they warn you that you have to donate every two weeks?"

"Or what, the Avalon Red Cross sends somebody named Guido to collect?"

"No, you pop a blood vessel and drop dead if there's nobody around to fix you." He watched her eyes widen and swore. "They didn't tell you. Somebody needs to be spanked."

"Dominic said I'm immortal!"

"You are. But along with giving you magical powers, Merlin's Gift allows you to feed vampires much more often than mortals can. Which means if you don't donate, your blood pressure spikes."

Worry drew down her dark, silky brows. "Couldn't I fix it with a spell?"

"'Fraid not. The Gift doesn't allow that. Merlin intended Majae to feed Magi, and he made damn sure they do it." He stubbed out his cigar in a crystal ashtray on the bar, then turned to her. "Come here, sweetheart."

Her eyes widened in an expression of alarm he would have found amusing if he hadn't been so damn hungry for her. "What? Why?"

"I'm a vampire, Caroline. Why do you think?"

3
❦

GALAHAD'S blue eyes simmered with a blend of erotic heat and alien hunger Caroline found both intimidating and perversely sexy. She backed up a pace. "Hey, I thought you didn't play those kinds of games."

"I don't." He followed, his gaze so seductive, she could feel her resistance melting. "I'm not offering you a sham romance, Caroline. This is about simple mutual need." As he spoke, she saw the flash of fangs.

God, she was tempted. What would it be like to feel those arms around her, that mouth on her skin? Would he be sweet and tender or rough and dominant?

Since they both knew what to expect, where was the harm?

But . . . "Believe me, I'd love nothing more than to play with all your jutting bits, but the bad guys are hungry, too. And they do hurt people. I don't think we have time for you to take a lunch break."

Irritation flashed through his simmering sensuality. "Do you have time to drop dead?"

Caroline blinked. "Not really, no."

"And I haven't fed in two days. Which is not the way I like to go into a battle to the death, particularly when I'm outnumbered. Just how long do we have before the bad guys start serving cocktails out of Geirolf's Grail?"

"I don't know. Probably not long."

His gaze locked on her mouth. "So we don't have sex."

Caroline licked her lips, trying to ignore the whimper of disappointment in the back of her mind. "No?"

"No. I'll just have to restrict myself to that pretty throat." He stepped closer, lids lowering over those blue, blue eyes as he lowered his head. "At least for right now."

She tensed, wondering if he was just going to grab her and snack, but Galahad was a lot more subtle than she'd given him credit for. He didn't take her in his arms. Only their mouths touched, his lips brushing over hers, damp, warm, maddening satin. Knowing she shouldn't, Caroline opened for him.

Mutual need. Yeah, she could do mutual need. That was safe.

Galahad caught her lower lip gently between his teeth and sipped at it. He was really good at that. With a groan, she slid her arms around his neck and buried one hand in the coarse black silk of his hair. The hard, cool contours of his armor pressing against her body made her wonder what he felt like underneath it. "You know," she said against his mouth, "this is kind of kinky."

"Oh, I haven't even gotten started." Galahad's tongue stroked boldly between her lips. He tasted of enchanted smoke and whiskey, a thoroughly masculine combination that tempted her into deepening the kiss. Instead, he drew back to lick and nip at her mouth.

She leaned into him blindly, craving the contact of his body, but all her hands touched was the cool, etched steel of his armor. Caroline moaned in disappointment and seriously considered zapping him naked just so she could rub up against him.

It had taken Dominic an hour of serious foreplay to make her burn like this.

Galahad tore his mouth free of hers and lifted his head, his blue eyes feral. "You sure we don't have time for more?"

Caroline stared blindly up at his extravagantly handsome face as she clung to his breastplate. "Oh, we've got plenty of time."

Fangs flashed in his smile. "Yeah?"

"What, you expect me to say I'd rather go fight vampires than have jungle sex with you? What are you, nuts?"

"Guess that answers that question." He stepped back and took her shoulders in his hands. Spinning her around, he pulled her back against his tall, armored body.

She stiffened. "What . . . ?"

"I'm losing it." Galahad's breath puffed warm against her ear. "If we stay face-to-face, I'm not sure I can resist the temptation." He pressed a burning, open-mouthed kiss to the leaping pulse in her throat.

Caroline caught her breath. "Is this going to hurt?"

He licked the straining cord in the side of her neck. "Did it hurt the last time?"

Nerves made her joke. "I'm not sure. About the time he bit me, I got lit up like a mosquito in a bug zapper by Merlin's Ugly Practical Joke."

Galahad chuckled, the sound wickedly suggestive. "Ah—a virgin." Tauntingly, he raked the very tips of his fangs over her pulse.

She shivered in an erotic blend of arousal and fear. "Galahad . . ."

"It won't hurt," he interrupted, his hands suddenly sliding up under her T-shirt to claim her breasts. "Well . . . maybe it will, but you'll be too hot to care."

His hands felt very warm as they squeezed her through the thin lace cups of her bra. Skillfully, he hooked his index fingers into the fabric and tugged just enough to pop her nipples free.

Caroline looked down to watch as Galahad's clever hands found the tight little peaks. Plucked, rolled, stroked. She squirmed, unconsciously rubbing her backside over his armored groin. The steel codpiece jutted against her ass, taunting her with the question of what his cock looked like.

"Sensitive little nipples you've got there," Galahad whispered in her ear. "Bet they'd be fun to suck." He rolled the hard nubs. "Mmm. Are they, Caroline?"

"You're asking *me*?" Panting, she threw back her head and let it rest on his hard, armored shoulder. She was starkly aware of his height. You'd think he'd be short, given the times he'd come from, but he was a full head taller than she was. An image flashed through her mind—Galahad naked, all sculpted swordsman brawn. "Oh, God!"

He inhaled sharply. "Ahhhh. Getting nicely wet now. I can smell it." Releasing one of her breasts, he reached down her torso, found the button of her shorts. Flicked it open. The zipper hissed.

She tensed at the erotic anticipation curling through her in shivering waves.

Galahad worked a hand down into her open fly and slipped into her delicate silk panties. As he found her sex, Caroline groaned helplessly. Two long fingers pumped their way between her tight folds, eased by the thick cream of her desire.

"Oh, yeah. You're wet." He scissored her clit between two fingers, and she arched her back, gasping.

"A little." Actually, a lot. She set her feet farther apart, knowing if he decided to push her down and take her, she'd welcome him. She was one deep breath from begging as it was.

"Mmmmmm. This is the good part." Galahad paused to trace his tongue over one of the whorls of her ear. "The anticipation. I'm going to take you right to the edge. And then . . ." He lowered his head to lick her pulse. ". . . I'm going to *bite*." Strong fingers stroked right up into her core as his thumb strummed her clit.

Caroline groaned. He'd discovered a delicate little bundle of nerves right over her pulse. He raked his fang tips across it as he played with her. She felt the orgasm building, teased to unbearable heights by those clever fingers. She arched against him as he pumped both fingers into her depths, squeezed her nipple with tender brutality.

And bit into her straining throat as he flicked a skillful thumb over her clit.

Her strangled gasp of pain spiraled into a cry of pleasure as her orgasm burst free. That first sweet wave was followed by a second, and then a third. Writhing mindlessly in Galahad's arms, she came in long dizzy pulses as he drank.

HER blood burned hotter than the whiskey had, flooding his mouth with its raw, intoxicating taste. Galahad tightened his grip in instinctive greed, wishing he were naked so he could feel every silken inch of her long, supple body.

He drank hungrily, drank until it should be time to start tapering off, drank until his cock ached. Caroline went right on pumping hard. It really had been way too long for her. She needed more drawn off, and he was delighted to comply.

Almost as delighted as he would have been to thrust into the tight, creamy flesh he could feel gripping his fingers. He was hard as a pole arm behind his armor.

But now was not the time, so all Galahad could do was work her with his fingers and drive her to another convulsing orgasm while he drank. Her nails raked the engraved steel of his armor as he fed.

Finally, after long, delicious moments, the pressure eased off. Galahad lifted his head, cradling her, knowing she'd feel dizzy from the sudden decrease in that murderous blood pressure.

"Thank you," he said in her ear. His voice sounded hoarse, and he cleared his throat.

"Oohhhh." She hung in his arms, panting. "That was . . . incredible."

Galahad grinned over her head. "My pleasure."

"I . . ." She stopped to swallow. "I've never come like that just from being . . ."

"Bitten?"

"That, too." She straightened in his arms as if making a deliberate effort to pull herself together. "Is it always like that?"

It had been pretty damn intense. More so than the last time he'd . . . Well, actually he couldn't remember the last time it had been that hot. "You needed it more than most." Yeah, that sounded good. He turned her carefully in his arms, made her meet his gaze. "How are you feeling now?"

She blinked, her cheeks a little flushed, her eyes glazed. "Good, actually. Better. Which is funny, because I'd expected to feel weak after losing that much blood."

"That's because you damn near waited too long. If you'd gone one more day without being milked, you'd have popped something that would have killed you." He laid a hand alongside her face to gather her floating attention. "Never do that again, Caroline. It's not something to fool around with. When you feel pain or weakness, don't just magic it away. Tell someone."

"Yeah, sure." She swayed against him. "Ummm. A chair would be good."

Galahad guided her over to one and tried to ignore the thoughts those long, bare legs inspired as she sat down. They had other fish to fry.

Bloodsucking vampire shark, in fact.

4

GALAHAD spent the next half hour grilling her about the vision.

So much for lazing in the afterglow.

Not that she could blame him. They had a nest of vampires to kill. *Focus, Caroline.*

But it was tough, and not just because the amazingly gorgeous man questioning her had just drunk her blood. She knew she must have climaxed harder at some point in her twenty-eight years, but damned if she could remember it.

And that was aside from the fact he was sixteen hundred years old *and* a knight of the Round Table.

What the hell was happening to her? This time last year she'd been trying to teach sentence construction to a bunch of bored high school juniors. Now she was supposed to help Sir Galahad clean out a nest of evil vampires and recover the Unholy Grail. What did she look like, Sarah Michelle Gellar?

Though she'd stack her eye candy against Buffy's any day.

Apparently satisfied he had as much of the story as he was getting, Galahad leaned against the bar and started scribbling on a notepad she'd conjured for him. His handsome face drew into a scowl of concentration as he wrote in long, slashing strokes.

He'd drank her blood. And she'd liked it.

Caroline was still mentally reeling from that when he finally lifted his head, running a harried hand through that silken hair of his. "Obviously, we need to clean out that nest you saw. The thing is, I don't particularly like going into combat based on intelligence from a vision."

"Yeah, I could see how that would be less than ideal." He looked all sexy and grim and determined. She, on the other hand, felt like a giant rag doll with all the stuffing sucked out. *Focus, Caroline.*

"That's putting it mildly," he said, turning to pace, apparently unaware of her dazzled gaze. "Visions only reveal the big picture, and in combat, it's the details that bite you on the ass. I'm damned if I'm going to just gate into some magical underground installation without knowing how many bad guys are going to object."

That particular mental image was enough to kill the last of her afterglow and start her stomach crocheting itself into sick knots. She rubbed it absently. "So how do you suggest we find out?"

"For one thing, we don't do this in one big go. It's going to take a series of strikes, just in and out. Fast."

Caroline nodded. It made sense. Not enough to keep her from wanting to throw up, but still.

"First order of business is to find that Grail you saw and secure it for Morgana to study," he continued. "Then we gate home to plan our next move. In the meantime, I want you to try to do a magical scan and get me a bad-guy head count. Find out where they are and what they're doing. Think you can do that?"

"I'll give it my best shot." Her palms were going damp. "Then what?"

"Based on that intelligence, we'll make a series of strikes to whittle down their forces."

Which was military speak for *killing people. Oh, God.* "Sounds good." An outright lie if ever she'd told one.

In her entire life, Caroline had been in exactly two fights. The first has been when she was ten and Jenny Peterson said she was a stupid head. She didn't remember much about the resulting catfight beyond hair pulling and being told she hit like a girl. Originality had never been Jenny's strong suit.

She'd gotten into the second one just a couple of years ago, when she'd tried to break up a pair of brawling seniors. Somebody shot an elbow into her face and she spent the next two weeks looking like Sylvester Stallone at the end of *Rocky*.

Now she was supposed to battle killer magic-users who sacrificed people and drank blood from cups. This was beginning to feel like a bad reality show. *Survivor: Vampire Vacation.* Somebody vote her off the island. Please.

But if they didn't do this, people were going to die.

"Your eyes are the size of bread plates." Galahad put a hand on her shoulder that was almost fatherly. "Look, this first time out, I'll do the heavy lifting. I don't expect you to do much real fighting; you haven't had the training."

Caroline licked her dry lips. "What if we're really outnumbered?"

He shrugged. "Toss a couple of fireballs and try not to hit me. Then gate us out of there." Apparently reading her sick anxiety, he gave her a reassuring smile. "I've been at this since Rome fell, Caroline. I know what I'm doing. Now, armor up and let's go."

"Armor. Okay." Tentatively, Caroline laid a hand on his

breastplate, closed her eyes, and reached for the magic. It leaped for her as it always did, almost joyously, surging across her body in a tingling, foaming wave. She envisioned what she wanted, and the energy settled against her skin, grew solid and cool. When she opened her eyes again, she was wearing a gleaming suit of magical plate that was an exact duplicate of his.

God, magic was fun. The rest of this sucked, but she did like conjuring.

Galahad looked down at her chest and grinned. "You do realize those runes spell my name, right?"

Feeling a flush spread across her cheekbones, Caroline looked down at the indecipherable designs scrawled across her breasts. She couldn't even read the symbols, much less write her own name in them. "Oh. Um . . ."

He laughed as he moved to put on his helm and gauntlets. "Don't worry about it, Caroline. Just create a gate to the cup."

GALAHAD watched Caroline square her shoulders. She'd gone pale as a ghost, yet she still seemed grimly determined to take out the nest. He had to admire that.

Besides, she looked really cute wearing that scaled-down version of his armor, name and all.

Gesturing, she drew the gate out of the air. It spiraled outward from a pinpoint spark to a glowing, man-shaped opening in the course of a blink. Not bad. The kid was green, but she had muscle.

Galahad stepped closer to see what was on the other side. The view showed a fountain cut from rough, red stone sitting in the center of a round room built of the same crimson rock. A clawed hand thrust from the center of the fountain bowl, holding something gold.

A cup.

And from it spilled . . .

"Is that *blood*?" Caroline demanded.

"Probably just looks like it. Geirolf's lot would never let that much go to waste. You sense anybody there?"

"Not right now. Which doesn't mean they won't gate in behind us."

"We'll have to risk it." Having dealt with more than enough raw recruits, he decided to remind her of the plan. "So we'll make it quick. I'll snatch Geirolf's Grail while you get me a bad-guy head count. Then we duck back through the gate again and decide how to clean house."

"Okay." Caroline's voice shook.

He threw her a smile as he lowered his visor. "You're doing good, kid. You'll be fine."

As he reached over to flip hers down, too, she gave him a sick smile. "Wonder if Custer said that before the Little Big Horn?"

"No, actually, he said, 'Indians? What Indians?'"

She snickered as the visor clicked down.

Satisfied, Galahad drew his sword and stepped into the gate. Magic rippled over his skin in a hot, tingling wave as it transported him across the dimensions to Realspace Earth. In a blink he was through, stepping out onto the smooth stone floor.

He moved aside to let Caroline through as he aimed a quick look around them, all his senses open. He didn't smell anything but damp stone and water. The room was silent except for the sullen patter of that disgusting fountain. "You feel anything?"

Caroline's helmeted head tilted as she went still. He could feel the magic rise around her. "We're underground," she said. "Somewhere in . . . Virginia? Out in the sticks . . ." She stiffened, her voice rising in horror. "Oh, God! They killed four people to work the spell! They sacrificed them right over our heads. I can *feel* them."

"It's okay, you're all right." Galahad touched her shoulder to bring her out of it. When her eyes met his through the slits in her visor, he told her, "These bastards can't draw on the energies of the Mageverse the way Majae can. They have to use death energy to work their spells."

"And what a fine source of power you're going to be," a strange voice said. Galahad whirled an instant too late.

BOOOOM!

The blast of magic took him full in the chest, knocking him across the room to slam hard into a stone wall. If he hadn't been wearing enchanted armor, it would have flash-fried him. Caroline screamed his name.

He hit the ground rolling and scrambled for the sword he'd dropped when the blast hit. The hiss and crackle of magic filled the air, shots volleying back and forth over his head. He grabbed his weapon and looked up to see Caroline exchanging fireballs with a tall, graying man in gaudy pseudo-priestly robes.

"You back-shooting son of a bitch!" she snarled, summoning another shimmering ball of energy. Judging from the glow, it had enough kick to melt a hole in a tank. She lobbed it at him, but the priest blocked it with a shield spell. His return blast splashed off her armor in licking tongues of flame.

She danced aside and hurled another ball at him like a major league pitcher with the bases loaded. He blocked it and started circling, looking for an opening.

Galahad knew Caroline would eventually wear the bastard down, since Geirolf's vamps ran out of magic when they used up the life force they'd stolen. Majae, on the other hand, drew on the raw energy of the Mageverse itself.

Unfortunately, she probably didn't have that much time. He was willing to bet the bastard's reinforcements were on the way.

He had to wrap this up.

Galahad leaped for the priest, bellowing a battle cry as he swung his sword with all his strength. The cultist spun, throwing up another one of those magical shields. The blade jolted in Galahad's hands as it hit the glowing barrier hard enough to rattle his back teeth. He ignored the sensation and started hacking, trying to batter down the shield before the priest could muster stronger defenses.

A burst of heat blazed against his back. *Hell, another one already.* Galahad ducked, glancing around for his new foe.

"Ooops!" Caroline called, a second fireball floating in her hand. "Sorry!"

"Watch it!" he growled and returned his attention to his opponent.

But the vampire had taken advantage of his instant's distraction to create a sword and armor. The priest now wore a suit of iridescent black mail, swinging the sword with skillful rotations of one wrist. Gierolf must have magically taught his worshipers how to use a blade; most moderns barely knew hilt from point.

Galahad wasn't worried. No spell could match his sixteen hundred years as a swordsman.

The only question was—how long before the rest of the cultists arrived?

CAROLINE watched anxiously, looking for an opening. The two vampires were so fast, she was afraid to try another shot for fear of hitting Galahad again.

Besides, he didn't seem to need the help. The knight moved in an oiled blur of gold, battering at his opponent with flashing strokes of his sword.

There! They'd whirled apart.

Magic rushed down her arm, tingling and stinging to coalesce in a white-hot ball. She hurled it at the priest with all the force she could muster. He screamed, the sound blending with an outraged female shriek.

"Bitch!"

A weight slammed into her back, knocking her flat on her face. Stunned, disoriented—where the hell had that come from?—Caroline felt something jerk off her helmet. She twisted around and threw up an arm just in time to block the fist coming at her head.

Britney Spears was sitting on her back.

Actually, it just looked like Britney. Blond, so young she could have been a cheerleader on the team Caroline advised. But her face was twisted like something out of a horror flick, and fangs filled her open mouth in curving spikes.

"You hurt my dad!" she hissed, fingers fisting in Caroline's hair. "I'm going to rip out your fuckin' throat and use the power to kill your boyfriend!" Fangs gaping, she bent toward Caroline's exposed throat.

"Get *off*!" Caroline grabbed for the power, twisted around, and shoved her fist into the girl's open mouth. Fangs raked her knuckles, but she ignored the sting and sent raw energy shooting down her arm.

The blast picked the girl up and threw her across the room like a straw in a hurricane. She didn't even scream as she hit the stone floor with a meaty thud.

Heart pounding, Caroline scrambled to her feet. The girl didn't move.

Swallowing, Caroline edged closer, only to recoil in horror. The kid was burned black, flesh seared to charcoal by that panicked blast. "Oh, Jesus."

"That your first?" Galahad asked, rough sympathy in his voice.

Unable to speak, she turned. He stood looking at her, his sword dripping blood. At his feet lay the priest, his body oddly stunted. It took her a moment to realize the object lying a few feet away wasn't the man's helmet.

It was his head.

Caroline whirled away and almost stepped on the girl she'd killed. She clamped both hands over her mouth and closed her eyes, fighting the rise of vomit.

"Shit," Galahad growled, his voice grim.

Mechanically, she turned her back on the body and opened her eyes. He was staring at the fountain.

Geirolf's Grail had disappeared.

5

"WHAT the hell happened to the cup?" Galahad growled, glaring at the empty clawed hand still gushing faux blood. "I know I kept that priest too busy to do anything with it."

"The girl must have transported it away before she attacked me," Caroline said, raking a shaking hand through her hair. She carefully did not look at either of the corpses.

He cursed in a language that sounded vaguely like Latin. "Is there any chance it's still in this complex?"

Caroline closed her eyes and concentrated, searching for the slightly greasy mental impression the cup had given her. Nothing. She swore in frustration and opened her eyes. "She must have sent it to her vampire buddies."

"Not necessarily. I've known Majae to create magical shields so strong, you could stand right next to it and not know it was there. We're going to have make a fast search." He turned toward the nearest of two corridors into the chamber. "And while we're at it, we need to make sure there's nobody else lurking around."

"I'm not picking up anybody."

Galahad jerked a thumb at the bodies. "You didn't sense them either, but they were sure as hell here."

That stung. "I'm sorry. I guess I screwed up."

He sighed and flipped up his visor. "No, that was uncalled-for. They probably gated in behind us. Either way, we're both still alive and two of the bad guys are dead. You didn't freeze when I was hit; you stepped in and started defending me. That was damn good for a first fight."

Unwillingly, her eyes tracked toward the burned and twisted body of the girl. "Yeah. Real good."

Galahad followed her gaze. "She'd have killed you, Caroline."

"She was trying to defend her father." She forced an insouciant shrug. "But hey, one less murdering vamp, right? Besides, she reminded me way too much of some of my bitchier cheerleaders."

"Cheerleaders?" He sheathed his sword. The blade scraped against the leather sliding in, the cave giving it a sinister echo.

"I'm a teacher. I was the squad advisor last year." Caroline's gaze drifted toward the girl's body before she snatched it away. "Did I tell you I was captain of my college cheerleading squad? We went state champion one year. I shake a mean pom-pom."

Galahad gave her a long, level look before stooping to pick up her fallen helm. "The first time you're forced to kill is never easy, but she didn't give you a choice."

"Not buying the act, huh?"

"No." He flipped up her visor so he could meet her eyes. "Whether she was defending her father or not, she wasn't blameless. You told me yourself that they murdered four people for the magic to build this complex. She was part of that. And judging by the way she tried to rip out your throat, I doubt she was as an innocent bystander."

Caroline shook her head. "I know, but . . ."

"Remember the string of cult murders earlier this year? The poisonings, the bombings, the mutilations? She and her fellow cultists did all that to provide Geirolf with the power he used to damn near wipe out Magekind. She had it coming."

"She could have been one of my students, Galahad."

"Klebold and Harris were kids, too, but that didn't stop them at Columbine."

She swallowed. The stench of burned flesh was making her queasy. "I know, but this is going to bother me for a long time."

"It's always going to bother you. You never forget the first one."

"That wasn't what I was hoping to hear, Galahad."

"What can I say? I'm like Superman—I'm always honest." He grinned. "Except when I lie."

She snorted, reluctantly amused. He was entirely too damn charming for her peace of mind. "Oh, that's comforting."

"I know." He clapped his mailed hands. "Okay, break's over. We need to find that cup and gate out of here before dawn. I figure we've got maybe two hours before the sun rises."

"We're underground. What difference does it make? It's not like you'd ignite. Dominic said that's a myth, like the thing about crosses and garlic."

"He left a few details out. No, I don't burst into flame, but when the sun comes up, I loose consciousness, and there's not a damn thing I can do about it."

"Well, that makes about as much sense as screen doors on a submarine. Why?"

He shrugged. "It's got something to do with absorbing energies from the Mageverse. Point is, I don't want to be here when that happens. If that cup's here, we need to find it. Now."

She sighed and snapped her visor closed. "You're the boss."

"You bet your tight little ass I am. And I'm telling you to get it moving." Drawing his sword again, he turned to lead the way down the nearest corridor. "Stay close."

THE good news was that they found no other vampires in the complex. The bad news was that they didn't find Geirolf's Grail either. Under Galahad's direction, Caroline scanned the walls and furniture carefully with a spell that was the magical equivalent of an X ray. She found nothing other than a nauseating collection of photographs in a drawer, apparently souvenirs from the cult's murders. The girl who'd attacked her held the knife in one of them, blood-spattered and smirking.

Caroline started feeling better about killing her.

The complex itself was laid out around a single cavernous central chamber like the hub of a wheel. Corridors spoked out to smaller chambers, most of them dormitories, though one was a den complete with a television set, an entertainment center, and a wide selection of porn DVDs. Galahad made a show of looking through them with such exaggerated lechery Caroline had to laugh.

But any amusement died a quick death when they stepped into the central chamber.

Galahad's vampire nose detected the reek of decayed blood coming from the pentagram-shaped altar that dominated the room. He turned just in time to catch Caroline as she staggered. Her open visor revealed a face as pale as paper.

"Death." Huge dark eyes met his. "I saw this. I saw this room. And now I see . . ." She gagged. "Oh, man, that's just disgusting. What is it with these people?"

"They're assholes?"

"Nah, that's an insult to assholes everywhere." She reached up and dragged off her helm. "Look, this is a waste of time. Geirolf's Grail isn't here, and neither are the vamps—thank God. I've scanned every inch of this place, and there's nothing. Besides, if anybody was here, they'd have jumped us by now."

Frustrated, Galahad glared around at the surrounding walls. "Then where are they? It's barely an hour until dawn. The cultists sleep during the day just like I do."

"Which means they'll be back any minute."

"That, or they'll go to ground somewhere else. Either way, I'm not waiting around to get ambushed. Look, could you work a spell to keep them out of here?"

Caroline's silky brows pulled together. "If I do that, they're going to know we're onto them."

"They'll figure that one out when they see the two bodies. Assuming Teen Bitch didn't just send them the cup and telepathically tell them what was going on."

"But if she did, why didn't they come back and blast us? Something else is going on here." She frowned and scratched her forehead through her open visor. "Think they've just decided to abandon the complex and build another one?"

"But you saw us fighting a whole bunch of them here in that vision. So they're going to come back." He drummed his mailed fingers on the hilt of his sword. "Tell you what. Set a spell to let you know when they return—without alerting them—get rid of the bodies, and gate us out of here. We'll come back when we've got reinforcements. Or at least a better idea what the fuck is going on."

"So what are we going to do in the meantime?"

"Get some sleep. It's not as if I've got a hell of a lot of choice."

THE priest was dead.

Marilyn Roth realized he was gone as she rose from the body of the rival cultist she'd just killed. His gnawing presence had vanished from her mind like a toothache. She licked the blood from her lips and grinned in pure, savage joy.

Alan Grange was dead, stripped of his stolen power, unable to dominate or abuse her any longer. She was free. Free to take control of his cult and enjoy all the benefits leadership would give her: safety and power and the fear of those beneath her.

And she had no intention of losing the opportunity his death gave her.

Her eyes tracked across the battlefield, where Alan's lieutenant was busy raping the leader of the eco-terrorists. Apparently Steve hadn't yet realized the priest was dead.

Good.

She plucked the blade from the heart of her victim and started toward him, detouring around a battling knot of vampires. She glanced at them long enough to make sure her people were winning. They were, so she kept going.

So much for the would-be grail thieves.

Just that night before, Alan announced he'd had a vision another cult had learned they had one of the cups. They'd all known what that meant.

War.

Only last month, all the cults had been united under Geirolf's leadership. That had ended when the demon god died and the vampires were forcibly scattered by Geirolf's lieutenant.

They didn't stay scattered. It wasn't long before the cult

leaders started searching out their original members. Alan had been one of them, armed with the stolen Grail he intended to use in creating fresh recruits.

Unfortunately, he wasn't the only ambitious priest with that thought. Anybody who had a grail was trying to hang onto it, while groups without a cup were trying to take one by force.

So far, Alan's cult had successfully defended its grail against another Satanist cult and a group of white supremacists. Next had come this bunch of eco-loonies who'd thought Earth would be just perfect without all the people on it.

Alan's decision to hit their would-be invaders first had handed them a victory, but they'd still lost several warriors in the process. Marilyn figured she was going to have to do something about recruitment as soon as she took care of Alan's second-in-command.

Of course, once Steve Jones was attended to, she'd have to deal with his supporters, not to mention whomever had killed the priest himself. That last might be a problem, since Alan had gasped something about the grail just before he gated away with his daughter.

But first things first.

Marilyn stepped up behind Jones as he pumped between his victim's thighs. She tapped him on the shoulder, the knife hidden by her side. "Oh, Steve," she purred, "I hate to interrupt . . ."

6

✦

"It's a good thing I'm not afraid of heights." Caroline stepped up to the edge of Galahad's bedroom and looked out over the moonlit mountains. She'd gated them there after he showed her a mental image of where he wanted to go.

Compared to the villas, chateaus, and castles of Avalon, Galahad's home was an exercise in minimalism. The semi-circular room jutted out from the face of a vertical cliff to hang, unsupported, a dizzying distance from the ground. It had no apparent walls other than the cliff itself—and, for that matter, no ceiling either.

That was an illusion, however. She could sense the magical barrier that protected the room emanating from runes cut into the stone. Nothing could get in he didn't want in.

She had to admit, the room suited him. The rough granite wall seemed a reflection of Galahad's uncompromising strength, just as his sensuality was reflected by the circular bed draped in white silk.

A heavy walnut armoire stood off to one side of the bed, its dark, gleaming wood heavily carved with more of those runes. She wondered what enchantment they cast—a cleanliness spell? An anti-wrinkle charm? Probably, since it was a good bet Galahad didn't do laundry.

Noticing a low, musical tinkle, Caroline looked around to see a little waterfall flowing through an opening in the cliff. It splashed down over the rocks to flow past the bed and into a tiny pool surrounded by plants and vines growing from niches in the stone. Other openings glowed with some kind of magical illumination that provided a soft, dim light.

Two rock doorways cut into either side of the cliff wall. Stepping over to one, she saw stairs leading downward. "Where do these go?"

Galahad dropped onto the bed and twisted around to reach into one of the stone niches. He pulled out a bottle and a couple of glasses. "There are two more floors below—a pool room and a library."

Caroline turned to look at him. "That's it? In the whole house?"

He shrugged, pouring the contents of the bottle into the glasses. "Hey, what else do I need? I don't eat anything that's not in the magic wet bar here. Any visitors who need something more substantial are probably Majae, and they can conjure their own food."

"You've got a point." She crossed the room to look down. Jutting from the cliff thirty feet below and off to the left was another circular platform. A pool shimmered in the center of it, its surface rippling from the waterfall tumbling down the cliff to splash into one end. "I've got to admit, this is impressive."

"Morgana built it for me." He walked over and handed her a glass.

Caroline took it. "How'd you get her to do that?"

"We were lovers at the time."

"You banged the dragon lady? You are brave."

"That's exactly what my brother knights said." He smiled a little dryly and took a sip. "We lasted an entire decade before I managed to piss her off. I still hold the record for longest-running relationship with Morgana Le Fay."

"Hey, better than I did with Dominic." Caroline swallowed a mouthful from her own glass, shuddered at the taste, and turned it into Pepsi. "Do you always drink like this?"

Galahad shot her a look. "I'm a vampire, Caroline. The only drinking problem I have is making sure I've got a date on Saturday night."

"You silver-tongued romantic, you."

His smile was wicked. "I didn't hear you complaining."

Caroline turned to watch as he walked back across the room in that muscular, long-legged stalk of his. Damn, the man looked good even wearing more metal than a can of tuna.

It was probably just as well it was so close to dawn. Given her romantic track record, it probably wouldn't be a good idea to yield to Galahad's potent temptation.

He sank down on the bed and slumped, looking tired. "Can you help me with my armor? I doubt I have time to take it all off before the sun comes up."

"Sure. Where do you want it?"

He gestured vaguely. "Over there's fine."

Caroline cast a quick spell, and the suit vanished from his body to take up residence in a neat pile. Her own joined it an instant later.

Galahad looked down at the pair of silk pajama bottoms she'd given him to replace it. "Nice. Thanks." He rubbed absently at his chest. "And I'm clean, too. Aren't you efficient?"

She shrugged and straightened the hem of her own cotton pajamas. "That's the nice thing about magic. It's a great time-saver."

As he rose to pull down the covers, it suddenly occurred to her there was only one bed. But before any real alarm could set in, she got a good look at his back and forgot about everything else. A rainbow of scrapes and bruises decorated his ribs. "What happened to you?"

He glanced up at her as he slid under the covers. "Got into a fight with a pedophile earlier tonight. Bastard had an axe. Armor kept it from cutting me in half, but the impact was a bitch." A pained grunt escaped him as he lay back.

Concerned, Caroline crossed the room to his side, frowning. "You want me to heal that?"

He shrugged. "My body will take care of it by sunset. It's one of the few kinds of magic I do have."

"But you're hurting now. Let me fix it." She could see the pain in his eyes, and it bothered her.

Reaching out a hand, Caroline rested her fingers against the side of his face and reached for her magic. Carefully, she sent it into him in the same gentle stream she used tending her own aches, seeking out his injuries and healing them. As she watched, the bruises faded and disappeared.

He sighed and relaxed. "Thanks."

Caroline shrugged and dropped her hand, feeling oddly shy. "Least I could do after you helped me with Father Fang and Teen Bitch."

"My pleasure, more or less." Galahad settled back against the mound of pillows. "You know, there's more than room enough for two in here."

"Honey, there's room enough for the Washington Redskins in that bed."

"Now there is a thoroughly unpleasant image."

Caroline gave him a wicked grin. "Depends on your point of view."

What the hell. She was too tired to conjure another bed anyway. She moved around to the other side and flipped the comforter back, then slid between the fine silk sheets.

They felt deliciously cool and smooth against her tired body.

With a sigh of pleasure, she snuggled in and looked at the horizon just beginning to pinken over the mountains. "Why don't you live in Avalon like everybody else? I figured you for a castle or something."

"I was never one for conspicuous consumption. Besides, sometimes I just don't need to be around people." He paused, and something a little dark moved behind his eyes. "I kill too many of them."

She bit her lip, painfully reminded of the girl she'd blasted. "Yeah. I guess I can understand that."

"It's nice to come here and look out at the stars and watch the dragons."

Caroline straightened. "You've got dragons? Here? You're kidding me!"

"Nope. They don't come around Avalon much. Too many people." He extended a brawny arm to point at a winged shape turning lazy circles out over the mountains. "There's one now."

She saw it breathe a long, lacy plume of flame. "Wow! Why did it do that?"

"Probably just target practice." He slid an arm around her.

She rested her head against his shoulder, watching the dragon. "What happens when the sun comes up?"

"The spell barrier filters out most of the light." Galahad rested his temple against hers. His late-night stubble rasped over her hair, the sensation oddly sensual. "Sometimes if I watch, I can just see the first little bit of the dawn."

They fell silent as the horizon slowly blushed rose behind the mountains. Another dragon came out to chase the first, dancing in the rising currents of magic. A sliver of bright disk edged upward.

"Look," Galahad said, his voice soft. "There it . . ."

But when Caroline lifted her head, his eyes were closed.

He sprawled halfway across the bed, his muscular arms flung wide, his dark hair tangled around his tired face. She caught her breath at his raw male beauty. Something in her chest contracted into a tight, aching ball.

Dammit, Caroline, don't you dare fall for him. Maybe she ought to conjure that second bed after all.

But before she could do it, she caught a glimpse of movement at the corner of her eye.

The dragon hung in the air looking in at her, its great wings beating lazily. Scales shimmered in the rising sun, green and blue dancing along the whipping tail. Its head was long and elegant and oddly delicate compared to the solid muscle of its body. Its eyes met hers, glowing iridescent in the light of dawn, intelligent and alien. Then it turned and flew away.

With a sigh, Caroline lay her head back down on Galahad's chest to watch.

THE dull gold of Geirolf's Grail was worked with naked human figures writhing together like a nest of mating snakes. They seemed engaged in every possible perversion. And a good portion of them seemed to be killing the others.

Fascinated, Marilyn turned the cup between her palms, studying it as she waited for the sun to rise. She'd found it on Steve's body after she'd killed him, along with a note from the priest's daughter.

Terri Grange had apparently had a little crush on her father's lieutenant, which was why she'd transported it into the pack he carried in case his magic ran out. The note she'd included said she hadn't warned him she was sending it because she was afraid of distracting him during battle.

The key to everything was slung around his waist, and he hadn't even known it. Marilyn rather appreciated the irony.

Now he and his supporters were dead. And so, her magic told her, was the priest and that little bitch, Terri.

The remaining members of the cult had been quick to see logic. They all knew Marilyn had a way with a spell. And between betraying Steve and the other kills she'd racked up, she had more than enough power for some very nasty magic.

Which didn't mean she had any intention of taking on the witch and the vampire knight Terri had described in her magic note. At least, not yet. For one thing, the cult's headquarters were located in Virginia—two time zones later than the Texas farmhouse they now occupied. The sun had already risen there, so it wasn't a good idea to gate back.

Besides, there were only fifteen members of the cult left. Marilyn wanted better odds when they went after their Magekind foes, which was why she decided the cult would camp for the night in their defeated enemy's headquarters.

Luckily she'd found several intriguing cages in the attic, stocked with pissed-off prisoners. To Marilyn's experienced eye, the ten men looked like a nice, beefy collection of potential warriors. Apparently the eco-terrorists had planned to magically recruit them once they got their hands on the cup.

Which gave Marilyn an idea. A little brainwashing, a shot from the cup, a murder or two for power and blood, and they'd be ready to give Arthur's idiots the shock of their lives.

She couldn't wait.

THE stench rolled out of the darkness in waves. Fear gripped Galahad, sick and cold, but he knew his duty. He took a deep breath, reached down, caught the rope handle of the trapdoor, and pulled. It creaked upward, carrying the smell of rotting meat.

Mentally bracing himself, he aimed the enchanted gem set in his gauntlet down into the hole and activated it with a whispered chant. White light spilled from it.

The little corpses lay naked, piled like dolls tossed aside by a sadistic child. "Oh, Merlin's Grail," he whispered hoarsely. "No."

As he stared helplessly, one of the bodies stirred. For a moment, his heart stopped, thinking perhaps the boy had somehow survived.

Then a face looked up at him that didn't belong to anything still living. "Why didn't you come in time?"

A hoarse scream tearing his throat, Galahad jolted awake.

7

"GALAHAD?"

He jerked around, his muscles coiling to strike out. Caroline blinked at him, her dark eyes wide and startled. His sleep-drugged brain jarred to full consciousness with a sense of relief.

A dream. It had been a dream.

He rolled out of bed and staggered toward the stairs, vaguely aware that she was hurrying after him. "Galahad? What's wrong?"

He didn't trust himself to answer. The sticky weight of fear and failure clung to his shoulders like a rotting shroud.

The minute he reached the exercise room, Galahad stripped off his pants and dove into the pool with the desperation of a man hungry to wash his demons away.

The shock of hitting the water blasted him fully awake, and he started stroking hard, trying to power his way through his lingering depression.

Sometimes he fucking hated this job. No matter how many battles he won, the war never ended. There was always another fight, on and on, world without end: Nazis, communists, terrorists, serial killers, psychopaths of every stripe.

And no matter how many bad guys he killed, he was always too late to save some innocent. The pit in his dreams had no fucking bottom. Gritting his teeth, he swam harder.

Finally he stopped pushing and rolled over on his back to float, his muscles jumping from the effort he'd demanded of them.

"You want to tell me what's eating you?" Caroline said.

Galahad looked over at her. She stood on the edge of the pool, watching him. The silky peach pajamas she wore emphasized the length of her legs and the sweet, high curves of her breasts. Hunger rose, sudden and violent. He tried to push it aside. She was still gun-shy from that asshole Dominic. "I hate the day-sleep," he told her finally over the patter of the waterfall. "I get nightmares like you would not believe, but I can't wake up."

Sympathy warmed her dark, lovely eyes. "I know what you mean. I had some nasty ones myself. I doubt I got more than four or five hours sleep." She sighed, making those lush breasts rise and fall. Her tight little nipples tented the fabric.

He remembered the way they'd felt hardening against his palms. Remembered the slick, tight grip of her sex as he'd stroked a finger inside. She'd feel impossibly good around his cock, which was suddenly rock-hard and aching.

God, he needed her. He needed the forgetfulness he'd find in her body. She was so damn clean. So innocent of the kind of shit he had to wade in every single day. He wanted to see the passion overtake that pretty face. Wanted to forget all the innocents he'd failed, all the men he'd killed. He wanted to plunge into her the way he'd plunged into the pool and just forget. His cock hardened in a hungry rush, arching over his belly as he floated on his back. "Caroline." His voice came out rougher than he intended, rasping with need rather than the smooth note of seduction he'd intended.

She took a wary step back. "As impressed as I am by that morning broadsword of yours, may I remind you we've got vampires to kill?"

Dammit, she had a point. "I assume they're back in their burrow by now."

"Actually, no. Not yet."

Galahad jackknifed upright until he could stand in the cool, shoulder-deep water. Despite both the temperature and the situation, his cock refused to get the message. He ignored it. "Any idea where they are?"

"No." She shrugged, a gesture that did marvelous things to those sweet, unbound breasts. "I spent the afternoon trying to figure out how to work a locator spell. No luck. But according to the vision that started this mess, they are coming back."

"So we wait." He gave her his best wolfish grin. "I have a couple of ideas about how to pass the time."

Caroline took another step back. "Pinochle?"

"How about a nice, rousing game of hide the broadsword?"

That pretty pink tongue crept out to lick her lips. "Don't do this to me, Galahad. I'm still recovering from Dominic."

"That prick needs his ass kicked," Galahad growled, frustrated. "My father was a court seducer before he met his new wife. They're supposed to keep it light, not convince you you're in love."

"Yeah, well, Dominic all but promised me a ring."

"You want me to beat him up?" He bared his teeth, meaning it.

She laughed, the sound throaty and impossibly seductive. "It's tempting."

Galahad stared at her, aching. "I need you, Caroline." The words emerged as more naked than he intended, but he didn't take them back. "Help me forget this. Just for an hour. That's all I need."

She looked at him. Her expression softened at whatever she saw on his face. "All right."

Light flashed, and the pajamas became a string bikini that made his dick rock-hard all over again. Before he could get the full effect of all those luscious curves, she dove in.

Galahad grinned, his heart lifting at the prospect of having Caroline to himself. Suddenly he was in the mood to play.

W HEN Caroline surfaced, the lights were out, leaving the room lit only by the Mageverse sky and moonlight reflecting off the water. Galahad was nowhere to be seen— not that she could see much anyway.

What's he up to now? Her heart began to pound as she looked around, expecting him to surface any second and pounce. The reflections on the water were so bright, she couldn't make out anything under them. Automatically, she tried to conjure a light.

Nothing happened.

"If I don't want you to use magic in my house, you can't use magic in my house," Galahad said from behind her, his breath warm on her ear.

Caroline jumped and whirled around barely in time to see the ripple as he submerged again. "Come back here, you big jerk!" She tried to levitate him out of the water, but he was gone. There must be a dampening spell built into the house he could order on and off. Which meant she was helpless.

All alone in the dark with a horny Galahad. A wicked little thrill ran up her spine.

This was going to be fun.

Which didn't mean she was going to make it easy. She had her pride. Drawing in a deep breath, Caroline ducked under and shot toward the other end of the pool, swimming in long, strong strokes. As she flashed through the water, male fingers brushed her ankle, just missing a grab.

Ha! Caught him off guard.

Not for long. Powerful arms closed around her waist and pulled her upright. Her head broke the surface. As she gasped in surprise, Galahad's mouth covered hers in a devouring kiss. He hauled her close against the hard strength of his body, one hand cupping her backside, the other stroking her breast, fingers teasing one nipple into aching erection. She leaned into him with a moan of hunger. He lifted his head, flashed her a triumph grin, and let her go.

And then he was gone.

Unsupported, she sank. Shutting her mouth barely in time to avoid sucking in a lungful of pool, Caroline looked around wildly. Underwater in the darkness, she couldn't make out a damn thing but dim flashes from the surface.

While vampires could see in the dark. Dammit.

Okay, so he had an advantage. They'd just see how long it lasted. Kicking twice, Caroline broke the surface, drew a breath, and dove under again.

Fingers tweaked her nipple through the thin fabric of her top. The fleeting pleasure almost made her gasp. Her heart pounding in a blend of atavistic fear and arousal, she kicked hard, trying to make it a little tougher for him to get those wicked hands on her.

But the minute she surfaced again, he grabbed the ties

of her bathing suit top. One ruthless jerk snapped it. Before she could turn, he freed the knot holding the top around her neck and pulled it away.

Caroline whirled in time to see the top disappear under the surface with him. "You're beginning to piss me off, Galahad!"

Arousal pulsed between her thighs. She licked her lips and thought of everything she'd like to do to him when she caught him.

Then she imagined everything he could do to her, and the heat increased even more.

Just behind her, he whispered, "I like to play with my food." Long fingers closed around her hips, dragging her backward.

Then she was plastered against Galahad again, her back to his brawny chest, his hard cock pressing her backside. His sword-callused hands slid up over her bare breasts to capture both peaks between thumb and forefinger. Pleasure spooled through her as he gently plucked them taut. "Breakfast," he purred.

Caroline panted as hot little flashes of pleasure skated across her nerves. "You've got a kinky streak, Galahad."

"Oh, yeah." He reached for the tie of her bathing suit bottoms. Tugging it loose, he started dragging the scrap of fabric off, raking sensitive flesh in the process. She gasped at the urgent clench of pleasure he triggered, and he chuckled, the sound deep and sexy. "In fact, maybe I'll just tie you up with your own bikini."

Caroline let her head fall back against his wet, brawny shoulder, impossibly turned on. "Yeah, you're kinky."

"Oh, darlin', you have no idea. Yet." Then those strong arms slid out from around her. She whirled, but he was gone. Again. "Tease!"

She could feel her sex swelling, throbbing. Evidently

Galahad wasn't the only one with a kinky streak. This was like being trapped in an erotic version of *Jaws*. And it was past time to turn the tables on the great white vampire.

Caroline really wanted to get her hands on his harpoon.

She swam for the side. If she could lure him out of the water, they'd be on more equal ground.

As equal as you could get with a guy who could bench-press a Cadillac, anyway.

Reaching the side of the pool, she caught the cool granite rim and prepared to lever herself out.

"Now where do you think you're going?" Galahad pulled her back into those magnificent arms, one hand taking possession of a hard nipple while the other slipped between her thighs.

A long, broad finger slid into her sex in a deep, breathtaking stroke. She gasped, arching her butt against his rock-hard cock. "There's a word for men like you."

He chuckled in her ear, the sound richly seductive. "There are lots of words for a man like me. Which one do you have in mind?"

Caroline whimpered at his lushly extravagant probes into her sex. "Tease."

"Nope, that's not one of them. Teases never intend to follow through." Scissoring her clit between his fingers, he raked his fangs across her pulse. "I do."

"When, exactly?" she panted.

"Now." He turned her around in his arms and lifted her out of the water. The next thing Caroline knew, she was lying on her back beside the pool edge with her thighs draped over his shoulders. Still in the water, he buried his face between her legs.

"Oh, God!" She came halfway off the stone floor as Galahad parted her lips and started feasting—licking, sucking, dancing his tongue over delicate flesh in seductive circles and swirls. His hands claimed her breasts again, stroking

the soft flesh, thumbing her nipples. Driving her insane
with breathtaking speed until she writhed on the stone,
begging for the climax bearing down on her with every
flick and caress.

But it wasn't enough.

She craved his massive cock, ached for his deep, driving
thrusts, burned to feel his weight spread over her, big body
surging against hers.

"Galahad!" His name was a desperate, pleading scream.

His only response was a growl.

"Please!"

He lifted his head, his eyes glowing red in the darkness.
"Goddess, I love listening to you beg." Fangs flashed in his
grin.

She groaned, panted. "Jerk!"

"Now is that any way to talk to a man who's got you
right where he wants you?" With a muscular surge and
splash, he levered himself out of the water. She whimpered
at the sensation of his wet body covering hers. His cock
pressed against her belly, hard as a blade.

"Yes! Now!" Her need leaped into a hot roar, and she
tried to wrap both legs around his backside.

"Not so fast." Galahad coiled his arms around her and
rolled her astride his hips, big hands spreading her thighs,
lifting her, positioning her so he could trust hard into her
slick, swollen core.

"Ooooh! Galahad!" Her eyes flared wide at the stark
sensation.

He chuckled in her ear. "Like that?"

"Jesus!" He felt so damn big.

"I'll take that as a yes." One hand clamped over her butt,
holding her in place as he started thrusting—hard, deep
lunges that raked her clinging flesh with delight. He fisted
the fingers of the other hand in her hair, pulled her head
back. She moaned in helpless anticipation.

The burning penetration of his fangs sinking into her throat made her yelp in a combination of arousal and erotic pain. Instinctively, she tried to pull back, but he wouldn't allow it. She couldn't move at all, held in those supernaturally powerful hands as he took her.

Then the pleasure rose, white hot and overwhelming, and the desire to flee drained away. Almost blind with it, she clung to his brawny shoulders as he stroked in and out of her slick flesh, his mouth hot on her throat.

The storm of sensation went on and on, blazing through her consciousness until there was room for nothing else. Then the climax hit like a velvet hammer, and she screamed. "Galahad!" The sound blended with the merciless slap of his hips on hers. As if her climax triggered his, he stiffened against her with a muffled growl of feral pleasure.

Helpless, lost, she lay in Galahad's arms as he pumped his seed deep and fed.

8

✥

CAROLINE lay in Galahad's arms as her heartbeat slowed its lunging pace, listening to the patter of the waterfall. Her muscles jumped and quivered with the aftershocks of his ferocious passion, and her throat stung. Clinging weakly to him, she let her eyes drift closed.

"Cachamuri's eggs, Galahad, have you ruined another virgin?"

With a start, she jerked her head off his chest.

A scaly head the size of her entire body stared at them from barely ten feet away.

With a terrified little shriek, Caroline tried to roll off Galahad—whether to run or throw a spell, she didn't quite know. He held her still, laughing. "Calm down, Caroline. It's just Soren. He won't hurt you." To the dragon he added, "Look what you've done, you overgrown gecko—you scared her!"

The dragon sighed gustily as it clung to the cliff looking in through the barrier spell. "I suppose it's just as well she's not a virgin. She's too high-strung for me anyway. Ah well. Let me in, would you? I'm getting tired of hanging out here."

"If you insist," Galahad said. "Just quit trying to scare the daylights out of my girl. Shield down."

Before Caroline could process being referred to as "his girl," the dragon snaked its massive head inside. Wide-eyed, she watched it maneuver its huge upper body through the opening. It was obvious the rest of the beast would never fit.

"He keeps promising me virgin sacrifices," the dragon complained to her in a rumbling basso. "But by the time they arrive, they're not virgins anymore. It's most frustrating."

"That thing actually *eats* women?" she hissed at Galahad, horrified.

The dragon's grin revealed teeth longer than Galahad's great sword. "Every chance I get." Magic streamed out of its glowing eyes to wash over its body and blaze painfully bright. When the glare faded, a tall, breathtakingly handsome man stood in the dragon's place. "But it's not as if I chew. And they don't seem to mind."

"No," Caroline said faintly. "I don't suppose they do."

The dragon man was dressed like a medieval courtier in a blue velvet doublet, an impressive jeweled codpiece, and hose that clung to long, powerful legs. His face was long-boned, with a majestic nose and sensual lips, and his head was shaved perfectly smooth, a faint blue tint just beneath the skin. "Very pretty." His iridescent gaze was hot and approving as he stared at her before he lifted a brow at Galahad. "I don't suppose you'd share."

"No." Giving the dragon a warning glare, Galahad added to Caroline, "Clothes, darling. Knowing Soren, something in a gunnysack."

Soren's sensual mouth shaped into a pout as she hastily

conjured jeans and T-shirts around both of them. "Selfish mammal. You know how I love seducing Majae."

Galahad rolled to his feet and gave his friend a dry look. "You might get more opportunities, if you hadn't indulged in the goat incident with Morgana."

"You'd be surprised. Anyway, you laughed louder than I did, you hypocritical egg-sucker."

He grinned. "I didn't say it wasn't funny." Catching Caroline's questioning gaze, he shook his head. "Believe me, you don't want to know. For one thing, if I told you she'd have to kill you."

"Then by all means, leave me in happy ignorance."

"Smart girl." He returned his attention to their exotic guest. "Speaking of well-cast spells, would you be willing to help us with a nasty little vampire problem?"

He described the situation, Caroline throwing in details of her own when she thought he'd missed a point. Soren listened, but when they'd finished, he shook his head. "Galahad, you know I cannot directly involve myself in mammal affairs."

Galahad sighed. "I know, but I thought it was worth a . . ."

"However, I do know of a spell that might prove helpful." He shrugged at the knight's surprised blink. "I never could stand Geirolf and his race of parasites. These vampires are no better."

"That's putting it mildly. What do we need to do?"

"You, nothing." Soren turned his shimmering gaze on Caroline. "You, come here. This is a complex spell; I'll need to transfer it to you directly."

Her heart gave a wary thump, but Caroline walked over to him anyway. He was even more breathtaking at close range, and she swallowed, looking up at him. "How, exactly, do you intend to do that?"

Soren gave her a wicked little smile, lowered his head, and kissed her.

She barely had time to notice his kiss wasn't as blazingly erotic as Galahad's when magic rolled over her in a frothing flood that rocked her back on her heels.

THE jealousy that flooded Galahad as he watched Soren kiss Caroline took him completely by surprise. It intensified when she sagged into the dragon's arms. Galahad knew her reaction was probably from whatever spell transfer Soren was doing, but his inner Neanderthal growled. It was all he could do not to stalk over there and make lizard pâté out of his friend.

Which, considering Soren's true form, said something about just how stupid his inner Neanderthal really was.

He'd never been this jealous of Morgana.

But just before Galahad's common sense went down for the count, Soren lifted his head and set Caroline back on her feet. She looked dazed, which only added fuel to the fire. The dragon gave him a toothy smile. "Lucky mammal."

"What the hell was that all about?" Galahad exploded. He knew he sounded like an idiot, but he didn't care.

Soren shrugged his broad shoulders. "It's the only chance I'm going to get to kiss the bride."

"You . . ." Galahad's mind belatedly processed what his friend just said. "What in Merlin's name are you talking about?"

Obviously enjoying his reaction, the dragon folded his arms. "You do know you're going to Truebond with this girl?"

He snorted. "You've been flying too high, Soren. That reptile brain is oxygen-deprived."

Caroline blinked, as though trying to shake off whatever Soren had done to her. "Truebond? What's a Truebond?"

"The Magekind version of marriage." A vast oversimplification, but it would have to do for now.

Caroline's jaw dropped in a gape. Even that looked good on her. "That's ridiculous. We haven't known each other twenty-four hours!"

"With a Truebond, that hardly matters." Amusement shone in the dragon's iridescent eyes. "You'll tap one another's memories, emotions, thoughts. You'll know one another better than if you'd been married a century."

"It's a mind-fusion," Galahad explained, glaring at his friend. The idea of exposing Caroline's bright innocence to his sixteen hundred years of corruption was repellent. It would destroy her. Hell, sometimes he thought it was destroying him. "And no way in hell are we doing it."

The dragon ignored him, looking into her eyes. "He'll be your conduit, Caroline. You'll free each other."

"I said forget it!" Galahad snapped. "I don't care what vision you had, it's not going to happen."

The dragon looked over at him in that infuriating way he had: wise, amused, tolerant of the hapless mammal's foibles. "Of course not." He gave Caroline a smile. "It was a pleasure to meet you, my sweet."

As Soren turned and started toward the edge, Caroline stopped him. "Wait. The Truebond thing. What else did you see?"

He smiled wickedly. "This and that." Before she could stop him again, he turned and leaped in a hard, long dive right off the edge. Caroline gasped as he disappeared, but an instant later, he shot past in dragon form, headed skyward, his massive wings beating.

She turned on Galahad, bristling. "Did you have to be such a jerk? I might have gotten some more out of him if you hadn't run him off."

He snorted. "Nobody gets anything out of Soren he doesn't want to give."

She stalked to the edge and looked up as if she were considering flying after the dragon. "Well, I'd still like to ask him when we're supposed to do this Truebond thing."

"We're not Truebonding," he gritted. "You have no idea what's involved, and believe me, you don't want to find out."

"Well, it sounds to me like we're not going to get a whole lot of choice."

"First off, visions have been known to be wrong. Second, Soren isn't above lying when it suits whatever game he's playing. Third, for all you know, if we do Truebond, it won't be for a couple of centuries. Either way, it ain't happening anytime soon."

Caroline glared at him. Even in his current enraged mood, he could see she was hurt. "Suits me just fine. I don't even know you." Whirling, she flounced off up the stairs toward the bedroom.

Galahad watched her go as irritation poured through him. Along with a healthy dose of fear.

Was the dragon right?

Merlin's Cup, he hoped not. He'd been around long enough to know they had the beginning of something good, something he'd never encountered in all his centuries seducing Majae. There was a warmth about Caroline he rarely saw in Magekind women, an honesty and lack of calculation. And, of course, there was that innocent sensuality.

Too often Majae seemed barricaded behind ennui, wariness or cynicism until almost nothing he did could reach them. But Caroline was so deliciously open, her uninhibited reactions aroused him as much as her pretty body did.

He wanted more time with her. He wanted to nurture and protect the fragile seed between them, watch it grow. It was going to be marvelous.

But only if she wasn't destroyed by a Truebond.

* * *

WELL, that had been pretty damn plain. Galahad wanted nothing whatsoever to do with a permanent relationship with her. After all his talk about being nothing like Dominic, he was cut from the same cloth after all.

The trick now was to maintain a strictly business relationship until they got Geirolf's little cult taken care of. She'd keep her distance and stay out of his bed, and . . .

"Caroline," Galahad said from behind her.

She straightened her shoulders, wiped the hurt from her face, and turned, determined to keep this light. "What can I do for . . . ?"

He snatched her into his arms, and his mouth came down on hers, hungry and devouring. Caroline stiffened instinctively, but he didn't let her go.

Oh, she thought, *he's going to be a pain in the ass.*

9

‖

OVER the next three days, Caroline discovered how right she was. She never found out if Galahad would take "no" for an answer; he made it impossible for her to get the word out of her mouth.

His centuries had taught him things to do to a woman's body that lit Caroline's up like the Eiffel Tower on New Year's Eve. He wove wicked spells with his mouth and his tongue and his big, hard hands that put to shame anything she could do with her magic. He whispered velvet threats that made her knees go weak, then carried every one of them out—bending her over, spreading her wide, pinning her against the nearest wall. All so he could work his thick erection slowly into her tight flesh, sink his fangs into her throat. And take her, over and over.

Those damn vampires didn't help. She'd set wards on the complex—a kind of magical burglar alarm, designed so that nobody but Caroline could sense them when they activated. But they never went off, and the vampires never came back. She kept checking, but the place remained empty of all but its ghosts.

While Galahad's home was full of him.

She knew he was after something. This felt almost like a feral kind of courtship, as if he were staking his claim on her.

Gaining possession.

But he'd said he didn't want her in terms that left no room for romantic illusions. So what the hell kind of game was he playing? And what should she do about it?

Because he was definitely getting to her—and not just with the impressive sex. Hot as he was, that wouldn't have done such a good job of chipping away at her mental barriers.

No, what got her the most was the lazy, drifting time just after he'd taken her and just before sunrise, when they lay in bed together watching the dragons play. That was when he'd tell her about the places he'd been, the times he'd seen, the amazing events he'd witnessed. Hearing the reality behind the legend never failed to enthrall her. It quickly became hard to remember why she needed to keep her distance.

Sunset on the fourth day found them nicely settled into their routine. She sat in bed polishing off a breakfast steak under Galahad's watchful eye—he said she needed the protein—while he did his evening sword exercises.

Chewing a piece of sinfully tender filet mignon, she watched him parry invisible attacks, sword flashing, his big, naked body moving with a dancer's grace.

The psychic buzz of her wards activating made her sit up an instant before the vision fell on her like an anvil.

Four of them held the naked girl spread across the altar. Over them stood a blond woman who held a snaking knife in one hand and the grail in the other. The blonde's face was twisted with savage anticipation that matched the black eagerness in the eyes of her followers. Caroline could feel their hunger to see blood spill. She froze, a scream clawing at her throat, unable to move or think as the poisonous images poured into her consciousness.

Then it was over, and the vision's hold snapped. Caroline flung herself out of bed so fast she fell on the floor. "Galahad!" Sick horror clawed at her as she scrambled to her feet, but she had no time for emotion now. "They're back!"

He stopped and lowered his sword. "The cultists?"

"Yeah. They've captured somebody. They're getting ready to sacrifice her on that damned altar."

His handsome face went cold. "Armor us up and open a gate. Let's see what's going on."

A gesture called their mail around them. Then carefully, she opened a gate just large enough to give them a view of the sacrificial chamber.

Just as her vision had predicted. Four cultists held the naked girl across the altar as the blond priestess lifted her knife. Galahad cursed softly. "I don't like this, but it doesn't look like we've got time to play it safe."

"I don't need much time," Caroline reminded him in a low voice. "Soren gave me that spell, remember? Keep them from killing the girl, and I'll do the rest. It'll take me sixty seconds, tops, to do the chant."

"Can you do it from here?"

She hesitated, her eyes locked on the struggling girl. "I don't think the gate could handle the energy flow."

"Yeah, I figured." Galahad drew his sword and prepared to leap. "Sixty seconds is all you get, Caroline. If you can't pull it off, they're going to be all over us."

She took a deep breath and expanded the gate to full size.

The girl screamed and bucked in her captors' hands as the blond female priest drew the point of the knife down her chest, just barely drawing blood.

"Go." Galahad growled.

Taking a deep, desperate breath, Caroline charged through the gate, aware even as she leaped that he had plunged in after her.

She emerged into Realspace at a dead run, Galahad roaring his war-cry at her heels. The vampires jerked toward them. Carline's full attention locked on the grail, she started chanting the first words of Soren's spell.

Black triumph flashed over the priestess's face. "Yes!" The blonde bared her teeth, threw the knife aside, and conjured a power blast.

Shit, the cultists had been expecting them. Caroline had to break off the chant to call a shield.

But even as the priestess's blast bounced off her magical barrier, something hit her hard from behind in a magical assault that sent agony slicing into her skull.

Galahad bellowed.

Caroline spun, ready to defend herself, but Galahad was already charging the three armored vampires who'd hit her from behind. She started to send a blast toward the nearest of them, but another spell hit her like a fastball pitch to the skull. The world pinwheeled as she went flying.

Caroline hit the stone floor with a teeth-rattling jolt. Struggling to rise, she lifted her head to see a ring of vampires closing in on her. Their hands glowed and smoked with magic. Desperately, she turned to look for the grail. If she could just hit it . . .

But even as she spotted the gleam of gold in the priestess's hand, the cultists opened fire.

GALAHAD saw Caroline go down under a hail of power blasts and roared a denial. Surrounded by vampire warriors, there wasn't a damn thing he could do to save her. Fear clutched at his chest with burning fists. He sent the nearest bastard's head flying with a single stroke of his sword and lunged toward her. Sensing something else coming toward him, he thrust his sword up in a parry. His frenzy gave him strength, and he knocked the vampire's blade aside, then buried his own in the man's chest so hard his victim's feet left the ground. Jerking his sword free, he ducked, avoiding another vampire's wild swing.

But there were just too damn many of them, and he knew it. At least thirty armored vampire warriors had gated in behind them the minute he and Caroline had entered. Even he wasn't good enough to take them all.

They'd been royally suckered.

Somebody dove for his legs. Galahad dodged aside, but a second warrior slammed into his hips, knocking him hard to the ground. He tried to roll away, swinging and kicking, but two of them landed on top of him. "That's it, fucker, you're done!" somebody sneered.

"I'm going to rip out your hearts, you whoreson bastards!" he roared, but then more of them piled on, crushing the air from his lungs. Brutal fingers clamped over his sword arm while others grabbed his left wrist. He felt his helmet being pulled off, but there wasn't a damn thing he could do about it. The steel rim raked the side of his face with a vicious sting. Hot blood rolled. He managed to choke in a breath. It smelled of old blood and rank bodies.

A female hand reached in and wrapped around his face. Before he could sink his fangs into her palm, she shot a blast into his head. Fire ripped along his nerves and the world went white.

GALAHAD came to naked, hanging in midair. Caroline was cursing steadily, viciously. For a moment, he felt a spurt of joy that she was still alive.

Then he opened his eyes and sucked in a breath.

She'd taken the girl's place on the altar. They'd stripped her of her armor—and apparently her powers, because one of the bastards was fondling her breast, and she hadn't fried him.

But she badly wanted to. That was evident from the rage and terror ringing in her voice. "Get your stinking hands off me!"

"Oh, I don't think so." The blond woman smirked down at her as the other vampires laughed. She held Geirolf's Grail in one hand and a dagger in the other.

"You've got very pretty tits, witch." She hefted the knife, grinning. "At least for the moment."

Furiously, Galahad fought the spell holding him, but he couldn't move at all. He knew they'd left him alive only so he could take Caroline's place on the altar when they'd finished with her.

The original victim lay bound and gagged on the floor off to one side. Evidently they were saving her for dessert.

The priestess bent over Caroline with the knife, crooning obscene threats the way another woman might promise pleasures to a lover.

Galahad's desperate, bitter gaze fastened on the grail. They'd been so damn close. If only she'd been able to complete Soren's spell. Hell, if only he could work magic . . .

He'll be your conduit.

Galahad jerked in his bonds, remembering Soren's prediction that they'd Truebond. *That's it!* Hope shot through his chest.

The cultists knew Magi couldn't work magic, so logically they hadn't bothered to place a nullification spell on Galahad. If he Truebonded with Caroline, she'd be able to send the spell through the link with him.

It could work. Soren had implied it would work.

But . . . a chill stole over him as he thought of what

contact with his mind might do to Caroline. It could destroy her as thoroughly as the witch's knife.

But what choice did they have? If there was any chance at all, they had to take it. He'd simply have to protect her somehow.

Assuming, that is, they could form the bond. It would be easier if Galahad had been the one to change her into a maja, but since he hadn't been, he'd need some other way to reach her.

Closing his eyes, Galahad sought inside himself, searching his mind for some trace of her.

"Arrhhh! Bitch!" Caroline screamed.

He flinched. *Running out of time . . .*

Don't think about that.

Caroline. Caroline arching beneath him, her eyes vague with the hot pleasure of her rising orgasm. The scent of her, pure femininity, the taste of her mouth, of her sex. Her wicked sense of humor. The terrified courage on her white face as she'd prepared to jump through that gate.

Caroline.

There she was—a delicate, ghostly presence in his mind. A fragile link, formed unconsciously when they'd made love.

That had better be enough.

Concentrating hard, Galahad sent his mind flying out along it, reaching desperately for her. He hit some kind of resistance—the blanking spell—but he forced his way through.

Contact.

When he opened his eyes, a ring of fanged faces grinned down at him, gloating lust in their eyes. Sick terror gripped his soul, mixed with a woman's helpless vulnerability. He could feel the pain of cuts slashing across Caroline's sensitive breasts. *They're going to kill me,* she thought in horrified despair. *They're going to torture me to death and kill me . . .*

Galahad sent his thoughts into the swirling terror that held her. *Caroline!*

Galahad! How did you . . . ? What are you doing?

We've got to Truebond, Caroline. If we bond, you can send the spell through me.

I can't! They've taken my magic! Galahad, they're going to kill me!

Despite his own fear, he sent a wave of calm authority along the link. *No, no, listen. Nobody can take your magic, they only put a dampening spell on you. But there's no spell on me. If we Truebond . . .*

I can send the spell through you! Oh, God. We've got to do it now! She gasped as the knife raked over her flesh again. The cut was shallow, but the sting was vicious and terrifying. *Jesus, Galahad!*

Reach for me, Caroline!

The link snapped into place with an almost audible click.

THE touch of Galahad's mind was like standing on the edge of Niagra Falls—a great, pounding mental presence, ancient and profoundly alien. *Come to me,* he whispered in her thoughts. *The Truebond alone isn't enough. You've got to be within my mind to work the spell.*

Despite her fear of the cultists, she knew a moment of even greater terror. The vast weight of his mind could rip hers to shreds. There was no way she could survive.

Sharp pain sliced across her ribs, and Caroline jumped against the hard hands that held her. "I'm getting hungry, Marilyn," one of the male cultists said over her head. "Quit playing with that knife and plunge it in. We'll feed while she dies."

"Patience, Roger," the priestess purred. "This is the best part."

And once they finished with her, Galahad was next. She was the only chance either of them had. With a mental howl of terror, Caroline plunged through the Truebond and into his consciousness.

Images bombarded her, too fast to process—faces she didn't recognize, whirling past like leaves in a hurricane; a blade biting deep into a man's neck; the reek of spilled intestines; a castle burning around her; flames leaping and crackling as heat seared her skin; a woman's throat beneath her mouth, the give of flesh yielding to her fangs; someone's sex gripping her cock; Morgana's voice purring lewd instructions; her own laughter . . .

Drowning, blinded, Caroline screamed.

"Listen to the gutless little slut," Marilyn laughed. "I haven't even started yet, Maja. Just wait."

But she knew in a moment it wouldn't matter. Galahad was destroying her.

Caroline! His voice spoke in her mind. She felt him fighting to protect her, to block the memories, to shield her from the black images roaring through her mind. Warm, soothing, strong, he cradled her. *All of this is just detail. It doesn't matter. Touch me.*

A bubble of silence formed around them like the eye of a hurricane. They were alone together. Even the cultists disappeared.

Suddenly he no longer seemed like some impossibly ancient predator, but a man. A man who struggled with a thankless, hellish job, yes, a man who despaired even as he continued to fight. A man she'd held and touched and loved. A man as vulnerable and lonely as she was.

Oh, a small voice said somewhere inside her. *It's you.*

Yes.

Caroline opened Galahad's eyes and looked across the chamber at the altar where the vampires held her pinned.

She was inside him. The barrier that had blocked her from her magic had been left behind.

"Isc aff argia t'ri ke per," she said in Galahad's deep voice. The vampires looked around, startled.

Marilyn realized what was happening first. "Oh, holy fuck!" She lifted the blade to plunge it deep.

But even as it descended, Caroline and Galahad roared, *"Ka avi ITA!"*

Magic exploded from them in a flaming, boiling wave, whipping the knife from the priestess's hand. Marilyn screamed as the spell hit Gierolf's Grail. She tried to throw the cup aside, but it was too late. The grail flared black and imploded, sending a blazing magical shock wave expanding outward.

The magical burst hit Marilyn and her vampire assistants first, vaporizing them instantly.

The watching vampire warriors bellowed and turned to run, only to vanish as the shock wave hit them, too. Even then it kept going. Caroline sucked in a breath as it shot over Galahad and slammed right through the complex walls.

The spell holding Galahad broke. He dropped to his feet with a grunt of satisfaction.

Caroline opened her own eyes and stared at the ceiling of the chamber, then lifted her head cautiously.

Galahad strode naked across the chamber toward her. She rolled off the altar and fell into his arms with a shriek of mingled relief and pleasure.

But just as he lowered his head to kiss her, they heard a tiny whimper. They stiffened warily and looked around. "What the hell was that?" Galahad growled.

The girl they'd come to save lay looking at them, her eyes huge over her gag.

"Oops," Caroline murmured. "Forgot." Reluctantly they drew apart and went to free her.

10

⚜

CAROLINE lay on her back on Galahad's bed. Gloriously naked, he leaned on one elbow swirling a strawberry in a bowl of frothy cream. "You know, I think I like this Truebond thing. Open up."

Lazily, she complied. He stroked the creamy berry into her mouth. She closed her lips around it and sucked gently, knowing the sight—and the mental image of what she imagined sucking instead—would drive him crazy.

"Are you goldbricking, or did you actually accomplish your mission?" Morgana demanded from the foot of the bed.

Caroline screeched and sat up. Only belatedly did she remember to zap jeans and T-shirts onto both of them. "Don't you knock?"

"No." The witch rocked back on her spike-heeled sandals, cool and elegant in a white suit that contrasted brilliantly with her black hair. "Nice conjuring. Next time set wards instead, and I won't be able to do this."

Bitch, Caroline thought.

That pretty much sums it up, Galahad agreed through

their bond. Aloud, he added, "What brings you barging in, Morgana?"

"Do you still need help taking that little nest of yours?"

Disgruntled, Caroline drew her legs beneath her to sit up. "No, it's taken care of. We returned the surviving victim to her family, and the police think the cult that kidnapped her died in a fire."

Turns out the Satanists had a house on the surface above the complex. Caroline had conjured it into charred rubble and added a few bones to give weight to the explanation.

The victim herself remembered nothing, thanks to Caroline's merciful alterations to her memory.

"Congratulations," Morgan said impatiently. "Where's my cup?"

Oops. "Ah . . . we destroyed it."

"What?"

One explanation later, the Liege of the Majae wore an expression of speculative pleasure that made Galahad more than a little uneasy. "So that explains it." Catching his lifted eyebrow, she said, "Remember the vampire nest in Peru I told you about? It wasn't going at all well when a wave of magic rolled across the battlefield. I estimate fully a third of the enemy simply disappeared on the spot. Vaporized. Same thing happened to the forces fighting Arthur and Lancelot."

Caroline's jaw dropped. "A third?" A wicked grin crossed her face as she considered the implications. "And there were three cups. My spell must have wiped out all the vampires who were turned from that particular grail."

"Obviously. You do still have that spell, I assume?"

"Sure." Remembering the way Soren had transferred it to her, she winced. "I'll . . . write it down for you." Hastily, she conjured a piece of paper with the spell and handed it over. Though why the dragon hadn't done the same for her was another question entirely.

Morgana accepted it with a smile of pleasure. "All we

have to do now is find the other two cups. Destroying them will be a hell of a lot easier than trying to kill all those cultists one at a time."

"Don't count your chickens, Morgana," Galahad warned. "They're not going to give up the cups without a fight."

The witch gave him a vicious grin. "Too bad." She turned, reading the spell and started absently toward a gate that had appeared in the middle of the room. Just before she stepped through it, she looked back at Caroline, her expression more than a bit smug. "I knew we needed you."

When the witch was gone, Caroline turned a disbelieving look on Galahad. "You stayed with *her* for a decade?" Then, reading an all-too-vivid memory of just what he'd found so appealing, she picked up a pillow and socked him with it. "You hound!"

"Now that's just offensive." Galahad plucked the pillow out of her hand. "I'll have you know I'm far more wolf than dog."

"We'll see about that when I make you sit up and beg."

But just as she was about to get her revenge, a deep rumbling voice filled the room. "Before you two start your mating ritual—I gather the spell worked?"

"Yes, Soren, thank you," Galahad said, pouncing on Caroline and wrestling her onto her back.

"Yeah, thanks. Galahad, cut it out!"

As they rolled and fought like puppies, the dragon, clinging to the side of the cliff, shook his massive head. "Mammals." Catching sight of a tempting shape standing above him on the edge of the cliff, Soren started climbing up the mountain face to meet her. "But it's not a bad idea. Come here, you."

CAROLINE squirmed as Galahad stretched her out and pinned her down, both wrists pulled up above her head by one of his hands. "Now," he purred, "are you going to get rid of this shirt, or am I going to eat it off?"

She glowered at him in mock temper before making it disappear. He lifted his head to contemplate her hard nipples with predatory interest. "That's better."

Caroline swallowed and licked her lips as he slowly lowered his head. The first hot flick of his tongue over the delicate peak made her jump. Through the Truebond, she caught an echo of how she tasted to him: slightly salty, deliciously feminine, uniquely Caroline.

He adored it.

And so he indulged, suckled, licked, nibbled. Slowly, enjoying the sensations she felt through the Truebond. *No wonder you like this.*

She moaned agreement and arched against him, then gasped at the feel of his hard, muscled weight while he enjoyed her lean, satin softness. "Let me go. I want to touch you."

"I don't think so." He tightened his grip on her wrists. "I like it just like this."

"Mmmmm." It did feel good. "But you're not fooling me. You're afraid you're going to lose it." Deliberately, she gave him a slow, sinuous wiggle, sliding her belly over his erect cock in a way that made him groan.

Oh, so that's how you want to play, he said through the link. *We'll just see who loses it first.*

Oops. Tactical mistake.

Too late. He reared off her and rolled over onto his back. His cock bounced, pointing cheerfully at his chin. *I'm challenging you to sixty-nine. Whoever comes first . . . Well, doesn't exactly lose.*

I was thinking that.

I know. Extending his arms over his head, he stretched, arching his back. The sight of that big body twisting against the sheets made her mouth water. "What are you waiting for? Mount up." He was thinking that a millennia and a half of kinky experience should allow him to blow her out of the water—so to speak.

Pride stung, Caroline glowered at him. "We'll just see about that, Sir Fangsalot." She sat up, swung a leg over his chest so her behind was in his face, and settled down to eye his cock.

Galahad simply grabbed her by the hips and pulled her to his mouth with such breathtaking strength she yelped. The cry became a gasp as he gave her a long, sampling lick.

She felt the smug satisfaction in his mind. *What are you waiting for? Get busy.*

Give me a minute. Caroline contemplated the length of his cock and swallowed. *I'm trying to figure out my plan of attack.*

Ha!

Hey, all you have to do is nibble. I've got to engulf this telephone pole.

He liked the description enough to reward her with a long, wicked swirl of his tongue. *Well, if it's too much for you, I'd be happy to tie you up and find somewhere else to put it.*

Pervert.

Not so. He sipped deliciously on sensitive flesh. *You're just a sheltered English teacher.*

Not anymore. To prove it, she took the thick shaft in one hand, angled it upward and swooped her mouth down over the head. Closing her lips, she began to suck.

He liked that.

So did she. In fact, she liked the startling sensation of wet heat so much that she stopped, just holding him in her mouth. That felt pretty good, too.

He slid one long finger into her sex and closed his lips over her clit. Sucking hard, he sent a sweet firestorm blowing up her spine. His cock jerked in her mouth in reaction to the glorious echo.

You know, he thought when the fierce sensation faded, *I think I'm winning. Where'd I put that rope?*

I wouldn't bring up the bondage idea to somebody who could chain you to this bed so fast your fangs would spin. Determined, she started suckling his velvety cock head again, trying to ignore the delicious sensations coming through the Truebond.

He licked. She worked another inch of cock down her throat. He suckled, swirling his tongue around her clit. She caught his balls in her free hand and cupped him gently as she bobbed her head.

A second finger joined the one in her cunt. He pumped slowly. She drew off him to lave the head of his erection while she stroked the shaft.

And every single caress from either of them sent delicious waves through both, the pleasure doubling and trebling.

The climax roared out of nowhere, so blinding and ferocious his bellow blended with her startled cry.

When the hot wave passed, she lay collapsed over him, dazed, vaguely aware of the taste of him. *Oh.*

Wow.

She twisted her head around and grinned back at him. *Did Sir Galahad, badass of the known universe, just say "wow"?*

A faint flush rose over his arrogant cheekbones. *That was you.*

It was not! You lying vampire! She rolled off him and grabbed the pillow. Before she could hit him with it, he grabbed her and dragged her beneath him.

Grinning, he settled down on top of her. "Oh, no, you don't. You lost. I'm claiming my prize."

"Hey, you came first! Yours triggered mine!"

"I don't think so." He lowered his head and kissed her

slowly, throughly. She opened for him with a breathy little moan.

When he broke the kiss, she threaded her arms around his neck. "You came first."

"I did not." He reached down and drew her legs apart.

"Did, too."

"Actually, the whole point is moot, because *I* am the big, strong vampire and I'm going to bang you like a drum."

"Well, I'm the witch and I say . . ." He thrust his cock deep. "Wow."

Galahad grinned and rolled his hips. "I aim to please."

"Ooohhhhh. You don't need much recovery time, do you?"

"Nope." Another breathtaking thrust.

The double sensation of her pleasure and his made her arch her head into the pillow. Hunger ripped over her, so sudden and hot the teasing mood died a quick death. She slung both legs over his working butt and grabbed his shoulders, sinking her nails deep.

Fiercely they ground against one another, the unbearable delight whipping through their bodies with every thrust.

Goaded, driven, they thrust and thrust and . . .

Detonation.

Hot, sweet waves poured over them, burning and delicious until they were left spent, curled together in a sweating heap.

Long moments went by before Caroline was capable of speech. "Damn. Is it going to be like that every time?"

"I hope not. I'll starve." He'd been so intent on taking her, he hadn't wanted to stop long enough to feed.

She laughed. "You romantic, you."

I love you.

The thought, coming out of nowhere, made her blink. She blinked again when she realized he meant it.

What was more, she loved him, too. Caroline sensed the wave of satisfaction from him at the thought.

But that's just not possible, she protested. *We've only known each other . . . the Truebond.*

Galahad rolled off her and pulled her onto his chest. *I'd have fallen in love with you anyway.* He grinned up at her, his smoky blue eyes wicked. "You're loveable."

"But I'm just a schoolteacher, and you're *you.* I . . ." She broke off, realizing she didn't even believe that anymore. If she'd been ordinary . . .

"You'd never have survived the Truebond with me. Hell, you wouldn't have come to get me to begin with. You'd have hidden in your little house and pretended you hadn't seen a damn thing." His expression grew grim. "And those bastard vampires would have handed Arthur, Morgana, and Lancelot their heads."

"Oh," she said faintly. Then her voice strengthened. "I love you, Galahad."

"I love you, Caroline." He drew her close, his eyes dark and deep as they met hers. "Marry me."

"Yes. Oh, yes." Hungrily, she kissed him.

NEITHER of them saw Soren fly past the barrier spell. Twisting his head around, he grinned at Morgana, who sat astride his neck. "I do good work."

"*We* do good work." She turned to look through the barrier at the couple entwined in passion, then gave him a wicked smile. "Would you like to do a little more?"

A hot light appeared in the dragon's eyes. "Oh, yes. But this time, *you* change form."

Morgana sighed. "Very well. But you make such a lovely man." She twisted, let herself fall from his back, and transformed, great wings beating.

He admired her sleek black scales. "You're not so bad yourself. Come here."

She gave him a toothy dragon smile and soared away with a tempting flick of her tail. "Only if you can catch me."

"Ah, I do love a woman who plays hard to get. . . ." He flew off after her into the glowing Mageverse night.

BLOOD LUST

Vickie Taylor

Prologue

❖

THE silver toe cap on the end of the black snakeskin cowboy boot gleamed under the harsh laboratory lights as it rushed toward Daniel Hart's face. He lurched away, but not before the sharp metal point laid open his cheek. His head snapped back. Blood arced above him, then splattered down on his lab coat like crimson rain as he rolled to a stop on the tile floor.

Bruised and battered, his stomach throwing up into his throat the remnants of the pizza he'd eaten at his desk an hour ago, he shifted to lay flat on his face and planted his palms out beside his shoulders, inhaling the mingled scents of industrial cleaner and blood while he gathered the strength to lever himself up.

Before he could move, another kick flipped him backward. He grunted, and another blow spun him in midair, then another.

His world became a blurry haze of stainless steel tables crashing to the floor, glass beakers shattering, instruments flying overhead in a whirlwind of violence and pain, and yet all he could think about was the work he'd dedicated the last three years of his life to. The delicate tests ruined. The data lost.

Well, almost all he could think of. There was the other matter of a few broken ribs, lacerations, assorted contusions and possibly some internal bleeding to occupy a small portion of his mind, but it all seemed far away, as if it were happening to someone else.

He rolled with another vicious kick, came to rest under the whiteboard filled with chemical equations on the far wall and curled his knees up to protect his abdomen. Something had torn inside him that time. His belly convulsed, his insides wringing like a dishrag. His breath rattled in his chest.

"Why are you doing this?" he asked clumsily, his tongue thick, bloody. "What the hell is wrong with you?"

"What is wrong with me?" The hem of Garth La-Grange's black duster swished over his boots as they scuffed the floor just inches from Daniel's face. He threw his hands in the air and cackled maniacally. "What is *wrong* with me? Nothing is wrong with me. For the first time in centuries, something is very, very right!"

Centuries? He'd known Garth was a little weird since he'd met him six months ago, but since the man with the penchant for black clothing and late-night business meetings had been the only one who'd stepped up to fund Daniel's research, he'd been willing to overlook a few . . . eccentricities. Suddenly he wished he'd taken the time to check out his benefactor more carefully. Looked into a few of the more pertinent details of his life.

Like the fact that he was whacked out of his mind.

Pain speared through Daniel, a lightning bolt that struck from his navel to his spine. He clenched his fist around the leg of the table near his head and rode the wave. "Why are you doing this?" he asked again. "What do you want?"

It galled him to lie helpless while Garth stomped through his lab like an angry child knocking over Tinker Toys, but at six foot eight, the guy had a good six inches on him, and who'd have guessed a man built like an underfed flagpole would have the strength of a bull ox? At one hundred and ninety pounds himself, Daniel was no featherweight, yet Garth had tossed him around the room—repeatedly— without breaking a sweat.

"What do I want?" Garth squatted next to Daniel and grinned wickedly. "I want it all. I want the world at my feet."

"You've lost it." Shaking his head, Daniel dragged himself sideways, along the wall. "You're nuts, man."

Garth's face darkened. A scowl scrawled across his lips as he tracked Daniel's progress toward the door. Dropping his arms to his sides, he took a measured step toward Daniel, then another. "You're right. I'm crazy."

He leaned over until his pasty face hovered at the end of Daniel's nose. His breath brought a new wave of bile up Daniel's throat. "After eighteen months of listening to your constant stream of mind-numbing, medico-scientific mumbo jumbo, I'M A RAVING FUCKING LUNATIC!"

Daniel couldn't disagree with that, though he took issue with the cause. He tightened his arms over his ribs, expecting another blow, but Garth spun away with a flourish of his long coat.

"*Oh Daniel, you're so smart,*" he mocked the praise he'd showered over Daniel so freely in the past. "*Oh Daniel, you're so dedicated.*"

Halfway across the lab, he turned. "I cozied up to you. I coddled you. When what I really wanted to do was—"

His face twisted in rage, he made a circle in the air with his hands, as if he were choking an invisible neck, and for the first time, Daniel noticed how long the man's thumbnails were. Thick and yellow, they curved out two inches beyond the ends of his digits, where they sharpened to pinpoints.

Gross, but Daniel didn't have time to contemplate Garth's personal hygiene, because he finally figured out what he should have known all along. Garth had never believed in his research. Never been as excited as Daniel about the potential to help people, to further the greater good.

The man had just been using him all along. "You want my blood."

Garth teased the rim of his lips with his tongue. "You have no idea how badly."

"You want the formula."

"I want what it can give me. Power. Control. A certain . . ." He flicked his chin up jauntily. His pocked cheeks looked more hollow than ever, his complexion more sallow, yet there was a dull gleam in his sunken eyes that made Daniel's stomach pitch. "A certain notoriety with women.

"It's not Viagra, man. It's blood. Synthetic blood."

"It's freedom. It's *life*!"

"You can't have it."

"I already do." He pulled a CD case out of the pocket of his coat, opened it carefully. Reverently. "By the way, this is now the only copy. I reformatted the hard drive on your PC and destroyed all the data backups."

Daniel's heart kicked on its first spurt of true panic. Getting his ass kicked by a freak with weird fingernails was one thing. Losing the work he'd dedicated his life to, work with the potential to save thousands of lives, was a whole other level of torture.

He could re-create the formula for the first non-organic human blood substitute, but it would take time. Reproducing the tests and documentation the drug manufacturers would insist on seeing before they committed their resources to the project would take even longer. Months and money he didn't have.

He found the strength to push himself to a sitting position. "You need me. And my medico-scientific mumbo jumbo. You'll never get a major pharmaceutical company's backing without me. You won't get in the front door."

"I have no intention of trying to get in the front, or any other, door."

"Even you don't have enough money to push a product like this to market yourself. It would cost you millions just to get it past the FDA. Tens of millions."

"The market I'm targeting doesn't require FDA approval."

"What market is that, the black market? Africa? Latin America? Where the people are too poor to afford the luxury of asking where their medicines come from, or in too much pain to care?"

Garth cackled again. "Such a humanitarian. But you overestimate my ambition. I was actually thinking of a consumer group much closer to home, and money is not an issue with them."

Nothing Garth said made sense to Daniel, but then his brains had been pretty well scrambled this evening. All he knew was that the man who had claimed to support his work was trying to steal it, and that the same man was more concerned about his own profit than helping humanity with a medical breakthrough.

Synthetic blood would save thousands of lives. Unlike the products most of the pharmaceutical companies had in development now, Daniel's brainchild didn't require any biological components at all. It could be mass produced on demand from simple chemicals, had an unlimited shelf life and none of the threat of blood-born pathogens such as hepatitis and HIV that accompanied the real thing. It had to reach the market—the legal market.

Clutching a set of metal shelves, Daniel dragged himself to his feet. "Bastard. You can't do this. I won't let you do it."

Garth smiled the way Daniel imagined a hunter would

smile at Bambi. Right before he shot him. "Oh, *do* try to stop me. *Please.*"

Daniel put his head down and charged, only to find himself flung back by an unseen hand. His back slammed into the wall behind him with enough force to knock a man-sized hole in the Sheetrock before he slid to the floor.

How had he done that? Garth hadn't touched him.

Shaking his head to clear it, Daniel braced his back against the drywall and pushed himself to his feet for another run, only to find himself knocked flat on his face.

Except there wasn't anyone behind him to knock him on his face. There wasn't anyone else in the room at all. Except Garth.

Okay, now this was getting spooky.

He raised his head to squint at his benefactor-cum-nemesis through burning, swollen eyes.

"You're finished. You have nothing left," Garth spat down at him. "I've got the formula. I've got the lab. I've got your house."

A groan tore its way out of Daniel's throat. The note he'd signed for the research funding. The collateral he'd put up, including the house that had been in his family for over a hundred years . . .

"I've got your car. That pitiful little savings account you call your nest egg."

Garth stretched his hand out toward the door to the lab, and what little breath Daniel had been able to draw into his aching chest caught in his throat.

Another black-clad figure sashayed into the room. Her leather pants squeaked as she rolled her hips. Her D-cup breasts spilled out of her leather lace-up bustier.

"Sue Ellen?" Daniel rolled to his knees, swayed sickly. Sue Ellen walked by as if she hadn't seen him. What was wrong with her? Why was she dressed like that?

Garth smiled as she stepped into his waiting arms and

rubbed herself against him like a feline. "I've even got your girl."

"Sue Ellen, get away from him!"

But she seemed to have no inclination to run. Instead, she flicked out a long thumbnail, scratching Garth's neck and scooping up a drop of blood. Then she brought the blood to her lips and licked it off with a dreamy look of enjoyment on her face.

God, what had he done to her? What sort of spell had he put her under?

Daniel watched, frozen in horror as Garth placed his hands around her neck, caressed the line of her jaw, then squeezed. Hard.

She should have struggled. He had to be hurting her, but she didn't seem to care. She seemed to be enjoying the pain. Eyes glazed over with anticipation, she let her head fall back as if he were caressing her like a lover, not choking her.

Daniel staggered to his feet. "What are you doing?"

Garth drew his thumbs over the column of her throat, licked his lips, and then dug his pointed nails into her flesh.

Daniel charged again, growling. Again the unseen hand stopped him, this time snatching him from behind and lifting him like a dog caught by the scruff of the neck. It pulled him up until he had to stretch to touch his toes to the floor, then beyond.

Garth pulled his thumbs back, and bright red blood bubbled out of the twin wounds he'd inflicted.

Daniel flailed in midair. "Let her go, you bastard. Let her go. I'll kill you for this. By God, I swear I'll kill you for this."

Garth flicked a careless look at Daniel. "You can't touch me. And neither can your God."

He winced as if he suffered some sudden pain, then lowered his head and suckled on the punctures he'd made on Sue Ellen's neck, a thin red stream of blood—her blood—trickling out the corner of his mouth as he drank.

1

❖

AT a corner table in the condemned warehouse that had been converted to a bar, at least for the night, Déadre Rue hunched over her tonic water and watched the throng of sweaty, drunken bodies on the dance floor gyrate to the sound of heavy metal rock with lust in her eyes.

Blood lust.

Sometimes the ache, the desire, the never-ending, sharp-toothed, razor-clawed, freaking *craving* for blood was so strong she thought she might die from it.

But then, what the hell? She'd died once. It hadn't been so bad. Infinitely better than coming back to life, actually. Oh, yeah. Rising as one of the undead—now that had been nasty.

Not that living, for lack of a better word, as one of the undead was much better, wandering the streets with a parched throat night after thirsty night, eyeing ready prey on every corner, yet forbidden to stalk it.

Raising her drink in a trembling hand, she drained the glass, but the cool, clear liquid couldn't quench the fire in her throat that had driven her out of her grave tonight and into the shadowy bump and grind of a rave party. The pulsing music had called her. The sweet smell of blood running just under the thin veil of human skin had drawn her.

And she needed money. Needed some token to bring her superior in order to be granted permission to take what she needed.

Damn the High Matron for putting a ration on human blood, anyway. Just because a few too many exsanguinated bodies had turned up on the streets of Atlanta this last year. Just because the mortals were starting to whisper, getting nervous. The Matron and her Enforcer had the vampires of the city starving themselves for fear of her punishment. Worse, she had them stealing and selling themselves to bring her bigger and better offerings every month, hoping to win her favor and a little larger share of blood. They were like those boys in a Dickens novel, thieving to earn their keep.

Déadre rubbed her right shoulder, which bore the scars of that punishment, inflicted because she'd dared to sip at the wrist of a drunk she'd stumbled over on a late-night walk three months ago.

She'd learned her lesson that night; she hadn't had a taste of blood since.

It wasn't fair. The old ones, like the Matron, could go years without feeding. Decades, if need be. But Déadre had only been undead since 1934. Like a kitten, she needed to nurse frequently, at least once every few weeks. She couldn't die from lack of blood, but she could grow weak from it. Sick. She could suffer.

Even now her limbs felt heavy. She couldn't gather enough saliva to moisten her lips. The scent of blood, heated by the tight crush of bodies in the club, made her dizzy with need. Her heart, if it were capable of beating, would have been racing, her pulse, if she'd had one, shallow but rapid.

As she watched one particular dancer, a blonde with skin so translucent that Déadre could see the veins in her neck when the girl tilted her head back, swaying with the beat of the music, her thumbnails began to lengthen, thicken. To sharpen to fine points perfect for perforating the jugular.

Déadre closed her eyes, rocked in her mind with the girl. Licked her dry lips. She imagined herself trailing her hands up the column of the girl's throat, feeling the heady pulse beneath her fingertips, searching for just the right spot—

"You look parched."

Déadre snapped her eyes open and jerked her hands beneath the table, thumbs tucked into her fists. While she'd been daydreaming, the music had stopped. The band was on break.

The dancers had disappeared, and a man loomed over her. Tall. Lean. Average brown hair gelled up in clumpy spikes. Leather pants, biker jacket with no shirt underneath. Studded dog collar around his neck. Nifty scar running diagonally across his left cheek.

He flashed her an easy smile. "Can I buy you a drink?"

She hesitated, considering. She needed a mark, and by all appearances, he would be easy enough to lure outside and separate from his wallet. All she had to do was return his smile, lean forward, and give him a glimpse down her shirt. He'd follow her anywhere. But something felt wrong about the man before her.

On the surface, he blended easily with the other Goths and punks milling around, but his posture—too straight—and his eyes—too guarded—said he didn't belong. Whatever he was up to, she wanted no part of it, even if blowing him off did mean losing a chance to beef up the paltry offering she'd gathered for the High Matron this month. Besides, getting close to a strong, vital body like his in her current state of need was not a good idea. She might forget about the High Matron and her blood rationing and suck him dry.

It took all her will to turn away. "No," she said, and made a point of looking bored, looking at anything but him and his surprisingly broad expanse of bare chest.

She couldn't look at that chest. Not without thinking of the heart beating inside it. Without hearing the swish of his blood through each of the four chambers, thinking how good it would taste.

He pulled out the plastic chair next to her. The legs scraped across the cement floor the same way his smile grated on her nerves. "Even if it's a Bloody Mary?"

She gasped at the offer. Her stomach tumbled as her gaze latched onto his. She'd love a Bloody Mary. Or a Bloody Tom, or Henry, or Heather . . .

She was so lost in her need that it took her a moment to realize he hadn't meant the offer literally.

Of course, he hadn't. He was mortal.

But she got the feeling, looking into the serene green of his eyes, that his choice of words hadn't been a coincidence. "Who are you?"

"Daniel Hart." He stuck out his right hand.

"What do you want?"

"To get to know you, for starters."

"Why?"

"You seem like an interesting person."

He seemed sincere enough on first glance. He had a handsome smile, full of straight white teeth. Even the scar on his cheek didn't detract from the personable expression he wore so comfortably. But on closer inspection, Déadre noted the fine red web in the whites of his eyes, the strain at the corners of his full mouth.

"Sorry. Not interested." She shoved her chair back and made for the door, the chain she wore as a belt jangling with every step.

Daniel swore under his breath. Picking up women in bars had never been his forte. Picking up a vampire was proving to be an even more elusive skill. He'd spent weeks researching her kind, finding them. He'd picked her out especially for his needs—a loner, young, female. Vulnerable to a man who paid attention to her, he'd hoped.

So she'd proved a little less vulnerable than he would have liked. He still couldn't let her go. In the days he'd spent in the hospital after taking the beating from Garth and throughout the weeks of recovery afterward, he'd searched for a way to kill the man—the monster—who had taken Sue Ellen's life, who held her undead body under his spell. Daniel had studied; he'd read. When he was able, he walked the streets and used the last of his money to buy information.

He knew what Garth LaGrange was, and he knew as a mortal he had no chance against him. There was only one way to win, to free Sue Ellen's soul, and it all depended on getting Déadre Rue to help him.

If Plan A didn't work, he'd go to Plan B.

He started after her, giving her space as she worked her way through the crowd and out the door, then caught up to her in the parking lot, where they'd have some privacy.

At least, he thought he'd caught up to her.

He stopped beside the red Jeep Wrangler in the last row and checked the plate. It was definitely hers. He scanned the darkness, the cones of light from scattered streetlamps. "Déadre?"

He felt a breeze, saw a blur of motion, and found himself flying backward to slam into the Corvette in the next parking space. His feet were on the ground, legs spread, but his back was bent over the rear quarter panel.

Déadre stood between his knees, holding him down with a fist clenched in the collar of his coat. Her pale skin looked as stark against her dark hair as a full moon against the night sky. Except the moon didn't usually scowl so fiercely. "How do you know my name?"

With her hands so close to his throat, now seemed like a good time for the truth. "I've been watching you."

"Why?" Her hands tightened. "Did the Enforcer send you to spy on me?"

"No. I mean, I don't know. Who is the Enforcer?"

"If you're not working for him, why are you following me?"

"I need your help."

"To do what?"

"To—" He hadn't planned to announce his intentions so soon, but he didn't see where he had much choice, at this point. "To become one of you."

For a moment, disbelief held Déadre immobile. *He knew what she was.* And he wasn't screaming in terror or running away from her.

The warmth of Daniel's body seeped into her. The feel of his firm thighs riding her hips gave her a brief reprieve from her craving for blood and stirred a long-unfed craving for another kind of fulfillment.

Then she whirled away from him. Disgust had her wanting to howl.

It happened once in a while. Mortals with terminal illnesses decided they wanted to live forever. Punks or Goths thought they wanted to do more than play at being creatures of the night. So they sought out a vampire and asked to be converted.

Some vamps were happy to oblige in the first part of the process, draining the mortal's blood to the point of death. But they often neglected the part that caused the conversion, giving some of the blood back.

The fools' corpses were usually found rotting in the gutter the next morning.

Before the rationing, that was. Now, the vampire would

be a fool to take human blood without the authority of the Enforcer.

She turned and sneered at the man pushing himself off the car and rubbing his throat. "Go home, little mortal. While you still can."

"I don't have a home anymore. Or a car, or a job, or anything else, for that matter."

"Aw, and you want me to feel sorry for you?"

"I want you to make me a vampire so I can kill the bastard who stole them."

A long moment ticked by.

Petty revenge. He wanted to give up his beating heart, warmth, sunlight, to rise as one of the undead just so he could get back at someone bigger or stronger or smarter than himself.

She shouldn't feel so disappointed. She didn't know the man well enough to have expected anything better of him.

But she had.

Strangely deflated, she turned her back to him and fished in her pocket for her car keys. So absorbed with her disillusionment was she that she didn't hear him move.

Didn't realize he stood behind her until she felt the sting of the needle he plunged into her shoulder.

2

❖

DANDELION fuzz floated on silver beams of moonlight as Daniel sat on a grassy hillside an hour north of the
city, Déadre handcuffed to his side. In the distance, the
lights of Atlanta blazed like so many earthbound stars.
Above them, the moon settled toward the horizon.

He dragged his free hand through the stiff spikes in his
hair. It would be dawn soon, and she was still out cold. He
checked for vital signs for the thousandth time.

She wasn't breathing. Had no pulse. But then, she
wasn't supposed to, was she?

He wasn't sure. All the research he'd done on vampires,
and he still didn't know a thing about their basic biology.
Apparently no one did, since most of the literature he'd
amassed had been based more on speculation and fear than
fact, as far as he could tell.

He glanced down at the unconscious woman—at least
he hoped she was just unconscious—at his side. *A vampire*.
It was still hard to believe. Not the fact that they existed.
Everyone knew vampires were real; they just weren't

talked about in polite company. Kind of like venereal disease.

What he had trouble believing was that she could be one of them and still be so beautiful. She had a heart-shaped face with bowstring lips. Her dark auburn hair was thick and shiny and slid through his hands like silk. Even though she wasn't a big woman, her body flowed from one enticing curve to another.

She was the kind of woman who had always attracted him before he'd met the long, leggy Sue Ellen. The kind of woman who still turned his head, though it made him feel guilty every time he did. Except this woman was a vampire.

Jesus, he couldn't have killed her, could he? Only exposure to sunlight, a stake through the heart, decapitation, cremation, or being completely drained of blood by another vampire could do that.

He hoped.

Her pale skin shone like marble. A cool breeze teased her bangs over her eyes and he brushed them back and tried shaking her again.

To his relief, her eyelids finally fluttered. She groaned.

When her eyes opened, he asked, "Are you all right?"

"Wha—What was . . . ?"

"Holy water." He let go of her shoulders when she stiffened. "Only a couple of CCs. It was just supposed to make you weak, not knock you out."

Wincing and arching her back, she rolled the shoulder he'd stuck with the hypodermic. "It burns."

"Burns? Is it supposed to burn?"

"Ohhhh."

"All right. All right. It burns. What can I do?"

She bit down hard on her lower lip. "Mmmmmmm."

"Okay." He picked her up, curving his shackled left arm

behind her back and lifting her beneath her knees with the other. "There's water at the bottom of the hill. Regular water," he added when she looked up at him with alarm.

She was definitely breathing now, shallow little gasps that tore at his conscience. Maybe she only stopped breathing when she slept. How the hell did he know?

At the moment, he didn't really care. He only cared about taking away the pain carved into her ivory-smooth face.

He set her on the creek bank facing land and peeled back her leather jacket, but he couldn't get it off over the cuffs, so he pulled it down her arm and then lifted her shirt over her head to join it.

She gasped and tried to cross her arms over her chest, but surprisingly enough, it wasn't her breasts that had him ogling. It was the jagged scar on her shoulder.

Surely to God he hadn't done that.

Please, don't let him have done that.

"How did this happen?" He reached out to touch the reddened mark in the shape of a cross, but she flinched before his fingers even brushed the puffy flesh.

"Please." Her voice was close to a whimper. "Don't."

He gave her one searching look, but found no answers in her dark eyes. Unable to stand her pain any longer, he leaned her back, holding her just above the water with his left arm and spooning the cool liquid over her back and upper arm with his right hand.

"Better?" he asked.

Her hair drifted on the current. Her face gradually relaxed. "Better."

She started looking around. Cicadas serenaded her from the trees. A toad croaked downstream. "Where are we?"

"Cherokee County."

She frowned and jiggled her wrist as if just realizing she was shackled to him. "Why?"

Avoiding her gaze, he dribbled another handful of water over the cross branded over her shoulder blade. "Because it's a long way from anywhere."

She shifted in his arms. "Did you bring me here to kill me?"

"No."

"Then what do you want?"

"I told you," he said mildly. "I want to be like you."

"No, you don't. Believe me, you don't." She craned her head toward the east. "It'll be dawn soon. You know I can't be out here when the sun comes up, right?"

"I know."

She scanned the hillside, left and right. "How did we get here? You—You have a car somewhere, don't you?"

"Somewhere." And just in case she decided to kill him and drive off in it on her own, he added, "But the keys aren't with it. They're hidden."

"You're going to hold me here?" She sat up, turned and tried to backpedal away, but didn't get far. She jerked the end of the short chain between their handcuffs. Her voice rose an octave. "You said you weren't going to kill me."

"I'm not. You're going to kill me." Tired of chasing her up the hill as she continued to back away from him, he pulled her to him. She wasn't strong enough to fight. Yet. "You're going to kill me and bring me back . . . like you. Then I'll get the keys, and we'll drive out of here together. Before the sun comes up."

Once he had the strength and speed of a vampire, he could fight Garth on equal footing. Kill him and free Sue Ellen's physical body from his evil influence.

What he'd have to do later to set his own soul free he wouldn't put words to.

Not yet.

*   *   *

THE moments before dawn were always the darkest, the quietest, the most peaceful for a vampire. These were the moments Déadre held on to when she thought she couldn't stand being what she was for another night. When she couldn't stand the hunger. These were the moments she'd always hoped would be her last, should her existence ever come to an end.

She pulled Daniel's coat tighter over her shoulders. After bathing in the creek and having gone so long without fresh blood to warm her, she had been chilled. He'd turned his jacket inside out and settled it over her shoulders. The gesture of simple kindness had touched her.

And confused her.

"Do you know what happens to a vampire in the sunlight?" she asked without looking at him. Pine and magnolia and jasmine all mingled on the breeze.

"I have a vague idea."

"The eyes go first. Our night vision makes us so sensitive to light that we're blinded."

A muscle in Daniel's jaw jumped. He jerked a blade of grass out of the ground and rolled it between his fingers.

"Then our skin begins to blister and peel. Our hair catches fire, and our internal organs start to liquefy."

"We don't have to be here when the sun comes up. All you have to do is . . . whatever you do to make me a vampire, and we'll leave."

"I don't like being used."

He turned toward her. His green eyes looked flat black in the darkness. "How is it using you to ask you to do what comes naturally to your kind?"

"I'm relatively young for one of my kind," she said. "But I've been a vampire long enough to know that I don't like it much. I won't curse another to suffer this existence."

"You'd rather die?"

"I died a long time ago, Daniel." She turned her face up to the sky. The moon was gone. The first pink tinges of dawn seeped up from the eastern horizon. Already she could feel her skin prickling. Soon the heat would replace her never-ending thirst as the source of her misery. "But I'd rather not burn. There are . . . kinder ways."

His face screwed up as her meaning sunk in. "You want me to kill you?"

"You're already killing me. I'm just asking you to do it mercifully."

"Jesus!" Daniel jerked his hand up to run through his hair, hit the end of the handcuff and winced.

He thought he'd planned for every contingency, taking care to hide the car and keys so she couldn't kill him and take off on her own. So she needed him to survive.

How could he have known she wouldn't want to survive?

Of all the vampires in Atlanta, he had to pick the one with a death wish.

He pulled her close. So close their noses nearly touched. Was her face already turning red from the sun?

"All you have to do is bite me, or cut me or whatever you do to get my blood."

She said nothing, just stared over his shoulder at the blushing sky.

He pushed her to her back, straddled her, not really putting his weight on her, but pinning her down as he fished a penknife out of his pocket.

"Here, I'll help you." He flicked the blade open and, hesitating only a second, gouged his wrist. Blood trickled into his palm in a steady stream.

"Go ahead. Drink." A drop of blood landed on the corner of her mouth. She pressed her lips together. "Drink, dammit! I know you want to."

More blood splattered on her chin, her cheek. She whimpered, and threw her arm up, but it wasn't to push his away.

It was to cover her eyes.

He glanced over his shoulder. The first bright sliver of gold shone from the horizon.

She writhed beneath him, struggling to turn away. He let her, sliding to one side, and she immediately curled into a ball on her side with her back to the sun. A spasm wracked her, then another, harder.

She covered her face with her hands, pulling his hand along, and his fingertips brushed her knuckles. They were hot. Cracking. The shell of her one exposed ear was raging red.

Christ!

He dove over her, wrapping himself around her, cradling her head. "It's all right. It's okay. We're getting out of here."

Taking only a second for one deep breath, he pulled his leather jacket up to cover her head, held the rest of her as close to him as he could, and pushed to his feet with her in his arms. Keeping himself between her and the sun as much as possible, he ran for the car.

Each step seemed to take an hour. By the time he reached her Jeep, the sun felt high and hot on his back. He retrieved the keys from the rock he'd hidden them beneath, then hurried to the Jeep parked behind a blackberry thicket, unlocked their handcuffs and settled her on the floorboard. He tucked his coat around her as best he could, then drove like a madman down the gravel road, dust and rock spewing up behind him like a monochrome rainbow. But where was he taking her? This had been his grandparent's farm years ago, but the house and barn were long gone. There wasn't a neighbor for miles, and even if there was—

"Hang on," he yelled to Déadre, and wondered if she was still coherent enough to hear him. To understand.

He slammed on the brakes at the entrance to the old lane, which had once led to a two-story frame house with gingerbread trim, and skidded into the drive. The house might be gone, but there used to be a storm shelter. A dank and dark concrete hole he'd been afraid of as a kid. He'd told his grandma he'd rather blow away in a tornado than crawl down in that grave.

He rolled to a stop beside the crumbling chimney, all that was left of his grandparents' lives. Twenty yards to his left was the split-trunked oak he used to climb. That meant the shelter should be . . .

There it was, the cement entry and wood doors nearly obscured by the overgrown grass.

He ran to the passenger side of the Jeep, pulled Déadre out and made a run for it. She was so hot he could feel her burning skin through the leather coat.

He kicked the door open and nearly fell down the stairs. He laid her in the shadows of the darkest corner and crouched over her.

Her chest jerked as she fought for breath. "The door." She moaned. "Close the door."

Cursing, he jumped up and grabbed the pull rope. The door banged shut behind him, plunging them into total darkness.

He felt his way back to Déadre, pulled her close. He couldn't see her, but he could feel her. Her whole body was shaking, her muscles convulsing. He smelled singed hair and scorched flesh.

His heart pounded against his breastbone. Blood and guilt roared in his ears. What had he done? God, what had he done to her?

"Déadre? Stay with me, baby. Stay with me." He rocked her gently but fiercely, afraid to hold her too tight lest he hurt her more. "Tell me what to do. How can I help? Can you hear me?"

She clutched at him mindlessly, clawed at him, practically crawled up his body, her fingernails scraping his shoulders and chest. Then she fell against him, panting, and knocked him back on his elbows, her hot face searing his bare skin.

Her tongue lashed out, swiped over one of the minor wounds she'd caused, and the touch was like a lightning strike in his blood. The heat transference was incredible. Every cell in his body sizzled.

She scraped him again, and again nuzzled the wound. He managed to string two logical thoughts together. "Blood? You need blood? Will it heal you?"

She didn't answer. She was too busy. Her hands were as quick as her tongue. They roamed and glided, scraped and tweaked. Pleasure and pain blurred.

This was what she needed. He could feel her getting stronger. More aggressive.

His body was electric, jumping and twitching at the intensity of the sensations her recovery was causing, and when she swung one of her hips over his to hold him down, he couldn't help but arch up into her as if she'd turned up the voltage.

He reached up to grab her, to pull her close, to hold her back, he wasn't sure which. His blood pounded so hard he thought his veins might burst. His mind overloaded. She ground her pelvis down on his engorged sex and he grunted, thrust as if they weren't separated by two layers of cotton and leather, his and hers. He found the hem of her shirt, slid his hands underneath and palmed her breasts, pinched the stiff nipples.

"Déadre, we've got to stop." But they were beyond stopping. Far beyond.

Some part of his mind knew this was wrong. Accused

him of betraying Sue Ellen. Betraying himself, his promise. Betraying Déadre, taking advantage of her when she was out of her mind with pain, with need.

Most of him didn't care.

He bucked and she rode him. Heat poured out of her core and over his erection like a lava flow. Her greedy mouth left a trail of fire over his jaw, his neck. He tensed, as her mouth paused over his jugular, but she traveled on, down his arm, where she snatched his hand and lathed his wrist with her tongue.

His bloody wrist.

Her mouth latched on over the open cut and she sucked as greedily as a newborn. She rubbed herself against him, mewling as she drew down hard on him.

He fought the urge to resist. She needed this; he'd almost killed her. And he wanted this. It was the only way he could kill Garth LaGrange and free Sue Ellen. But now that the moment was here, panic swelled. He could feel the life force being drained out of him by the pint.

His head spun. He felt like a drunk on a three-day binge. The blood loss should have rendered him incapable of maintaining an erection, but he grew harder and thicker than ever and wondered if his stamina was a result of the thrall the authors of his research material had speculated about. The sexual excitement that stole a vampire victim's senses, made him unaware he was being fed upon until it was too late.

If so, he could understand where vampires got their reputation as masters of eroticism.

They'd earned it.

His limbs went numb. His heart stuttered, restarted, stuttered again like an engine running out of gas. He was dying, and it didn't seem to matter. He was almost there. Ready to climax.

Déadre was ready, too. He could feel it. Her thighs quivered on each side of his hips. She tilted her head back and took one long, last draw from his wrist, then dropped the limp appendage. With his blood smeared across her chin and cheeks, her jaw slack and eyes glazed in ecstasy, she sat down on him hard and pushed her pelvis forward, trapping his shaft in her body's natural channel. Her upper body stiffened, hung suspended above him for a long moment, then fell forward, kissing him with a gusty sigh, and Daniel let go.

The last living things he knew were the fiery eruption of his body, the sound of her name in his throat, the taste of his blood on her mouth.

He managed to mumble four words against her slick lips. "Bring me back. Please." But in her fevered state, he wasn't sure she heard them.

Then with one final, shuddering pulse, his heart stopped, and his life ended.

Spent.

3
⚜

DÉADRE woke up with a muzzy head and a bad case of cotton mouth. She couldn't quite figure out why she was awake at all. It was daytime, even in the dark she could feel the sun in the warmth of the air, the dry heat of her grave.

Except this wasn't her grave. This place was larger, deeper underground, and she wasn't lying on the freshly turned earth of her homeland. She was sprawled across a broad male chest.

A still, cold, broad male chest.

It all came back to her in a rush of pain. Heat. Arousal. *Daniel*.

She snapped upright. "Daniel?"

With her excellent night vision, she could see his pallor was gray as stone. Though his lips were parted, she could discern no breath passing through them. She couldn't hear his heartbeat or the blood swishing through his veins.

Terror clawed at her.

"Daniel?" She shook his shoulders, but got no response. She'd killed him.

No, no, no, no, no. *Yes.*

He was dead. In her fever, she'd drank his blood until he had no more to give. None to sustain himself.

She'd murdered him.

She scrabbled backward until her shoulders hit the rough cement block wall, and stuffed her fist in her mouth. She hadn't killed a mortal since 1934, when she'd been made a vampire by the elderly gentleman down the row from her to whom she sold milk and eggs twice per week.

One week, dairy and poultry hadn't been enough to satisfy his hunger. He'd taken her blood. And initiated her into the ways of the undead.

When she was strong enough, he taught her how to hunt, to feed. He'd picked victims for her that were weak so that they wouldn't pose a threat, for she believed old Jonathan Rue had loved her in his way. He didn't want her hurt.

In her inexperience, she had taken too much from one old grandmother, a neighbor of Jonathan's. She hadn't realized the woman was bedridden and in frail health even before Déadre had slaked her thirst at the woman's throat. She hadn't realized she was killing her until it was too late.

Jonathan had comforted her, told her they all made mistakes at first, but Déadre would never forget the slack expression on the grandmother's face, the open mouth, as if she'd tried to cry out and couldn't. The lifeless eyes that looked just like Daniel's did now.

She could put life back in those eyes, or a semblance of it.

No. She'd never made a vampire. Wasn't sure she knew how.

It was what he wanted. What he died for.

Daniel, with the body to rival any Greek statue. Beautiful Daniel, with the body cold and gray as stone.

No. Yes. She had to do it. Had to try.

He'd saved her life. He'd fed her.

He'd hurt her. Almost killed her.

He'd come as close to making love to her as any man had in decades, since Jonathan had been staked through the heart by a mob in '46.

She couldn't leave Daniel here to rot. It might already be too late. How long had it been? How long had she slept? She had no way to tell.

"Don't let it be too late," she pleaded to no one and crawled forward. Cradling his head on her lap, she extended her thumbnails and pricked her index finger, then squeezed a drop of blood onto his tongue, then another. "Come on, Daniel. This is what you wanted. You can do this."

She closed his mouth, worked his jaw, simulating a swallow. When she'd repeated the process three times with no effect, she slapped his cheek. "Don't you give up on me, dammit. You started all this. Don't quit on me now!"

She opened a bigger gash on the palm of her hand, let the blood stream freely onto the back of his throat for a full minute, then closed his mouth and worked his throat again.

Tears welling in her eyes, she rubbed his chest, pounded on him with her fist, threatened and begged and pleaded with him to move until his left hand twitched.

She froze, watching, hoping.

His fingers clenched rhythmically. His eyes rolled to white, then back to murky green as his chest bowed. His back arched off the floor as if he'd been defibrillated and he dragged in a deep, rasping breath.

Remembering too clearly the confusion he would feel as he regained consciousness, the pain, the inexplicable rage and the blood lust, she backed away. The next few moments would be worse than death, worse than a thousand deaths, but there was nothing she could do to help him. Not until his rage was spent.

Eyes wide and lips snarling, Daniel rolled to his knees, then staggered to his feet. He rushed the cement block wall of the storm shelter as if it were a demon after his own soul. He pounded the concrete with his fist. The flesh split, bone shattered, but he didn't bleed. He had no blood left.

She hated to see him hurting himself, but it didn't really matter. The pain of transformation was so great that he'd never notice a little thing like a few broken bones, and once he was undead, he would heal quickly.

Eventually his temper died to the point where he became aware of her. He cocked his head and stared at her with insensible eyes. Animal eyes.

She beckoned him with a motion of her hand. "Come to me," she said softly.

He growled and rolled to the balls of his feet, ready for attack.

"Come to me."

His shoulders sagged. He slid one foot forward as if he were too tired to lift it.

"That's it. Come. It will get better soon. I have what you need."

He stumbled forward and fell into her arms. Gently, she lowered him to the dirt floor, their backs against the wall, and opened her shirt. With a flick of her thumb she sliced the side of her breast, pulled his head down and stroked his hair as he fed.

DANIEL had a vague notion that time had passed, though he couldn't guess how much. Time seemed elastic now. Hours rushed by in the blink of an eye. Days were a blur of sleep, warm, coppery drink and soft hands.

The hands were on him now, pressing something cool and damp to his forehead. He opened his eyes and found her studying him.

"Daniel? Are you there?"

Arms shaking, he pushed himself up on one elbow. "Of course I'm here. Where else would I be?

She wrung out her cloth and laid it across the sports water bottle he remembered from her Jeep. "Never-never land, maybe? Or wherever you've been for the last three days."

"Three days?" He levered himself to a sitting position, leaned back against the block wall. "Jesus, I—"

He winced. It was like someone set off a firecracker in his head. He dug his fists into his eyes. "Christ."

Bam. Bam. Bam. Bright white lights exploded in his vision.

"You might want to choose a non-religious expression," Déadre said. "Vampires and Him don't mix too well."

"Vampires? What do you—" He pulled his hands away from his face and looked down at his chest. Had he always been so pale? For that matter, how could he see his skin tone at all in the dark?

His gaze flew to hers. "Did you . . . ? Am I . . . ?"

Biting her lower lip, she nodded.

"I don't feel any different."

Never taking her eyes off his, she walked to him, picked up his hand and laid his palm over the left side of his chest. "Feel that?"

"No."

"Exactly."

He slid his hand side to side, searching. "My heart's not beating."

"You'll learn to make it beat when you want it to, later. Comes in handy when you have to get close to a mortal. I'm sorry."

"Sorry for what?"

She stared at the floor. "For killing you. I didn't mean to. I—I lost control."

He grabbed her by the upper arms, made her look at him. "I asked for this."

Her glistening eyes tore him apart inside. Amazing how

his heart could be dead in his chest and still cause him so much pain.

Her bowstring lips quavered, and he couldn't stand to see them tremble, so he stopped them the only way he knew how. He captured them with his own.

She stiffened, but only momentarily, then she leaned into him with a pleading mewl. He slipped his tongue past the seam of her lips and answered with a groan. Their mouths fused, he tugged the hem of her tank top out of her leather pants and slid his hand underneath.

She might have been a creature of the night, but she felt more like an angel filling his palm. He backed her up to the wall and, pinning her there, slipped a second hand under her shirt.

There were advantages he hadn't thought of to this vampire business, like not having to breathe. He could ply her with kisses endlessly, never breaking contact, while his stealthy hands kneaded her, memorized her shape and texture.

The underslopes of her breasts were soft as clouds, the nipples tight as rosebuds. The tear-shaped sides were—

Bloody. A sticky mess.

He pulled his head back and yanked her shirt up. "Jesu—" he squeezed his eyes shut as a cherry bomb went off in his head. "Ow!"

"I told you—"

"I know, I know." The flash of pain already receding, he squinted at her chest. "What the hell happened to you?"

She hesitated only a moment. "You are a voracious eater."

"I did this?"

"Not exactly. I opened the wounds so you could feed."

Very tenderly, he lowered her shirt and then took a step back. "Thank you. I won't be feeding off you any longer."

He turned his back to her, but she stopped him with a hand on his shoulder before he could walk away.

"Whatever you're thinking, get over it. Feeding is a fact of life for vampires."

He wheeled. "Maybe it's time the facts of life changed."

Already he could feel the hunger gnawing at his bones, though. He was so thirsty he thought he might dry up and blow away like the ashes of a cold campfire. He trembled with raw, powerful need.

Jesu—

Ow!

He had to learn not to do that.

Clenching his fists, he fought the urge to go to Déadre. To take what she offered, no matter what the cost to her. Or to his self-respect.

For the first time, Daniel began to understand what synthetic blood could mean to these people. To him. He began to see why Garth had been so desperate to have the formula.

But if he'd stolen the formula to feed his people, why didn't they have it already? Garth had walked out with the discs more than two months ago.

Garth. Thinking about Garth was good. Anger staved off the hunger. Raised a different kind of blood lust.

He stoked the rage inside him, used it to do what he needed to do. It was time. Time to leave Déadre and time to do what he had to do. He climbed the short staircase to the door.

She called out to him in a high voice, "What are you doing?"

"I have to go."

"You can't."

He bowed his head, telling himself to go on. He couldn't turn back now.

"I made a vow, D. To—" He flicked a gaze skyward.

"Him who shall remain nameless, and to myself. I can't give it up now."

"You're not ready."

"I'll never be ready, if I stay here."

He didn't need Déadre anymore. She'd fulfilled her purpose. He probably should kill her—she was a vampire, after all—but he didn't kid himself. He'd never be able to bring himself to do it. He couldn't stay with her, either, though. It would be too easy to lose sight of his goal. To be distracted by her, by this awful, aching thirst that never seemed to go away.

Rallying his resolve, he flung the overhead door back on its hinges. Cool, night air rushed in, full of the heady smells of summer. The stars shone overhead, each one bright as a moon to his newly heightened senses. He heard a tune playing on a car radio that must have been miles away, felt the strength in his muscles as he sprang out of the shelter and into the grassy meadow in one easy leap and smiled.

It pained him to leave Déadre behind, it really did, but he couldn't think about that now. He was finally ready to fight Garth LaGrange, take back what he'd lost. To free Sue Ellen.

He was a vampire, and at long last, vengeance would be his.

4

IDIOT.

Déadre rolled her eyes. Did he really think he could just walk away from her?

She could have tried to explain that he was newly made. That he was bound to her, at least for a while, as she was to him, but she doubted he'd have listened. Some lessons one had to learn for oneself, and this was going to be a particularly painful one, if Daniel Hart was as stubborn as she believed, which she was sure he was.

He'd left her the car—probably being chivalrous—and set out on foot, but she couldn't drive after him. Now that he was undead, he'd hear her coming for miles. Besides, it didn't matter. He wouldn't get far. So she gave him a ten-minute head start and then marched down the road after him.

He wasn't hard to follow. His footsteps sounded like a stampeding herd of elephants to her sensitive ears, which reminded her to keep her step as light as his was heavy. Even with his new super senses, he wouldn't have a clue he was being tailed.

Poor boy, he had a lot to learn about being a vampire.

She wasn't sure how she felt about teaching him. Creating a life, or un-life, in this case, was a big commitment. The vampire equivalent of having a child. Until he learned the ways of the undead, his safety was her responsibility.

But there was a very un-childlike side to their relationship as well. Vampires were, by nature, sensual, sexual creatures. Biologically speaking, the taking of blood meant a sudden increase in volume of blood. Increased blood volume meant increased blood flow to the sex organs, resulting in arousal.

Some vamps couldn't get off without gorging themselves. Some couldn't gorge themselves without getting off. Either way, it made the exchange of blood a very personal, and often intimate, interaction.

So far, Daniel had been too weak to feel the full effects of the blood she'd given him. His body had been focused on survival, but he was getting stronger by the hour. Sooner or later, he was going to want more from her than blood, and she had to decide how much she was willing to give him.

Lost in her thoughts, she didn't notice until she rounded a bend that the road stretched out long and straight before her. Long, straight and empty.

Where was Daniel?

She stopped, scanning the trees on either side of the lane, listening for him. She finally heard his breathing, harsh and labored, and knew that he'd reached the end of his endurance. New vampires needed to feed every couple of hours. He would be weak, sick. The blood lust would be on him like a horse master's whip, driving him forward, driving him to feed.

This was a difficult time for a new vampire. A test period, during which he would find out if he had the mettle to control the blood-sucking urges, or if he would go rogue and have to be put down by his own kind.

A farmhouse rose out of a grassy meadow to the south. Potted geraniums on the front porch added a splash of red to the silvery moonlit scene. Daniel stood in the driveway beside a pickup truck, his head turned up to the curtains fluttering in an open, dark, second-story window.

There were mortals inside. Even from this distance, Déadre could smell them. Ready prey.

She crept toward the house, willing Daniel away. "Come back to me, little vampire. Back to me."

But when she broke out of the tree line, Daniel was nowhere in sight. Her stomach clenched. He wouldn't do it. He was a moral man. That wouldn't be lost in the vampire he'd become. He hadn't been able to kill her, he wouldn't kill the mortals in this house, either.

The blood lust was strong, though, and he hadn't learned control. He might not want to hurt anyone, but he could make a mistake, the way she'd made a mistake so many years ago with that poor old woman . . .

She had started toward the house after him, hurrying now, not caring if he heard her, when the bleat of a goat drew her attention toward the barn. She stopped, her senses alert, and heard more animal snuffles, a rustling of hay. Normal barnyard sounds.

Or not.

She glided to the barn without a sound and found Daniel on the floor bent over a puddle of vomit, a decapitated chicken in one hand and blood trickling out both corners of his mouth.

Daniel turned his face away. He didn't want Déadre to see him like this, on his knees, puking his guts up.

"I was so thirsty," he said. "I couldn't stand it. But the people in the house . . . I couldn't do it."

"You need to feed every few hours when you're newly made. Later, you can go longer."

He shook his head. "Something is wrong. I can't drink

the blood. It comes right back up. Maybe I'm not really a vampire. Maybe it didn't work."

He hadn't heard her move, but suddenly she was crouched beside him. "It's the animal blood. You can't have it. It isn't compatible."

He coughed, choked, spit. "Oh, God—*Ow!*—No kidding."

Gently she pried the chicken from his fist and, holding one wing between her thumb and forefinger, deposited it in a muck bucket next to the horse stall.

He worked up the nerve to glance her way and was relieved to see she wasn't laughing at him. "You couldn't have told me about this animal thing?"

"You didn't ask."

Still on his hands and knees, he laughed sardonically. "Guess there are a lot of things I didn't ask."

She knelt next to him and dabbed the chicken blood from his lips with the hem of her T-shirt. "There's still time to make up for that. But first you need to feed."

She sat with her back against the wall and pulled him to her. He was too weak to resist. The barn spun around him like a gyroscope.

She lifted her T-shirt, but he brushed her hand away from her breast. "Wait, wait. One thing I have to ask first."

She frowned down at him. "What?"

"Is it normal for me to get totally turned on when I drink your blood?"

"Very normal. Although you'll learn you do have the ability to control it, if you want to."

He thought about that a moment. "Like if I decide to take a nip from a ninety-year-old crone with the face of a weevil?"

"That would be a good time, yes." He could tell she tried to suppress her smile, but it broke through.

He was still contemplative, though. "Is it . . . as good . . . for you, too?"

She brushed her hand through his hair. "Not as good as for you, at this point. But when you're stronger, we'll exchange blood, and then it will be."

He nodded, feeling queer about contemplating a future with her. A future had never been in his plan. He was going to kill Garth, and then himself and Sue Ellen so that they could rest in peace. Wasn't he?

He thought it would be simple. He would become a vampire, and he'd have super strength and use it to kill Garth.

Unfortunately things hadn't worked out quite that way. He'd become a vampire, all right, but he was about as strong as a newborn lamb, and Garth was the big, bad wolf.

Obviously, he had some recalculating to do. Not tonight, though. Tonight, he needed to feed. He needed blood to quench the fire that threatened to consume him. He needed Déadre.

He rested his head on her shoulder and she beamed such a beatific smile down at him that this time, he extended a thumbnail and opened the wound on her breast himself.

The scent of fresh blood was like the smell of the ocean to a sailor. It cleansed him. Stirred him. His skin tingled and a low throb pulsed in his sex.

Lying next to her, he turned to his side and hooked one leg over her, rubbing with his calf, pressing himself into her hip. He smoothed his palm down the soft planes of her belly and under her waistband to the nest of curls between her legs.

She drew his head down with her hands, offering nourishment, offering her blood, but tonight he wouldn't just take. He would give as good as he got.

As good and better.

*   *   *

"How long until I don't have to feed so often?" Daniel asked.

Hand in hand, they walked on a footpath through the woods behind the farmhouse. Nocturnal eyes peeked at them from branches and scrub brush, then scurried away.

Déadre couldn't remember the last time she'd felt so at peace. When she'd still been mortal, maybe.

"It's different for everyone," she said. "But most of us are able to sustain ourselves for at least a day or two after the first couple of months."

His face twisted. "Months?"

"In vampire years, a month is hardly the blink of an eye."

"Vampire years. Is that kind of like doggie years?"

"Yeah, except a lot longer."

"Hmmphh."

The path ended at a pond polka-dotted by floating lilies. Daniel skimmed a stone across the moonlit surface. "How often do you need blood?"

"Every few weeks or so. But it's been a little longer this time."

He had raised a rock for another throw, but he paused. "Am I hurting you by taking your blood when you haven't fed?"

She shrugged, hoping he wouldn't see the weariness in the gesture. "I'm a little weak, that's all. I'll feel better once we're back in the city."

In truth, she wished she never had to go back to the city. To face the Enforcer.

"Once you take a mortal's blood," he said, the words tinged with revulsion.

"I don't kill my donors. I only take enough to sustain myself without harming them."

"How do you do it?" He lifted his head. His green eyes looked black, bleak, under the quarter moon. "I tried. I was so desperate for blood, I wanted to go into that farmhouse, drink from whoever lived there, but I couldn't. It made me sick to think about it."

He sat down in the grass, pulled his knees up and hooked his arms around them.

She lowered herself next to him, mimicking his position, and grazed her fingertips over the nape of his neck, down his spine. "Eventually you'll have to take blood from someone besides me."

He stared out over the water for so long that she thought he wasn't going to respond. That he wasn't ready to face that reality. But finally he said quietly, "What if there was another way? Could you give up mortal blood? Would you?"

"What other way? Snapping the heads off chickens?"

He winced. "No, no animal blood. That's a lesson I won't forget."

"Then there is no other way." Daniel sighed, and got such a faraway look on his face that Déadre wondered where his thoughts had taken him. "Daniel?"

He stood and brushed himself off, then offered a hand to help her up. "We'd better get back. It'll be dawn soon."

Déadre's own thoughts did some wandering on the way back to the farmhouse to collect the jacket she'd left in the barn. "Let's don't go back, Daniel. Back to Atlanta, I mean. We can sleep today in the storm shelter, then head out tomorrow night for wherever we want to go."

She'd never thought about leaving her home city before. Vampires congregated in clans and to be separated from the clan was risky. They supported each other, watched each others' backs. Clans tended to be wary of strangers, especially strange vampires. The clan in a new city wasn't likely to welcome them with open arms.

More likely they would brand them as rogues, cut off their heads and bury them facedown.

She'd rather take her chances with a strange clan than with the Enforcer, though. She couldn't go back to Atlanta and face the High Matron and her thug. She couldn't take Daniel there.

Her excitement grew with every step. "California, maybe. I've always wanted to see the coast."

"I can't."

"Or the mountains. What do you think about the mountains?"

At the back of the farmhouse, he stepped in front of her, stopped her with firm hands on her shoulders. "Déadre, I can't. I have to go back to Atlanta."

She jerked away. The goats in the pen against the barn bleated. The mommas ran back and forth across their corral, their babies at their heels. The cattle next to them joined the ruckus, mooing and snorting.

"Because some man stole your house and your car and your work," she said bitterly, remembering his words from the rave club. "And you have to kill him."

"Because he killed someone I care about. My . . ." His voice broke. "My fiancée."

"Your *what*?"

"He's not a man, Déadre. He's a vampire. And he . . . he made her one, too."

She shook her head, not believing any of this. "So you used me to make you a vampire so you could win her back?"

"I used you to make me a vampire so I could set her free. She is—was—sweet and gentle. She wouldn't want to live like that. She wouldn't want me to leave her a—"

"A what?" She raised her hands out to the sides. "A monster, like me?"

He didn't answer her question. He straightened his back and looked her straight in the eye. "He's a vampire. As a mortal I had no chance against him. He's too strong. Too fast."

"What will you do if you manage to kill him, huh? Then you'll still be a monster? What will you do then?"

He looked her straight in the eye, his face solemn and sad. "Then I'll set myself free, too."

Her eyes went wide. Her stomach pancaked on the floor of her abdomen.

He'd used her. To find his fiancée, a vampire, so he could kill her.

And then he was going to kill himself.

Her beautiful Daniel.

Her mouth rounding in a silent, "No", she ran around him into the barn and nearly mowed down a sleepy-looking elderly man in a bathrobe and rubber boots. The farmer held a double-barreled shotgun, and her momentum sent him stumbling back. The stock of the gun connected with a support beam. His hand jerked on the trigger. There was a tremendous explosion, then a flash of flame from the end of the gun.

And two loads of double-ought shot tore through Déadre's chest.

5

❖

DANIEL felt the concussion of the shotgun blast all the way outside the barn. He charged through the back door in time to see Déadre sway once, her spine straight and arms at her side, then topple backward like a domino. A red stain the size of a dinner plate bloomed between her breasts.

The farmer dropped the rifle and backed up until his shoulders hit the wall. His eyes were huge and round, set deep in his face, his complexion waxy. "Whaa—? No. Oh, no. I thought it was those wild dogs in the barn again, botherin' my stock. I didn't know. I didn't mean to do it. It was an accident."

Daniel stood immobile for a long moment, then dropped to his knees beside Déadre. He was pretty sure a gunshot couldn't kill her, but it was still quite a shock seeing her fall, seeing her lying on the ground, still and pale.

He checked her vitals quickly. She wasn't breathing, had no pulse. By all outward appearances, she was dead.

The farmer shuffled toward the door, mumbling. "Nine-one-one. I gotta wake the wife and call nine-one-one."

"No." Daniel touched Déadre's lips once before he rose, both a plea and a promise. He hoped she heard both in that deep sleep vampires went into when they needed to heal. Just because she couldn't die from a gunshot wound didn't mean she couldn't suffer from one. Feel the agony of torn flesh and splintered bone.

He needed to get her out of here, take her somewhere where he could help her. Where he could hold her, if nothing else. But first he had to deal with the farmer.

"You can't call anyone," he said, moving slowly and kicking the gun away as he approached the farmer.

The man shook like a child who'd played too long in the snow without his mittens. "B—but she's . . ."

"She's going to be fine."

He could see how hard the farmer tried to believe that. But the man shook his head sadly. His voice broke about the same time tears sprung to his eyes. "She's dead."

"She's not." He advanced on the man slowly, trying not to spook him.

"She . . . She's not?"

Daniel felt his confusion. He was sorry for the old guy, but a call to the cops could cause him and Déadre a lot of trouble. The last thing he needed was the police on his tail when he took her out of here. If they found her, they'd take her to the morgue, do an autopsy.

He suppressed a shudder. What if they cremated her afterward? Then she really would be dead.

No, he couldn't let the old man call the cops.

"You didn't shoot anyone," Daniel said firmly, holding the man's gaze. He wasn't quite sure what he was doing, but there had to be a way to convince the man it was in his best interests to forget what had happened tonight.

If that didn't work, he just tie the geezer up and leave him for his wife to find in the morning, after Daniel was long gone.

"I didn't shoot anyone," the farmer repeated. His voice was going flat and his eyes took on a faraway sheen.

"There was no one in the barn."

"No one in the barn."

Daniel raised his eyebrows. That was easy.

Too easy.

"It was just a couple of wild dogs bothering your stock. You scared them off."

"I scared off some wild dogs."

Daniel waved his hand in front of the guy's face, but he didn't blink. He'd suspected from his research that vampires had some way of mesmerizing their victims, making them forget. Now he knew for sure.

He just didn't know how he'd done it.

As long as he had, though, he might as well take full advantage. "I need to borrow your truck," he said.

The farmer stared off into space with unfocused eyes. "Keys are under the floor mat."

Excellent. "Go back to the house and go to bed. If your wife is awake, you'll tell her that you scared off the dogs."

"I'll tell her I scared off the dogs."

The old man turned to shuffle back to the house, but Daniel called out to him before he reached the door. "Wait!"

Daniel looked from the old man's slack face, to Déadre's pale one, and back. He figured he had less than two hours of darkness left. Enough time to get Déadre to Atlanta, where he could help her, before sunrise, but he was going to need all his strength to do it.

Daniel couldn't feed off Déadre. In her condition, he risked draining her dry and killing her. But she'd said he couldn't go more than a few hours without blood, either, newly made as he was. Already he was feeling light-headed and clammy.

The solution to his problem stood at the barn door in a

natty bathrobe and rubber boots. Could he do it? Could he drink the blood of a mortal? A living, breathing man?

The thought repulsed him at first, but he was also curious. Was he mortal or was he a vampire?

He couldn't straddle the fence forever.

He couldn't straddle the fence and build the strength he needed to fight Garth. Not quickly.

His stomach flipped and he realized his heart was beating, fluttering really, in his chest. He looked back at Déadre, her pale, elfin ears and the way her long lashes lay so still over her cheeks.

He forced himself to relax by thinking of her. Doing what he needed to help her.

He began to hear his own pulse in his ears. The blood lust beat a rhythm that couldn't be ignored. With his breath coming in short strokes, his thumbnails lengthening, he turned back to the farmer. He saw fear deep in the man's eyes, behind the veil of the thrall in which he held him, and smiled to ease his dread as he punctured the farmer's jugular and lowered his mouth over the wounds.

Daniel moaned, lost in the pleasure as the essence of life poured down his throat, sweet as honey with a coppery tang, and he drank long and deep.

Much to his surprise, he liked it.

DRIVING south down I-95 toward Atlanta in the farmer's rattling old pickup truck, Daniel suppressed the urge to wipe his mouth with the back of his hand for the thousandth time. He could still taste blood on his tongue, feel the man's pulse beating beneath his lips. He still reeled from the heady rush of heat suffusing his dead heart, his veins.

He was dead, and yet he felt more wonderfully alive than ever. Taking blood made him strong, invulnerable. Immortal.

It was a high far beyond anything he imagined cocaine or PCP could induce. If it was like that for all vampires, and he assumed it was, it was a wonder there were any mortals at all left in the world. How easily that kind of trip, that surge of power, could become an addiction.

He had to respect, if grudgingly, the control it must take for the undead to walk the streets night after night, surrounded by ready sources of that magic elixir, and not go on a rampage, drain the city dry.

More control than he had, he feared. If Déadre hadn't stirred as he'd been gulping down the farmer's life force, Daniel didn't know if he could've stopped, or if he would have kept drinking until the man had no more blood to give.

Until he'd killed him.

But she'd moaned, and her hand had twitched. Her eyes had scrunched in pain, and her pain had called him back from the dark edge he'd been teetering on.

Thank God.

Ow!

He really had to stop doing that.

One of Déadre's hands clenched his pant leg and he glanced down at where she lay curled up on the seat of the truck, her head resting on his thigh. Her fragile shoulders looked narrower than ever as she hunched them and moaned again. Her eyelids fluttered again.

Daniel tightened his fingers on the steering wheel. She was going to wake up soon, and when she did, she was going to hurt like hell.

She was also going to need blood and lots of it.

Turning his gaze back to the road, he punched the accelerator and sped through the darkness.

By the time he slowed down to cruise by the two-story brick warehouse that had once been his lab, he figured he only had about forty-five minutes left before the sun rose. If he was wrong about the lab still being relatively intact, he wasn't going to have a chance to find another hidey-hole.

Luckily, he wasn't wrong.

The windows had been boarded up to protect against vandalism, but that would work in his favor. The wood would hold the sunlight at bay, give him more time.

He carried Déadre to the stoop, set her down while he easily shouldered his way through the double dead-bolt locks on the door, then lifted her against his chest and took her inside.

He felt disconnected from himself, a sort of out-of-body experience as his Nikes crunched over broken glass and kicked aside a fallen chair. This lab had been his life once. All he cared about. Now the only value that history held for him was its ability to help him help the woman in his arms. To take away her pain and make her whole again.

In the middle of the room, he righted a table and stretched her out on the stainless steel. Her body bowed. She bit her lip and mewled, and he eased her back down.

"Easy, baby. Easy. I'm gonna help you now. Just a few more minutes."

There was no need for lights. His newly acquired night vision allowed him to work in the darkness—it was easier on his eyes, anyway—gathering the supplies he needed and repairing the equipment Garth had damaged. Had it really been eight weeks ago?

It seemed more like a lifetime.

Actually, it had been a lifetime, he supposed. His lifetime. Sometimes he forgot he was dead now.

As the first pink fingers of dawn crept around the edges of the boards over the broken windows, he stood back and studied his work: a full liter of synthetic blood in an IV bag, and more cooking.

He had the rubber tubing and large bore IV needle ready, but as he listened to Déadre whimper in the dark, her head thrashing side to side, he realized he couldn't do it. He couldn't pump it into her.

He hadn't gotten anywhere near the point of human testing in his research. Even if he had, that wouldn't have proven the synthetic blood safe for vampires. The last thing he wanted to do was cause her more pain.

His decision made, he yanked the tourniquet tight around his left arm by holding one end with his right hand and pulling the other with his teeth, then probed the inside bend of his elbow with the needle until he found a vein, and ran the IV wide open.

He watched as the dark liquid flowed down the clear tube. The synthetic blood hit his body with a sizzle that made him jolt, then made him dizzy.

Whoa. Head rush.

Fire poured through his veins. A sweat broke on his forehead. His vision swam. His insides swooped up to his throat, then plummeted to the pit of his abdomen. It wasn't an entirely unpleasant sensation, just . . . unsettling. Like riding a roller coaster without being quite sure there really was an engineer behind the controls.

Panting, he lowered his head and went with the flow. It was too late to turn back now. As if he'd want to. The liter bag was nearly empty and every cell of his body felt gorged with life, with oxygen, with energy.

At last he understood why Garth had gone to such lengths to get the formula. It hadn't been for his people, to save them having to take human blood. It hadn't even been about money.

No, it had been about one thing: power.

If Daniel had been stronger after feeding before, he was Superman now.

Smiling, he disconnected his IV and hung a fresh bag.

All he had to do was bring his Lois Lane back to life, and he'd be unstoppable.

6

⚜

DÉADRE awoke on the back of a giant black stallion galloping through the dark of a moonless night, galloping straight toward a cliff, the booming sound of waves crashing against rock rising up to her from far below. Her muscles rippled with his. Wind whistled through her clothes, tore at her hair. All she could do was wrap her fingers tighter in his mane and hang on for the ride.

Hooves clattered over stone. She felt his haunches gather for the leap, heard a scream and realized it was her own, then she was flying, soaring through the night, but doomed to fall, to break against the rocks below like the next wave.

She opened her eyes for one last look at the world, the night . . . and found she wasn't riding a giant horse through the sky, wasn't falling. Daniel held her, safe in his arms.

He sat on the edge of a cold metal table, cradling her head against his chest, rocking her. "Shh. Shh, now. It'll get better in a minute. A lot better."

Her heart was beating, she realized, beating hard without her even trying, and she was breathing without any effort at all. Fresh blood flowed through her system, pooled between her legs and rushed her toward fulfillment.

She clutched at Daniel's jacket, grabbed his hair by the handful and bent him back over the table, her greedy mouth latching on to his, sucking and kneading, while her hands raked over miles of hot, silky skin and hard muscle. He mumbled something that she sure hoped wasn't "stop" because she couldn't have stopped if she'd tried. Even if her life, or her unlife, had depended on it.

Lost in a frenzy that was somewhere between the fury of an erupting volcano and the big bang of a new star being formed, she pulled Daniel to her and rolled. He landed on the floor beneath her with a thud, but she didn't think he was going to complain. He grabbed her T-shirt by the neck and tore it in two as easily as if it had been made of paper. Absently, she noted that the gunshot wound had healed. Her breasts were pink and perfect, bobbing over his face while she pressed her thigh against his erection and rubbed encouragingly.

Not needing much encouragement, he fumbled her zipper down and peeled off her leather pants, then she straddled him.

He brought his hand to her, feathered his fingers through her curls, but she pushed his wrist away. "I can't wait. Can't wait."

She jerked down his fly, pulled him out, squeezed once and then lowered herself until she'd taken him to the hilt.

Her eyes closed. Her head fell back. Her hair brushed her bare shoulders as he put his hands on her hips to hold her down and then bucked beneath her.

She was back on the horse, the black stallion, galloping, the wind in her hair, the night air in her lungs. His muscles rippled with hers. He lifted, she clenched. They both groaned.

She quickened the pace, rode him hard. This time, the crashing she heard wasn't waves against rocks, it was her own blood in her ears. She spurred him on, knowing the dark cliff lay ahead, insane for it, mad with the need to fly off it with him. She urged him faster with her hands, her heels, then leaned over and used her teeth, her tongue.

She wanted more; he gave her more. Another powerful stride. Another powerful stroke. He tensed beneath her, gathering himself. She clutched his mane, holding on. Blind. Deaf. But able to feel. Feeling every shudder, every gasp, every ripple as they catapulted off the cliff together. Fell, arm in arm.

She landed on top of him—again—this time splayed across him like a piece of limp spaghetti.

"If this is how you recover," he said, his warm breath fanning her damp forehead. "I'm going to have to shoot you at least once a week."

She lifted her head weakly and grinned at him. "If this is how I recover, you won't have to bother. I'll shoot myself."

A laugh rumbled beneath the ear she had pressed to his chest. "Maybe we should think about a little less bloody form of foreplay."

"Bloody." Her heart skidded to a stop. "Oh, damn. I've taken blood." No way she could have recovered so quickly—or so passionately—otherwise.

She grabbed his neck and scanned for every inch of earthy-smelling male skin. "You don't understand. You can't give blood yet. If I take too much, it'll kill you." Her hands trembled on his trachea. "How much did I take? Are you okay?"

"You took plenty." He wrenched his head away. "But it wasn't mine."

She looked around the room, not convinced, still afraid she'd hurt him. "Whose? How?"

"No one's. It's synthetic. A product I've been working

on for three years. I'm a microbiologist, Déadre. It's what I do."

"A microbiologist." She hesitated, wanting to believe him but not quite daring. If he was trying to protect her from the truth. . . . If she'd hurt him. . . . "And you've made fake blood?"

"Completely non-organic. Doesn't even require human hemoglobin like the products the big drug companies have been working on. It's so simple I'm amazed no one thought of it before. All I did was compound perfluorocarbons."

"Perfluoro-whats?"

"PFCs. Flourine and Chlorine." His eyes lit up and he laughed. "I knew it would work. I knew it would. The PFCs are even more efficient than real red blood cells because they just absorb the oxygen, instead of bonding it to iron the way blood does."

"If you say so."

He clasped her shoulders. The touch zingéd through her hyperstimulated nerves.

"Can't you feel it?" he asked. "The PFCs are forty times smaller, so they can fit into the smallest capillaries, literally reach every cell in your body, yet they carry twice as much oxygen. Can't you feel how strong it makes you? How alive?"

She did feel different. Warmer. Not so tired.

He lurched to his feet, fastened his pants and threw her jacket and pants to her. He didn't bother with the ruined shirt.

Pacing, he dragged a hand through his hair while she dressed. "This stuff is powerful mojo. Not only will it help mortals, but it could mean a whole new life for vampires."

She zipped her pants and shoved her arms in the sleeves of her jacket. "New life?"

"No more feeding off mortals. No more killing, accidental or otherwise. And the power it will give us, it's tremendous."

It sounded good, so why was her stomach turning. "You know what they say about power corrupting."

He stopped, turned to her. "Son of a bitch."

"What?"

"That's why you and every other vampire in the city haven't already heard of the synthetic blood. He wasn't going to share it with the rest of you. He wants it for himself. He wants to be the biggest, baddest-ass fucking vampire in Atlanta."

He picked up his own coat and punched his arms into the sleeves. "Well, I've got news for him. He's not the only vampire who can cook up a pot of this joy juice, now. Garth LaGrange is going down. For good."

She dropped the test tube she'd been holding. Glass shattered at her feet. "Garth LaGrange?"

"The one who wrecked my lab and stole my work."

"The one who turned your fiancée."

"Yeah." He looked down at his feet, then raised his head. Color spotted both cheeks as if he'd just realized, as she had, that they'd made love while he was engaged to another woman, but she couldn't think about that now.

"The one you're going to kill," she said flatly, already knowing how he would answer.

"Tonight. Right after I drink so much synthetic blood that an M-one tank couldn't stop me."

Oh, God.

She winced, the pain flaring instantly. *Crap!* She hadn't done that in decades. Rubbing her temples, she hoped it would be decades, or longer, before she did it again, assuming she was around that long.

Which she might not be, since the vampire she'd just made—the man she loved—was determined to try to kill the evilest, cruelest, most powerful being in Atlanta.

Garth LaGrange, the High Matron's Enforcer.

7

IT was a good thing Daniel was dead already, because he didn't think he could live with himself after what he'd done.

Bad enough he'd kidnapped Déadre, used her to make him a vampire and then fed off her while he gained his strength.

But to make love with her, that was an unpardonable sin.

This whole quest was about Sue Ellen. Finding her. Setting her free.

Getting tangled up—literally—with another woman hadn't been part of the plan. Still wasn't.

Except every time he tried to picture his fiancée, to shore up his resolve by remembering her sweet smile, her shy, tinkering laugh, all he saw was Déadre in black leather. All he heard were her moans, her sighs. He felt her hot hands around his—

"You can't kill him," the object of his rumination said stubbornly. "He's like the Terminator on steroids and immortal to boot."

He glanced over to the passenger seat of the borrowed

pickup. He and Déadre had passed the day in the basement beneath his lab. He'd cooked up a couple more batches of blood, and now that night had fallen, they were heading west, to an old restored plantation home about twenty minutes outside the city limits. The home Garth had stolen from him.

"Vampires aren't immortal," he said, switching his gaze back to the road. "Not really. They're tough to kill. But they do die."

She cocked an eyebrow at him. "You've been made what, three days, and you're an expert on vampires now?"

"I told you you didn't have to come."

"Oh, and miss seeing all that blood spilled? Are you kidding? Of course, all of it is going to be your blood, but I'll try not to let that spoil the fun."

She crossed her arms over her chest and turned her head to stare out the side window.

Aw, hell. What was he supposed to say? She wasn't going to understand. He wasn't sure he understood anymore.

"If you really think he's going to kill me, all the more reason for you to stay behind."

She turned her head. At least she was willing to look at him again. Her dark eyes burned with angry fire. "I told you once already, life as a vampire sucks. And yes, I mean that figuratively as well as literally. Don't you get it? You're the only thing in my miserable undead existence that hasn't sucked. Why would I want to stay behind without you?"

Of all the things she could have said, things that would have made him stop, force her out of the truck, leave her behind for her own good, that was the one thing that disarmed him.

In her own, ineloquent way, he thought she'd just said she loved him.

Jeus—

I mean, Holy Hell.

He smiled. He was learning.

"Just for the record," he said. "I don't think you suck, either."

Her gaze snapped up to his. "Oh, yes, I do. Take me back to the lab and give me some more of your mojo juice, and I'll show you how hard."

He laughed out loud. That was his girl.

"Hold that thought, okay? Maybe we'll give it a go later. First, I've got a vampire to kill."

Not to mention a fiancée, though he kept that part to himself, because once he put a stake through Sue Ellen's heart, there would be no later for him.

THE thumping in Déadre's chest was slow and sad. Fine time for her heart to start beating on its own, she thought. When all it wanted to do was pound out a dirge.

Her eyes were hot and wet and felt swollen in their sockets. This is what it's like to want to cry, and to force yourself not to, she thought, and the fact that she remembered the feeling from so many years ago, when she'd been mortal, brought more tears to her eyes.

She'd been remembering a lot of things about her mortal years since she met Daniel. What it was like to care about someone else so much that his injuries made her hurt. What it was like to need someone. To love someone.

Now she was afraid she was about to remember what it was like to lose someone.

She swallowed past the lump in her throat and looked at Daniel. He had a strong profile. Noble. Determined.

Stubborn as a jackass in a field full of clover.

She'd tried every way she could think of to talk him out of this fool mission of his without luck. All she could do now was pray, and how was she supposed to do that when she couldn't think—much less say—His name?

"Here we are." Daniel killed the engine and the headlights on the pickup truck and coasted to a stop in a grove of pecan trees beside a long, narrow drive.

At the end of the drive, a white house rose up from the green turf like the pearly gates from a cloud. The white wooden pillars lining the porch shone like marble in the spotlights turned on the porch. A magnolia tree bloomed in the front yard, scenting the air with the signature smell of a Georgia summer.

"This was your house?" she asked, whispering though she wasn't sure why. Even with super-hearing, Garth couldn't hear them at this distance.

Daniel nodded. "I inherited it. Grew up here. Haven't really lived here since I was a kid, though. It's been in my family since the Civil War, one of the few plantations spared when General Sherman took Atlanta."

"It's beautiful."

Daniel supposed it was. He'd never thought about the house much before. He'd been too busy with his work. His research. His life.

Funny how he had to die to see that he hadn't really been living at all. He'd been holed up in his lab day and night, obsessed with the quest for synthetic blood. He'd told himself there would be time for the rest later. Even when Sue Ellen came along, she'd always been second to his work. It was a wonder she'd agreed to marry him. A wonder he'd thought to ask. But then, he hadn't really asked, as he remembered.

He'd forgotten that until now.

They'd been talking over pizza in bed after an evening of so-so sex, and she'd asked him if he thought maybe he would ask her to marry him someday. "Yeah, sure," he'd said. "Maybe someday."

The next thing he knew, she was telling his lab assistant and the security guard and everyone else they ran into that they were engaged. He'd felt sort of obligated to get her a ring.

Why not? She was good-looking and a nice-enough girl. Who else was going to put up with his weird work habits and obsession with blood? It was what people did, right? Grew up, earned medical degrees and Ph.D.s in microbiology. Got married. Had kids.

Looking back, he could see what a mistake he'd made. How he'd taken the easy way. He felt like a fool for it now, looking at that big front porch and seeing himself old and gray in a rocking chair with Déadre, not Sue Ellen. Déadre's kids and grandkids puttering about, but what was done was done. That future wasn't to be. He'd made a commitment to Sue Ellen. He couldn't abandon her now. He had to put her soul to rest, and once he did, he couldn't go on living himself. It just wouldn't be right.

Wrenching his thoughts firmly back to the here and now, Daniel turned to Déadre. "Looks like Garth's having a party."

Two or three dozen cars lined the circle drive in front of the plantation house, among them several long white limousines and a couple of hearses.

"Not a party." She flicked her tongue out to moisten her lips nervously. "High council."

"High council?"

"It's the end of the month, isn't it? Time to settle affairs, collect offerings, and mete out punishments."

"What punishments?"

"You really don't know much about being a vampire, do you?"

"Apparently not."

The more her fingers twined in her lap, the more his own nerves jumped to life. He had a bad feeling about this.

"At the end of every month, the vampires of a clan—in

this case, the clan Atlanta—are called before the High Matron to pay homage. Some bring gifts. Some share the wealth they've stolen from their victims."

"You think Garth gave my formula to this High Matron?"

"Undoubtedly. Whatever he has belongs to her. *He* belongs to her. He is her Enforcer."

Daniel narrowed his eyes. "What, exactly, does he enforce?"

"The rationing, mostly." She rubbed her scarred shoulder. "We aren't supposed to take mortal blood without permission. They say it's because too many suspicious neck wounds gets the mortals riled up, makes them talk about witch hunts, but I've always thought it was because the less blood we have, the weaker we are."

"And the more powerful they are. The more control they have."

"The landowners starving the peasants so they won't revolt. The bigger the offering we bring, the more blood they give us permission to take."

"Son of a bitch. So that's where he gets his money." He put his hand over hers on her shoulder. "Did he do that to you? Give you that scar?"

"I—I took blood when it wasn't my turn." Her gaze jumped to his beseechingly. "I was so thirsty. I can't go as long as some of the older vampires. I only took a little. I didn't kill the man."

"I know. You wouldn't."

She swallowed, lowered her face. "Garth knocked me down and held me there with his foot on my shoulder."

Daniel's throat closed. "The metal cross embedded in the sole of his boot." So that's what it was for.

"He's so old, as long as there's leather between it and his foot, and as long as he can't see it, it doesn't bother him."

"But he uses it to keep the rest of you in line."

"The rest of *us*. He'll use it on you, too, if you interfere with him."

He reached into the cooler behind the seat and pulled out two plastic Coke bottles he'd washed out and refilled with his *wünderblud*. One bottle, he opened and handed to her. The other he kept for himself, then knocked his container against hers in mock toast. "From now on, you can have all the blood you want."

Turning his gaze toward the brightly lit house, he drank deep, then wiped his mouth with the back of his hand. "Garth LaGrange is *never* going to put a hand, or a foot, on you again."

She followed his lead and downed her blood with gusto. When she finished the bottle, her eyes were fever bright. In medical terms, he'd say she was feeling no pain.

She slid her hand over to his lap, and he felt the building arousal in her, and in himself. It would be hard not to feel it, since it was currently threatening to bust the seam on his pants. If they were anywhere else, they'd be going at it like minks already.

"Killing Garth can wait one more night, can't it? He'll be more vulnerable when he's alone. And tonight . . ." Her tongue curled in his ear. "We have better things to do."

Come to think of it, what did it matter where they were? No one knew they were here. No one could see them.

He took her hand and started to pull her closer, but the headlights of another car sliding past them down the long drive had him blinking and throwing his hand up over his face.

"A late guest?" he said.

"Not likely. No one would dare be late to Council." Raising her head, Déadre watched the car pull up to the walk and stop. Four people got out, two of them huddled together and wearing dark hoods, the other two flanking them on either side.

Daniel's expression darkened. "You didn't tell me this was a costume party."

"It's not." She shook her head. "I guess now would be a good time to tell you that sometimes, when the High Matron is feeling particularly generous, they invite guests to the High Council. Mortal guests." She had to pinch her lips together to keep them from trembling. "Most of the time they don't survive."

8

❖

DANIEL'S face twisted. "They kidnap innocent people and bring them here . . . to feed on?"

She shrugged, but there wasn't a hint of carelessness in the gesture. "The vampire equivalent to a gang bang. Everyone who's been good gets to take a turn."

"That's sick."

"I told you it was a miserable existence."

He slung the satchel he'd packed full of deadly goodies over his shoulder and reached for the door handle. "We've got to help them."

"There are thirty or forty vampires in there. Are you going to fight them all?"

"If I have to." He swung the door open and jumped out of the truck.

Swearing under her breath, she followed, beseeching whatever deity would listen to her—if any would listen to her—to save her from fools and do-gooders. More importantly, save him.

"Wait." She caught up to him at the edge of the trees,

tugged on his sleeve. "They won't get to the . . . refreshments until after the ceremony. They'll stash them somewhere until they've finished their business."

"Where?"

"Somewhere with only one way in or out so they can't escape. Near the assembly—that would be in the largest open area, probably, so there'd be room for everyone."

Daniel took her hand and skirted along a hedgerow, careful to stick to the shadows. "Sounds like the ballroom."

"You have a ballroom?"

"It's an old house. There's a big pantry between it and the kitchen. No windows. One door into the hall."

"Which will surely be guarded. How will you get in?"

He looked back at her and smiled encouragingly. "I told you this house was built before the Civil War, the slave era. It has service tunnels running all through it. One of them leads right to the pantry close to the ballroom."

"And if they aren't there?"

"Then we'll try somewhere else."

They found a ground-floor window open at the back of the house, the gingham curtains barely fluttering on the still air. Inside, they heard voices. Raucous shouts and pleas for mercy. A few screams. Daniel's jaw ticked and his hand tightened around hers, but he said nothing. Just led her deeper into the mansion. Into trouble.

They entered a narrow passage behind a stairwell and followed it as it twisted and turned around the house. At one point, they were so close to the assembly that she could make out the individual voices: Maximillian and Tomása, Gretchen and Alexi, and Garth's mad screech.

Her breath stuttered and quit. Spiderwebs caught in her hair, and she had to flick something big and black off her forearm twice, but Daniel seemed unaffected, so she stumbled along after him as quietly as she could.

They went down a few stairs, into a cellar. There were racks on the walls. What looked like wine racks, only . . .

Daniel stopped and stared at the bottles, finally lifted one from its cradle, shook it, squinted at the label and smelled the cork.

"It's blood, isn't it? Your synthetic blood."

He nodded.

"So all this time Garth has been making it and hoarding it. Making the rest of us go thirsty. Punishing us for taking mortal blood while he gorged himself."

Daniel put the bottle back in the rack, gave her a hard stare. "Looks like it."

She exhaled noisily. "Let's get the bastard."

"That's my girl."

They walked on through the musty cellar, finally stopping under an old-fashioned service lift. Daniel pushed the box meant to wench goods up into the pantry from the cellar out of the way and dragged over an old crate to stand on. Stretching up, he wrapped lightly on the ceiling above him.

"Shh," he warned in a harsh whisper. "I've come to help you. Keep quiet."

Then he slid the hatch aside and leaped straight up into the pantry with no more than a mild fluttering of air to mark his travel. Déadre followed close behind.

She pulled the hoods off the young couple curled together in the corner while Daniel untied their hands.

"Are you hurt?" he asked.

The young man's finger flew to his lips. He made the symbol for two and then pointed at the door.

Guards.

Daniel nodded and helped them slide down into the cellar without a sound.

"What now?" Déadre asked when the hatch was back in place above them.

"Take them to the truck," he answered. "Get them out of here."

"What about you?"

His gaze slid up and back to right about where the assembly would be. "I have unfinished business."

"You can't do it alone."

"I can't do it with them in harm's way." He looked from the frightened mortals to her and brushed her jaw with his knuckles. "Or you."

With only a few false turns and backtracked steps, Déadre retraced her path back to the truck with the two mortals in tow, shoved the keys into their hands and told them, "Go!"

Damn Daniel Hart to hell and back. He deserved to live the rest of eternity as a vampire for this. But he didn't deserve to die, which was what was going to happen if he faced Garth alone.

Probably what would happen if they faced him together, too, but there was nothing she could do about that. Or about the fact that even if they did survive, by some miracle, he would have his precious Sue Ellen back, and wouldn't need Déadre anymore.

She was head over dead stupid heart in love with the man, so what's a girl gonna do?

Probably get herself killed, too, that's what. But then, it wouldn't be the first time.

As the pickup's taillights disappeared in the distance, she crept back into the shadows, back toward the house.

Back toward Daniel.

If she'd only smelled a little sooner the smoke the guard taking a break by the side entrance puffed out, or stepped a little lighter, so that her foot hadn't snapped that twig, she might even have made it.

* * *

DANIEL put the hood the man had been wearing over his head and looped the rope that had bound him loosely around his wrists, then waited. The goings-on in the other room seemed to drag on forever, and he willed the vampires to hurry. With every minute that passed, the advantage he'd gained from the synthetic blood waned, and his chances of success lessened.

Finally, the pantry door opened. He heard footsteps shuffling in, was jerked to his feet.

"Where's the girl?" a man's voice asked. "Where'd she get to?"

Someone else growled. "Take him out. We'll find her." Daniel found himself stumbling along in the grasps of two strong men-vampires.

He felt the press of bodies around him when he entered the assembly, the excited surge of static electricity through the air as he was pulled onto a raised platform at the front of the room. He could almost hear them licking their chops.

The vampires were hungry, and he was the main course.

A hand yanked off his hood and he found himself staring into Garth's insane eyes. "Surprise," he said.

Shock flashed across Garth's face, then amusement. "Well, Dr. Hart. How nice to see you again."

"Good to see you, too. So I can send you to Hell, where you belong." The room was dim, lit only by candles in the four corners. He scanned the crowd for Sue Ellen, didn't find her.

"Been there, done that. Got the blood-stained T-shirt," he said and laughed. "But I'll take great pleasure in passing the favor on to you, instead."

Daniel's heart thumped like he was alive again. He threw the ropes off his wrists and pulled out the sickle jammed under his coat between his shoulder blades. The crowd of vampires gasped, took a step back as a unit.

"Sorry," Daniel said, flashing the razor-sharp blade in the candlelight and circling Garth. "Not interested."

"Well, well, Daniel. You do surprise me."

"I'm going to do a lot more than that to you." He spoke over his shoulder, keeping one eye on the crowd and one on Garth as he moved. A still target was a dead target.

Garth's hand lashed out at supersonic speed. Daniel dodged left, swiped the blade down hard. It was only a glancing blow, and still it sliced his wrist to the bone. He lifted the bloody limb and gaped at it.

"Yeah, that's right," Daniel said. "I'm as fast as you. I'm one of you. It's a fair fight, now."

Garth screamed out at the assembly, "Take him!"

Daniel wheeled, swung the sickle at neck level, the threat of decapitation—one of the few sure ways to end a vampire's existence—obvious. No one moved.

"He's been holding you hostage with blood and his punishments," Daniel said, his gaze roaming from face to haggard face in the crowd. There wasn't one among them without sallow bags under their bloodshot eyes, hollow cheeks. They were thin to the point of emaciation. "For how long now? How long have you let him torture you, starve you while he has all the blood he needs stored right here in the house?"

"Kill him!" Garth yelled, holding his injured wrist.

No one moved.

"I know where he keeps the blood," Daniel told them. "There's enough for everyone. You don't have to take it from mortals. You don't have to ask his permission."

A ripple of murmurs spread round the room.

"Don't listen to him. He lies." Garth took a step forward.

Just then the double doors to the ballroom banged open and two burly vampires dragged Déadre in.

She lifted her head and looked up at him with ravaged eyes through the hair that had fallen over her face. "I'm sorry."

He jerked his head sharply once. "You have nothing to apologize for."

She'd come back for him. He couldn't quite wrap his mind around that fact. He knew how afraid she was of the Enforcer, and yet she'd come back to help him.

"Ms. Rue. How nice of you to join us. Bring her up here," Garth ordered. "I presume since you're skulking about instead of joining the assembly that you're with him." He jerked his head toward Daniel.

The guards laid her on the floor on her back. Garth lifted his boot over her and she turned her head away, hissing in pain.

"You know what this is?" he asked Daniel without waiting for Déadre to confirm or deny his assumption. "What it does?"

"I've seen your handiwork," Daniel answered.

"Ah, then the two of you have been . . . close. If I touch the metal cross to her skin, she burns. If I hold it there, it burns all the way through her." He moved his boot until it hovered inches above her chest. "If it burns through her heart, she dies. Permanently, this time."

"Let her go, asshole." Daniel swung the blade, but Garth ducked. "I'm the one who came to kill you."

"Kill me?" Garth laughed. "I eat bugs like you for breakfast, boy. You're not going to kill—"

As he was talking, Garth took his eyes off Déadre. She took the opportunity to slide a small wooden stake out of the sleeve of her coat and jam it upward, right about where his testicles would be.

He swayed, his hands moving to his crotch and his boot inching closer to Déadre's chest. As if moving in slow motion, he leaned. His boot came down.

And Daniel lopped off his head with one clean swipe before he could put his weight on it.

Grabbing her by one arm, he dragged Déadre away from the corpse, which decayed to dust in seconds.

The crowd hushed for a moment. Then one of the vampires fell to his knees, crawled forward and bowed his head, holding on to Daniel's pants leg and calling him "Master."

"Leggo," Daniel said, shaking himself free.

A few of the vampires broke into sobs. Others began to crowd around him. Unsure what they intended, he waved them off with the sickle.

"You said you knew where there was blood," someone yelled.

"Plenty of blood."

"I do," he answered, still backing toward the door, one arm looped around Déadre's waist. "Enough for everyone."

"We need blood."

"We need it now."

"Get ready to run," he whispered in Déadre's ear, and then told the crowd, "It's in the cellar. Bottles of it, and it's more powerful than anything you've known. Once that is gone, I can make more. But only for those who don't abuse it. Only for those who don't take blood from humans, or harm them in any other way."

Then he made for the door, towing Déadre along with one hand. They skidded into the hallway, around a corner, then another, while the mob fought each other to get downstairs.

At the back of the house they ducked out the same window they'd come in, and ran across the lawn, not bothering with the shadows this time, until a voice from a second-story window jerked Daniel to a stop as if he were a dog on a leash.

"Daniel?" Sue Ellen's pretty voice called. "Daniel, is that you? Help me, Daniel. Please, I need your help."

9

"DANIEL, no! You can't go back in there." Déadre tugged on his hand once and gave up, the futility of her efforts written on his face.

It was useless; she'd lost.

"Daniel, please," the sickeningly sugary voice in the window said. She couldn't see the face in the darkness, but Déadre just knew it would be a pretty face. Women with voices like that were always pretty.

"Don't leave me here," the woman called. "I'm afraid."

Daniel turned and walked slowly back to the house. He didn't seem to know where he was, or what he was doing. He sure didn't seem to know Déadre was with him.

She talked to him anyway. "This is crazy. There are two dozen ravenous vampires in there."

He kept walking, one slogging step after another.

"Without the Enforcer to control them, who knows what they'll do. Once they've had a taste of your synthetic blood, they'll be powerful, and they'll be angry at what's been done to them all this time. What they've suffered. Who knows who they'll decide to take that anger out on."

He pulled away, and she let him go. His eyes never wavered from the dark window, the gauzy curtains fluttering around the silhouette of a female form. He stumbled through a side door almost as if he were sleepwalking.

Or . . . the woman upstairs held him in thrall.

How could that be? She was a vampire, yes, but she was almost as newly made as him. She would had to have had a relationship with him—vampire to mortal—before tonight for her to control him from this distance, with just her voice.

How could that be . . . unless . . .

No!

Déadre hurried to catch up with Daniel. She tried to tackle him as he climbed the stairs, but he threw her back. Her head smacked the wall and she had to take a moment to clear the little birdies before she could go after him again.

On the landing, she tried to get in front of him, to block him. "Daniel, she's not who you think she is. She's not *what* you think she is!"

"Sue Ellen?" he called and shoved past Déadre as if she didn't exist.

"Here, baby," the woman crooned. "Here, Danny. Come to me."

Déadre followed him into a huge bedroom. The walls were draped with black and red satin. Night and blood, the curse of the vampire. The bedcovers and curtains were all dark. Heavy wooden shutters were folded back against the wall on each side of the window, ready to be pulled closed at dawn to block out the sun.

Daniel didn't seem to notice the unusual decor. He stared transfixed at the shadowy figure in the corner until finally, holding out her arms to him, she stepped into the light cast by the gas hurricane lantern on the sconce by the door.

Déadre sucked in a breath, barely resisted the automatic urge to drop to her knees, press her cheek to the floor with her arms out to the side in the position of subjugation. "High Matron," she said, her voice breathy.

The High Matron of clan Atlanta stopped, folded the velvet hood back from her head. "What are you doing here, little girl?" Her voice had lost the sugary tone and taken on the rasp Déadre associated with the queen of the vampires.

"Sue Ellen?" Daniel said as if he hadn't heard either of them.

The High Matron beckoned him with the curl of one finger. Daniel took a step forward.

Déadre stopped him, grabbing hold of the back of his jacket. "You can't have him!"

The High Matron smiled as he pulled free of Déadre's grasp and stepped into her arms. "I already do," she said again in Sue Ellen's sweet voice, and then hooked her thumbs into his throat and lowered her lips to the two bubbling wounds she'd made.

A moment later, she raised her head. Daniel's blood trickled out one corner of her mouth. She swiped the drop away with the tip of her tongue. "Mmmm. Good. Strong. Powerful."

She lowered her head to suckle on him again.

Déadre's arms went stiff at her sides. Her fingers curled into her palms. Her skin went cold and her blood boiled. "You tricked him. You knew about his research all along and you pretended to fall in love with him."

"Of course I did, darling." She lapped at Daniel's neck like a cat at a puddle of spilled milk.

"He loved you. He came here to save you!"

The High Matron raised her head, patted Daniel's cheek. "Did he now? Then I shall have to make him my special pet. With Garth gone, Daniel will make a fine new Enforcer."

No. Déadre couldn't let this happen. Daniel wouldn't want to live like this. She wouldn't let it happen.

She grabbed the kerosene lantern from its hangar on the wall. Before the High Matron could raise her head in surprise, Déadre threw the lantern. Fuel splashed all over Daniel and the woman. Flames engulfed them.

Yelling, "No!" but not sure any sound actually came out of her closed throat, Déadre reached into the flames and pulled Daniel back. She threw him to the floor and slapped at his burning pants leg, the cuff of his coat, smothering the flames with her body. "No. No, no, no!"

"You bitch!" The High Matron stumbled backward into the satin-draped wall. The wall covering ignited. She swatted at the cloth, but only succeeded in tangling herself in it further. Screaming, she spun, and the burning cloth encased her like a shroud. A moment later, her whole body burst into flames and disintegrated.

Daniel's eyes snapped open as if he'd awoken from a nightmare. His arms closed around Déadre as his lungs dragged in a ragged breath. He rolled with her, away from the fire. Away from the pile of ashes that was all that was left of the High Matron.

"Sue Ellen!" he yelled, but Déadre heard the difference in his voice. The betrayal. "Sue Ellen," he said once more, quieter, before he pulled Déadre to her feet and down the stairs, out the door and into the fresh night air.

"NICE digs," Daniel said. He sat on what he supposed doubled as both dining room and coffee table since it was the only table in the twelve-by-twelve crawl space underneath the maintenance shaft to Track 11 of Atlanta's metro rail system. The walls were bare, the only furniture besides the table was a coffin lined with dirt in the center of the room.

At least the ceiling had some décor. If you could call heavy metal rock posters and stick-on glow-in-the-dark stars décor.

"Don't be a funny boy." She spooned a glob of burn medicine out of a blue jar with her finger. "Or I'll have to mix a little holy water with your salve."

He leaned away from her approaching finger. "You wouldn't."

She daubed the glob on the end of his nose, then swiped it down his chin. "No, I wouldn't. But it wouldn't hurt for you to show a little respect."

"Honey, after what you did to Garth, I'm downright afraid of you."

Her chin wobbled. "It's been a long time since I killed anyone. And I've never done it on purpose."

"You didn't kill Garth. I did."

She ducked her head. "The High Matron . . ."

"She was using me. Pretending to be mortal, dressing in prissy outfits and playing sweet and helpless and dumb, when all along I was the stupid one. She was just waiting for me to perfect the synthetic blood. She had to have been working with Garth all along. She's the one who introduced me to him, said he could fund the research. She would have made me into what he was, eventually."

He captured Déadre's chin between his thumb and forefinger and brought her face up to his. "You saved me from that. A fate worse than death."

"You don't want to die, now that her soul is free?"

He touched his lips to hers, tasted her fear and her passion, and whispered, "Not when I have you to live for."

She looped her arms around him and pressed herself into him. Their noses bumped. Burn salve squished across their cheeks and brows as they nuzzled and kissed each other. That didn't matter. They'd both been burned.

"We have a lot of work to do, getting your blood to the vampires of Atlanta—everywhere, for that matter—so that they can live and thrive without feeding off humans," she said between biting his earlobe and running her tongue over the crease of his eye.

"I want to get it into human hands, as well. There's still a lot of need there."

She wiggled her hips against him. "Maybe we can keep enough for ourselves to keep life interesting at home, too."

"We'll keep plenty."

He felt her smile on the side of his neck. "I love you, Daniel."

"I love you, too, Déadre."

He opened his legs and she stepped into his body where she belonged, where the blood lust beat intimately between them.

For eternity.

#1 *New York Times* bestselling author
LAURELL K. HAMILTON

"What *The Da Vinci Code* did
for the religious thriller, the Anita Blake
series has done for the vampire novel."
—*USA Today*

It's hunting season with
Anita Blake, Vampire Hunter.

penguin.com